Final Reckoning

BABYLON 5™

Final Reckoning

The Fate of Bester

By J. Gregory Keyes

Based on an original outline by J. Michael Straczynski

A Del Rey® Book
THE BALLANTINE PUBLISHING GROUP • NEW YORK

This book contains an excerpt from the forthcoming edition of *Babylon 5: The Long Night of Centauri Prime* by Peter David. This excerpt has been set for this edition only and may not reflect the final content of the forthcoming edition.

A Del Rey® Book
Published by The Ballantine Publishing Group
TM & copyright © 1999 by Warner Bros.
Excerpt from *Babylon 5: The Long Night of Centauri Prime* by Peter David copyright © 1999 by Warner Bros.

www.randomhouse.com/delrey/

Library of Congress Catalog Card Number: 99-90606

ISBN 0-345-42717-3

Manufactured in the United States of America

First Edition: October 1999

10 9 8 7 6 5 4 3 2 1

For

Tom Deitz

acknowledgments

J. Michael Straczynski and Walter Koenig

Nancy Delia

Min Choi

— *prologue* —

Joseph Begay caught the scent of monster and grinned. He fired his thruster and drifted deeper into shadow. One uneven edge of the asteroid gleamed like a thin seam of silver in the darkest of all mines. The bare suspiration of carbon dioxide he had just released moved him into total eclipse—the silver thread vanished, and the huge rock became a gaping hole in a sky full of stars, the black maw of the underworld. And in that hole was his prey, lurking.

The comlink in his helmet crackled. "Begay. Where are you going?"

He frowned in irritation. The channel was guaranteed secure, but nothing was more guaranteed than silence. And even P12s leaked sometimes when they spoke aloud—vocalizing triggered the part of the brain that 'cast. Only long years of Corps training enabled suppression of that tendency. It was like trying to revolve one's arms in opposite directions—to the thirtieth power.

"I've made him," he replied.

"Herbst and Cortez are already down there."

"Yeah? Have they scented him?"

"No."

"I have."

"Give the position, then, but keep the high ground."

"No way. He's mine."

"Begay—"

He cut the link. The last thing he wanted now was distraction. Sure, he'd get a reprimand later, but it wouldn't go far. He was the best, and after this hunt no one could ever doubt it.

He had come a long way from being that punk in Ganado, nothing better in his future than the leadership of a smalltime gang and an early, violent death. Whatever its faults, he owed the Corps for that. They had plucked him out of that life, given him a chance to do some good.

He drifted down into the shadows and recalled the stories of his Navajo ancestors—the ones his crazy uncle Hatathli had told him when he was a kid. Those tall tales were starting to make sense, the ones about the Monster Slayer, who had rid the People of their enemies. After years of laughing at them, he finally understood that the finest thing a man could be was a hero, one of the ones who fought the monsters, who made the Human race better.

This was an age of heroes—Sheridan, Delenn, Lyta Alexander . . . He would find his place among them. Today.

There, the scent again.

Space was the perfect hunting ground. Planets were full of voices—thousands, millions—on Earth, billions. Prey could hide in those voices as a rabbit might in dense brush. But space was quiet, simple, with nowhere to hide. He knew all of his fellow hunters with the intimacy of many hunts, and he could tune out their voices until there was only silence and the breath of the hunted.

That breath was near.

He flipped on his night vision, and the asteroid reappeared. It was cold, the backside of this lump of nickel and iron, but the side facing the sun was hotter, and metal was an excellent conductor of heat. The landscape reflected that: the higher elevations were colder than the low. A firefly appeared, too—Herbst or Cortez, probably. Space suits had to shed heat or their occupants would bake alive, and no technology had been invented that could overcome the basic laws of thermodynamics.

So where were the prey and the other hunter? There ought to be three bright dots.

The answer was simple enough. The prey was hiding someplace—they already knew the asteroid was hollow. That might also mean that one of his teammates had found the monster's bolt-hole and was holding out. Everyone wanted to be the hero who caught this fellow.

Well, Joseph didn't need to see him. He *felt* him. The others were P12s, too, but not all P12s were created equal.

The almost inconsequential tug of the planetoid gripped him now, and he let himself drift toward the surface, guided by small bursts from his thruster. He knew what he was looking for, and soon he found it—a regular, circular opening. One of the old mine shafts. He angled toward it.

The tunnel dropped down straight, perpendicular to the surface. He drew his PPG and went in feet first, the weapon aimed between them.

A reddish blob of heat appeared, and again he grinned like a coyote.

But only for a moment. With line of sight it was simple to read a psychic signature. The blob below was Herbst, not their quarry.

With line of sight it was easier to send and receive without leaking, too.

Herbst?

It's me. I thought he was in here, but I lost him.

Are you sure?

Yeah. The shaft goes down another three hundred feet and dead-ends. Nobody there.

Where the hell did he go?

I don't know. It must have been a false trail. I've heard spooky things about this guy. Maybe—Gott! *Above you!*

Joseph snapped his head up. At the same moment a psychic attack cracked into his shields. Only yards away, a man-shaped blob dropped toward him.

The attack was strong and simple, aimed at paralyzing. Even as he tried to close the contact of his PPG, he found his finger wouldn't move.

He had killed a boy once, before Psi Corps had found him. He didn't remember much about the fight, only that he had been losing until the anger woke in him, a fury so cold and brilliant it made him feel like a giant. When they had pulled him off the older kid, he'd already pulped in his head with a

rock. Begay had been twelve, a minor, and so had been re-
manded to juvenile court. That's when his psi powers were
discovered, and that's when the Corps had given him absolu-
tion, and a new life.

Ten years ago. He was a new man.

Except for the anger. It came now, a sheer shuddering blast,
meeting the dark wind that was slamming into him head-on
and pushing it back, back. The monster was terrifically strong,
but he didn't have to win the psychic duel, he only had to move
his finger. Just a little, a fraction of an inch . . .

The shaft lit with green light, once, twice. In the second
blast he saw a nebula of ice crystals, already billowing out
from one rupture.

And that hideous monster's mind—went out.

"Ya-heeeeee!" he shouted. "I got the bastard!"

I thought we wanted him alive, Herbst 'cast.

*Well, maybe if you'd helped! He had me. In another second
he would have been on me, taken my weapon, killed us both.*

You didn't give me time!

*There wasn't any time. Besides, this saves the trouble of a
trial, doesn't it? Swift justice.*

He felt Herbst's disapproval. *That's not the way we do
things. That's the way* he *did things.*

You were here. You saw I had no choice.

Yeah. He's dead, right?

As dead as lead. We'll take the body back.

He flipped on his headlamp and the sudden illumination
made him blink. His first shot had split the faceplate open,
and what he could see through the mirrorlike surface was a
real mess. The second shot had taken him in the chest, from
which mist still drifted.

Moments later, they were back in open space, navigating
toward the distant transport. He noticed Herbst was favoring
his left hand. Joseph reactivated his link.

"—Begay, for the last time—"

"Easy, boss. We got him."

There followed a satisfying pause. "Really?"

"Yeah. I had to take him down, but it was him, all right."

"Well—well done. Is that Herbst or Cortez with you?"

"Herbst."

"He was having comlink trouble earlier. Where's Cortez?"

"I don't know. He was on the surface."

"Well, he isn't there now."

"Must have gone around to the sun side."

"He would have reported."

"Maybe not. Or maybe . . ."

He didn't want to say it. Maybe the monster had claimed one last victim.

"We'll find him. Let's get this stiff inside."

"I'm starting the lock cycle now."

By the time they had reached the transport, the outer air lock was open. They drifted in, and Joseph closed the hatch and cycled it. A few moments later the inner door opened and they were surrounded again by friendly, breathable air. Joseph unlatched his helmet. It popped out of its gasket with a sigh.

The corpse floated, ghostlike, its blood now liquid and drifting into tiny beads. Joseph remembered other stories now, of *chindi*—the evil spirits of the departed, which caused illness. Maybe he should arrange to have a ghostway done when he got back home. He didn't exactly believe in that stuff, but he didn't exactly *not* believe it, either.

Still, *chindi* or not, he couldn't resist. While he fumbled at the collar of the monster's suit, he heard the soft hiss of Herbst taking off his helmet.

The PPG had done a lot of damage, frying skin and carti- lage, and explosive decompression had done even more. It took him a few seconds to piece together Herbst's features.

"What?" *Chindi!* his mind shrieked.

"Simple, really," a voice said from behind him. "An old trick, transposing. I did it the first time when I was only six, to win a game of cops and blips."

Joseph went for his PPG, but this psi assault was even stronger than the one before. He managed to twist enough that he could see the man standing over him. Then everything froze.

It was the monster, looking much as he did in his photographs, except that his face was composed, serene. His dark eyes were touched, not by anger or madness, but by quiet melancholy. He was holding a PPG.

"I masked the switch with that earlier attack. As I said, simple. And now you've let me on your ship. Thank you."

Joseph felt his hand inching toward his weapon. He could do it again. He could . . .

"I kill you filthy," the monster said, and then chuckled, as if it were a joke instead of nonsense. Then everything flashed green, and something hot stabbed Joseph in the chest, and he tasted fire in his mouth.

Alfred Bester considered the dead man and shot him again, in the head. You could never be too sure. Then he moved quickly to the hallway.

Their teammate Cortez was already dead of a seizure, lying at the bottom of the shaft. According to what he had gleaned from Begay, that left only two, both P12s. He looked back at the corpse and shook his head sadly. Why did they insist on sending these *children* after him? Maybe the other two would present more of a challenge.

But they didn't. Ten minutes later he jettisoned the four bodies into space, disabled the tracking devices on the transport, and sat contemplating where he wanted to go.

Michael Garibaldi woke with a dry mouth, blurred vision, and a serious sense of disorientation. He cracked one eye and saw a blinking red light. He put it together with the insistent *brreeep* that had disturbed his sleep, but couldn't figure out what it meant.

He sat up, and his body protested. It was a sickeningly familiar sensation, one he had hoped and sworn and prayed he would never feel again.

"God, you stupid . . ." He was talking to himself. Not a good sign. He couldn't remember drinking, not even one drink, but that was how it was sometimes, with blackouts.

His heart was pounding. He couldn't do this again. He couldn't.

Then the details of the day before started to return. He remembered a morning full of pushing paper, lunch with that smug CEO from Amtek, then racquetball with the same little smartass—beat him, too. More pushing paper, a call from Lise, who was on Earth for business, a movie with his daughter, another movie without her, then bedtime.

Everything accounted for. No drinks.

The noise hadn't stopped, but at least he realized what it was now. It was his red-line comlink, which meant it was important. The clock on it solemnly and silently informed him that it was 5 A.M. Martian standard time, February 15, 2271.

Like the months on Earth had anything to do with Mars. Wasn't there some legislation in the works to do something about that?

Five o'clock?

He hit the switch. "Yeah. Garibaldi. This better be *so* good—"

"It's about Bester, sir." The voice was Jim Hendershot, his head of very special security.

"Is he close enough for me to shoot?"

"No, sir."

"Call back in five minutes."

If it was about Bester, he needed to be a little more alert than this.

He went to the bathroom, splashed some water on his face, and looked in the mirror. There he saw the same handsome guy who had been looking at him for fifty-odd years. Some grey in the eyebrows and beard, sure. But he didn't look hung over.

Racquetball. That was it, wasn't it? Jeez, was he *that* old, *that* out of shape, that a game of racquetball against some twenty-five-year-old punk left him feeling like he'd been on a two-week bender?

That was almost more depressing than the prospect that he was in the bottom of a bottle again.

Almost.

He got a cup of coffee and settled down in front of the link. Hendershot called back, right on time.

"Tell me you got him," Garibaldi said.

"Sorry, boss."

"He wasn't at his asteroid hidey-hole? I paid damned good money for that information."

"Oh, we think he was there. An EABI transport— Metasensory Division—went out there on your tip. Their last transmission was that they had him. Then nothing. And the transponder in the transport went quiet."

"No!" Garibaldi exploded. "Who the hell did they send out there, the three stooges?"

"Sir?"

"Nothing. We should have known better than to trust the Bureau, especially their telepaths. We should have sent our own team. Hell, I should have gone myself."

"We didn't have anyone in the area. By the time we could have got there—"

"Yeah, yeah. I just don't trust them. Half the people in the Metasensory Division were folded in from the old Psi Corps."

"From the side that split against Bester. Nobody wants Bester more than they do."

"Nobody? Nobody? Man, you don't know *me* very well, do you? Hendershot, Bester *trained* most of those guys who are chasing him. He knows everything about them, and I don't doubt he still has men on the inside. I don't doubt it for a second. Old Psi Corps, no Psi Corps, rotten-to-the-Corps— you can't trust telepaths, not when it comes to one of their own." He put his head in his hands and smoothed back hair that wasn't there. It had been receding since he was twenty and he had finally figured, why wait? Beat it to the punch. Now he had almost grown into it.

Yep, he was getting old, like it or not. Which meant Bester was older. The thought that that son of a bitch might die in his sleep was the worst thing he could imagine. He could almost hear the Psi Cop's triumphant, cynical last laugh.

"Listen, Hendershot. I've had it with playing coyote to this guy's roadrunner. I run one of the ten wealthiest corporations on Mars, and I don't ask for much. But—I—want—Bester. Make me happy."

"I understand."

"And next time, I want to *be* there, *capisce*? No more tips to the Psi Corps hunt squads or whatever nicey-nice name they've given them now. Surface cooperation, yeah—they can still be useful. But I want to be two steps ahead of 'em, which oughta put me only two steps behind Bester."

"Yes, sir."

Garibaldi closed the link and stretched. Tortured, feverish muscles complained.

Bester!

The trick was not to be even one step behind your quarry. The trick was to figure out where he was going, and be one step ahead. To do that, you had to know what he wanted.

He stood and went to the window, opened the metal shield so he could see the beautiful, stark landscape of Mars. The sun stood just above the horizon, throwing all of the shadows on the plain toward him.

"What do you want, Bester?" he asked, gazing at the still-dark sky. "What do you want?"

part i

Homecoming

— *chapter 1* —

"I want to go home," Bester said. "I'm tired."

He took a sip of the red wine, resisted making a face, and set the crystal flute back on the stand next to his chair. He managed a smile for his host, a narrow-faced woman with ebony skin and a barely managed shock of gunmetal hair. Her eyes widened.

"Mars? Mr. Bester, I don't think—"

"Not Mars. Earth."

"Earth? Even worse. Mr. Bester, you're wanted on every world and station in Human space, and on quite a few beyond. To return to Earth itself would be—"

"Unexpected," Bester finished. "It's how I survive, always doing what no one expects. They've done their best, tried every trick in the book, but I *wrote* the book. Still, I'm sick of all this. I've never been able to stay on a colony world for more than a year or two. How can I? In a population of hundreds or thousands, I tend to stand out. But Earth has billions. It's easier to hide in a crowd."

"Yes, but things are more *lax* in the colonies, too, Mr. Bester. Earth! The risk of getting you there—of forging the necessary papers, of passing you through quarantine—phenomenal!"

"What quarantine? The Drakh plague is gone."

"Oh, indeed. And EarthGov has no intention of letting another one slip through, intentionally or accidentally. Traffic to ancient and little-known worlds has increased tenfold in the wake of the *Excalibur*'s explorations. Public opinion and a lot of scientists claim it's a disaster just waiting to happen."

"Fine. So I'll go through a screening. What of it?"

"They'll discover you're a teep. They'll have your DNA—everything they need to identify you. You think all off-world teeps aren't compared to the tribunal lists?"

"I am confident of your ability to manage it, Sophie."

"Mr. Bester—the risk isn't just to yourself."

"Oh, that I understand, Sophie. If I'm caught, I doubt I can stop them from finding out whatever they want to. I would never turn in an associate, but they have ways. Yes, if I'm caught, I doubt very much that I shall stand trial alone.

"You and I know that everything we did was justified, but in any conflict, the winners have the privilege of writing its history. We did not win, you and I, and history does not look kindly on us."

"Are you threatening me, Mr. Bester? That isn't very gracious, considering all I've done for you. And as *you* know, I am not wanted by the tribunal. Unlike yourself, I didn't commit any acts that can be construed as war crimes."

Bester broadened his smile a bit. "Ah, truth," he said, taking his glass and studying the play of light in the burgundy fluid. "It's all so . . . relative. Once I was a patriot, an example of everything that was good about the Corps. Now they say I am the most terrible criminal who ever lived. And who better than me to tell them who the other criminals were? After all, I was the evil mastermind."

"You wouldn't."

"Sophie, I want to go to Earth. Get me there with a secure identity. Get me through or around this quarantine. I'm asking nicely, right now. But as I said, I'm weary, and cranky, and I'm tired of cheap off-world wine. Once I'm there, I doubt very much that you will see or hear from me ever again. Oh, the occasional postcard, maybe . . ."

He thought she would relent there, but she went for another round. "I've heard you still have the black ships," she said. "The ones EarthGov and the Corps couldn't admit existed. What about them?"

"Your information is a little outdated," Bester countered coldly. Then he softened his voice. "Sophie, you were a good intern. And I was good to *you*, wasn't I? Wasn't I there for you when things got tough at Kerf?"

Her eyes darted about, like those of an animal seeking escape. But there wasn't any, not from him, and she knew it.

"Very well," she said at last. "I'll do what I can."

"I knew you'd see things my way."

"Mr. Bester, you have a way of making certain there's no other way to see them."

He nodded condescendingly. "Another thing," he said as he rose. "I'll need a supply of choline ribosylase—untraceable, of course."

Her face suddenly transfigured, and he felt a hint of pity. "I'm sorry," she said. "I didn't know."

"Save your sympathy for someone who needs it, Sophie," he replied, more brusquely than he intended.

Not much later he retired to his room, but found that he wasn't tired enough for sleep. He decided to take a walk. After all, he had never been to the Maui colony, and if things went well he would never be back.

He selected a suit of black silk twill and a caudric shirt the same color, fastening the top button with a brass-colored over-cap. He studied himself for a moment in the floor-length mirror. His hair was almost white, as was his beard, though his eyebrows still kept a reddish brown tinge. His face seemed to have more lines each time he looked at it, but all in all he looked pretty good for a man of eighty-two.

Except for his hands, which jarred him every time. Pink, gloveless—naked. He flexed his right hand, the good one. When he was a teenager, he'd had nightmares now and then that he was out in public, without his gloves.

Telepaths didn't wear gloves anymore, so he couldn't either, not without being noticed. It made him feel dirty.

But, he mused, one adapted.

A few moments later he stepped from Sophie Herndon's rambling abode onto a quiet street. A few natives were out walking, too. The air was cool but not cold, very pleasant except for the faint smell of the sea—fishy, but subtly different from any ocean on Earth. Maui was mostly water—from space you couldn't really see anything else. From what he had seen of it, it was rather charming. It had character.

The original settlers had been mostly Polynesian romantics, bent on recapturing a lost past. Of course you couldn't really do that. And children rarely inherited their parents' infatuations, especially when it meant living in grass houses on a planet somewhat chillier, even at the equator, than Earth.

Still, the architecture had certain South Sea touches, and the streetlamps resembled paper lanterns made in fanciful shapes, a legacy of the second wave of mostly Chinese immigrants. The people seemed pleasant enough and minded their business. Not a bad place to settle for a while. Until they found him again.

Maybe Sophie was right. Maybe going to Earth was too dangerous.

The street took him to a dockside stretch, and as he walked up that, he felt the tickle of minds around him. Somewhere near, tentative lovers were embracing. A man on a boat was silently cursing his mangled nets. An old woman was remembering that the nights had been warmer when she was a girl.

He smelled something cooking, and his stomach reminded him he hadn't eaten in a while. The lights of a restaurant appeared ahead, welcoming, and on impulse he entered. Inside, it was warmer, in temperature and in mood. The walls were of polished, reddish wood—or, no, maybe coral, or whatever passed for it here. Candlelight provided the only illumination.

A girl at the door asked him to remove his shoes and showed him to a long, low table with mats on either side—no chairs. He sat cross-legged, an act his bones protested a bit. There were others farther down the table, who nodded at him as he sat. He nodded back.

The girl brought him a sweet, mildly alcoholic drink that tasted like sake with a green-tea aftertaste. It wasn't bad, so he took a few sips.

"Something to eat?" she asked, in lilting Anglic.

"Please," he replied. "Whatever's good."

She nodded and left, but returned a few moments later with a young man, whom she seated across from him.

He figured it was probably the custom here to seat together strangers who came in alone. But he wanted to be by himself. He smiled at the young fellow, and was just about to say so, when all the hairs on the back of his neck prickled up.

The man was wearing a Psi Corps badge.

No, that wasn't right. It looked like the old badge, but there was no Psi Corps anymore. This badge merely identified a telepath who was working professionally within some other organization.

"I—ah—guess this is how they do it here," the fellow said hesitantly. He couldn't be more than twenty, a square-faced boy with auburn hair and an infectious smile. He was wearing an EarthForce uniform. Bester felt nothing alarming in his surface thoughts. Could this be a coincidence? He didn't really believe it. Carefully, carefully, he tightened his blocks while at the same time extending his senses.

"My name is Derrick Thompson," the fellow offered.

"Nice to meet you," Bester replied. "I'm Fred Tozzer."

"It's good to meet you, Mr. Tozzer. Are you a native?"

Still not even a whiff of deception. It would take more than a P12 to hide that from him. "No, actually," he replied. "I'm a tourist."

"Where from?"

"Oh, Mars originally, but I suppose you could call me a citizen of the galaxy. I've traveled all of my life, and now that I'm retired, I find that I can't break the habit."

"What brought you to Maui?"

"Oh, I heard the fish was good."

Derrick laughed politely.

"And you? I assume you aren't from around here."

"Nope. Earth, Kansas City. You might have guessed from my uniform that I'm in EarthForce. I'm stationed here, on the base at Bue Atoll. Right now I'm on leave and thought I'd take in the sights."

"You must be pretty disappointed to be seated with an old man rather than a young girl. And me not even a local."

He shrugged. "I have a girl already, so this'll keep me out of trouble. I—ah—saw you staring at my psi badge. Telepaths don't make you uncomfortable, do they? I won't take offense if you want me to sit elsewhere."

"No, not at all, it's just—well, I'm an old man. I'm not used to seeing that badge on that uniform. And I haven't been back to Earth since before the—crisis, did they call it?"

"Yep. Well, things are different now. Better. Before the crisis there were a lot of things we weren't allowed to do. Be in EarthForce, for instance. Now the world is wide open."

The waitress arrived with their food, one big bowl and two small plates.

"That looks like boiled shrimp," Al said.

"It is. They farm it off the coast."

"I was hoping for something native."

Derrick smiled. "You want a bowl of plankton? The native life is all microscopic. Anything big enough to see came from somewhere else. But you'll find the shrimp has a unique taste, since they feed on the native stuff."

Al tried one. It *was* unique, if not exactly good. A bit sulfury, like the yolk of a boiled egg.

Derrick smiled at his expression. "Takes a little getting used to. How long are you staying?"

"A few days."

"And where next?"

"I'm not really sure. Just playing it by ear."

"Well, that must be the life." He lifted his cup. "To seeing the universe."

Bester raised his cup. They clinked and drank.

As the night wore on, Derrick and Bester talked of the places they had been and the things they had seen. Bester had more stories, of course, and Derrick listened with fascination. Bester kept buying the younger man drinks but sipping his own, so that by the time the place closed, Derrick was more than a little tipsy. They left together, ostensibly to find someplace that was still open.

Derrick stopped outside, stood swaying slightly and looking at the stars. "Not a single famil'r constellation," he murmured. " 'S the way I like it. Like you, huh? I guess we're two of a kind."

"Actually," Bester said, "I wouldn't mind seeing the Big Dipper again. It's been a while."

Derrick didn't seem to notice the remark. They continued up the dockside walk.

"Y'know," Derrick said, "I have to tell you, you seem awfully familiar to me. Like maybe we've met before. What's that called? Déjà you?" He chuckled at his own joke.

"No, it just means you've seen my picture. I'm really Alfred Bester, the notorious war criminal."

Derrick laughed at that, then became serious. "That's not funny, really. Bester is the worst of the worst, everything that was bad about the old Psi Corps—" He stopped, suddenly, eyes widening as he turned to look at Bester.

"Oh, shit! You *are* him."

Bester nodded sadly and struck hard and fast, blowing through the young man's drink-deadened guards as if they weren't there. Derrick collapsed, and Bester dragged his limp form to a nearby bench. A man and woman, walking some thirty feet behind them, stopped.

"Is he okay?"

"He'll be fine. He's had a touch too much to drink."

"Can you manage him?"

Bester smiled. "It's the story of my life. I'm always the baby-sitter. But thanks for your concern."

The two walked on, seemingly satisfied.

When they were gone, Bester went to work, snipping out the parts of Derrick's memory that included him. But he didn't erase them. Instead, he walled them up, buried them. In time, the memories would return—first Bester's face, then their conversation. And in that, as carefully as one might set down a bird's egg in a pile of glass shards, he placed a destination. When he was certain everything was right, he called a cab and had Derrick taken to his hotel.

In a week or so, Derrick would remember he had been attacked, and like a good little soldier he would have himself scanned so his brave new Corps could learn all of the facts.

One thing they would learn was that Bester was headed out of
Human space altogether, things finally having got too hot for
him. It amused him to think of the hunters, certain that in his
old age Bester had finally slipped up.

He went back to Sophie's house, pleased with himself. He
could still find the opportunity in any situation. And now he
was sure—he had what it took. Dangerous or not, he was
going home.

— *chapter 2* —

"Ah—Paris in spring," Bester said to the cab driver. He meant for it to sound cynical, and maybe it did, but to his own surprise, he didn't feel that way. It *was* lovely, the green track along the Champs-Élysées, the blossoms and golden sunlight, and the sky of that peculiar blue that—impossibly—didn't exist anywhere else on Earth, much less on any other planet.

But what made Earth home was its smell. Spaceships and stations, no matter how much they strove to duplicate planetary atmospheres, always smelled like the inside of a can. Planets each had their own peculiar complex of scents—different incidental gases that mixed in different proportions.

Scent was the most primal and least intellectual of the senses, triggering instincts older than the Human race as inexorably as it did childhood memories. A whiff could bring back a buried memory more vividly than could any other sense. That had been a useful thing for him to know, as a Psi Cop.

Yes, Paris smelled like Earth, and it smelled like Paris. Suddenly he was fifteen again, seeing, smelling, *feeling* the city through the astonishment and wonder of the boy he had been, so long ago.

It felt almost like happiness.

The cabbie, however, was unimpeded by such sentiment. He had caught Bester's original intent.

"Ah, yes, the spring. When great flocks of silly birds descend on the city with their cameras and their 'which-way-is-this' and their *'je-ne-comprends-pas.'* My favorite time of year, to be sure."

21

"I would think it a lucrative time of year."

"Yes, yes. I make lots of money. But when should I spend it? When should I enjoy it? In the dreary months, when no one wants to come here? When I am old enough to retire?"

"Yes, I can see you've drawn a very sorry lot in life," Bester said. "But at least you have a ready audience to inflict your angst on, whenever you choose."

"You are offended by my opinions? Monsieur, there is quick relief for that. I can put you out here, on this sidewalk—"

"Yes, why don't you do that."

The driver's mouth dropped open for a second. "Monsieur? We are still very far from your hotel."

"I know the city—well enough to know you're taking a somewhat roundabout route. I prefer to walk."

"Very well."

They were only a block or so from the Place de la Concorde. Bester paid the cabbie with his forged chit and got out. The cabbie drove off, complaining loudly to himself about crazy tourists.

Bester took a deep breath. He had only a small shoulder bag that contained his forged documents and a hand computer. His only clothes were a black leather jacket, black gabardine slacks, and a yellowish brown shirt.

He felt—free.

He started walking, back up the Champs-Élysées, toward the Arc de Triomphe. He had made reservations at a hotel, but suddenly he didn't particularly care if he went there or not. It was morning, and the whole day lay before him.

There was a sense he had not indulged in yet, the best of all. He found a bench lightly shaded by trees, then closed his eyes.

And felt the mind of the city. It was in Paris, as a boy, that he had made an important discovery. Each city, he discovered, has its own psionic fingerprint, a combination of thoughts and conversations and interactions of all of its citizens, emerging into something as distinct and complex as a fine vintage of wine.

He recognized it. An odd thing, really—how many people living in the city today had been alive when he was fifteen? Not many. And yet it was the same, as if the city were a Human body, retaining continuity and integrity even though the individual cells that had made it up one year before were mostly dead and replaced.

Oh, it was a bit different, the mind of Paris. Somehow, inexplicably more vital, more alive than ever. Younger.

He started walking again, and vaguely heard someone whistling. He had gone fifteen steps before he realized that the whistling was coming from him.

Now, this is going too far, he thought. *I can't lose all my perspective, not if I want to survive.*

Nonetheless, a few minutes later he was whistling again.

He stopped at a crepe shop and got one of the pancakelike desserts filled with hazelnut paste. He felt very much like a tourist, but he didn't really care. He topped the snack with espresso, and then continued on.

Hemlines were up, he noted—way up. He seemed to remember reading somewhere that that tended to happen after wars and crises, and humanity had certainly had plenty of those lately. Clothing in general was flashier, more colorful than he remembered. The stereotypical Parisian beret, rare when he had last been here, seemed ubiquitous, though he suspected those who were wearing them were mostly tourists, or those pandering to the tourist trade.

He had the same skepticism about the antique feel of the city—that it was tourist-driven. Oh, Earth in general, and Paris in particular, were conservative, in terms of technology. But Paris actually seemed to have stepped backward in time since he had visited it last. One had to concentrate to see what was being hidden—the phones and personal computers woven invisibly into shirt collars, the electronic-ink displays in shop windows that mimicked disposable paper signs, the police hovercraft that looked like groundcars until they almost apologetically took to the sky.

He wondered if the pretense was some gestalt decision on

the part of Parisians or more specifically the result of legislation. If the latter, it wouldn't be the first time that well-
meaning laws had been passed to make sure Paris remained
Paris. As if it could ever be anything else. He imagined the
city snickering at such efforts.

He left the broad avenue and wandered deeper into the
heart of the city, gradually working uphill toward the Sacré
Coeur. By midday he found himself in the Pigalle, which had
once been the red-light district and still had something of its
old reputation. Here, where few tourists went, was found the
real life of the city. He passed a small, run-down café where
two grizzled old men were playing checkers. Children, just
out of school, playing soccer, reluctantly parted to let the occasional delivery truck through narrow streets—some still
cobblestone—bordered by brick buildings pitted by centuries
of rain.

The residents of the Pigalle were a genetic cross section of
Earth. For centuries, immigrants from every corner of the
globe had settled in Paris, and Paris, in her own inexorable
way, had made them Parisian. They always seemed in a hurry.
They walked with shoulders square, arms close to the body
and usually in front of them, their faces masks of neutrality.
But just when you were tempted to think of them as automa-
tons, someone would explode in a burst of laughter, or hurl a
stream of obscenities at a car that had come too close, or stop
to scold a child.

He was starting to think about supper when he turned a
corner and was greeted by shouting. A woman stood in front
of a small hotel—the Hotel Marceau. She was petite, perhaps
thirty-five, with pale skin and curly brown hair chopped just
below her ears. Her stance was defiant, one hand on her hip
and the other shaking in front of her as a fist.

Her voice was defiant, too. She apparently didn't go in for
the short skirts of the day—she wore denim pants and a T-shirt.

"—not another cent from me, you hear? Five customers
you've chased away from me this week. You say I must pay to
protect my business. But when I pay, you ruin it anyway."

For all of her defiance, Bester could feel fear beneath the

surface. It was no mystery where that came from. She was shouting at five men, most teenagers, but one of them was an older brute who bore a massive scar on one cheek, a crooked nose, and putty-pale skin. He leveled a thick finger at her.

"You *pay* us because I say to. And I'll tell you another thing—I'm used to better treatment than this from my friends. You *are* my friend, aren't you, *cherie*? Because now that I think about it, you haven't been all that friendly to me."

Bester couldn't help it—he uttered a single, dark laugh. He had seen death and deceit on a cosmic scale, waged wars of empire, battled alien races that possessed godlike powers. Watching these stupid normals, fighting over their little scrap of turf, struck him as unutterably ridiculous.

His laugh got their attention.

"What the hell are *you* laughing at?" the big fellow grunted.

Bester shook his head and kept walking. The question wasn't worth answering. If they didn't understand how absurd they were, they wouldn't notice it just because he pointed it out.

"Yeah, that's right, old man," the fellow called. "You just keep on walking. Nothing to see here."

Bester was planning on doing just that. For a few short hours he had forgotten how much he hated normals, but his mood had done an about-face. Now he remembered. The woman was stupid for standing up to men she had no power against, and if they beat her, or raped her, or killed her, it would make no difference to him. Or to the world at large. If she had been a teep, then he might have helped.

Though given what the rogues and the new-and-improved Psi Corps had done to him, he didn't particularly care for his own kind, either. All his life he had worked for his people, his telepaths. He had saved them more times than they knew, yet in the end they had turned against him, pitched in with *normals*.

He was a man without a people, now—orphaned, divorced, exiled. Maybe that was why he had felt so free. He no longer felt the slightest responsibility to anyone or anything except himself.

And none at all to this stupid woman.

Still, he paused, to see what would happen. It was like watching a train wreck.

The bravos had turned their attention back to her, though one of the younger ones noticed he had stopped, and was glaring at him.

"Be a smart girl, Louise. Pay me my money."

"Or what? Are all of you big brave men going to beat me up? Tear up a few of my rooms? Go ahead, then. I can't stop you. You can take, but I won't *give* you anything anymore."

"That mouth you got ain't doin' you any favors," the man warned. "Best you put it to some better use. I got some ideas about that—"

"When Mars has oceans."

"Ooh!" one of the younger boys said. "She told you, I think."

The big man turned on his smaller companion. "Shut up," he demanded, and then he noticed Bester, still watching. "I thought I told you to keep walking, you old scab."

"The zoo was closed today," Bester replied. "I didn't get to see the ape house, so I'm making do."

The big man blinked as if he didn't understand, then strode menacingly toward Bester. "You ain't from around here, I don't think. 'Cause if you were, you wouldn't still be standing there. And you sure as hell wouldn't be mouthing off to me."

Bester smiled. "Please know, I find you *truly* terrifying. The fact that it only takes five of you to threaten such a dangerous young woman—well, it puts me in awe. I wouldn't dream of crossing you."

The man grabbed him by the collar and lifted, his face reddening. Bester glanced down at the fist knotted in his shirt. "That's expensive material," he said, calmly.

The man pulled back his other fist, and Bester watched it, unblinking. He could kill the fellow, of course, without lifting a finger, but not without arousing suspicion. Still . . .

"Put him down, Jem," a new voice said. "Put him down right now."

Bester couldn't see who was talking. Jem could, however, and his face set in a sort of sullen resignation. He hesitated for a moment, then lowered Bester back to the street.

"There ain't nothin' goin' on here, Lucien," he grunted. "Not a damn thing."

"I'll be the judge of that."

Al turned slightly, so that he could see that the new voice belonged to a policeman, a stocky fellow in his early forties.

"Have you got a complaint?" the policeman asked Bester.

Bester smiled at Jem, then turned back to the policeman. "Yes. This man doesn't smell good at all. Other than that, everything is just fine."

The cop looked him up and down, made a disgusted noise. "Louise?" he asked.

She hesitated for a moment. "No," she said.

"See?" Jem said. "So why don't you go bother someone else?"

"Why don't you?" the policeman said. "Run along."

Jem glared at him, then shrugged. "Come on, boys. We've got business elsewhere, anyhow." He directed a nasty look at Bester. "Nice to meet you, grandpa," he said. "Too bad you're just passing through."

"It is a shame," Bester agreed. "I'll miss your stimulating conversation."

As he watched them leave, he sent out tendrils of psi, just enough to know their signatures, to recognize them in the dark.

The cop, meanwhile, was confronting the woman.

"Louise, I can't do anything for you unless you make an accusation."

"You know I can't do that, Lucien. I have to live here. And suppose you managed to arrest Jem and his bunch and keep them—not that I think you could, but just suppose. Another bunch would just move in, and they would take care of me in advance, so I wouldn't repeat my mistake with them."

"Then pay them what they ask. Otherwise—well—I can't be here twenty-four hours a day."

"I know that, Lucien," she said.

"Though I could be here more than I am," he hinted.

"I know that, too." She sighed. "You know I'm grateful, Lucien, but I'm just not—"

She suddenly noticed that Bester was still there. "What are you waiting for? Do you want some of my money, too?"

"No."

"I don't know who you are, but you shouldn't have gotten involved. They're like sharks, those men. A little blood and then the frenzy. Why you want to commit suicide, I don't know, but go do it someplace else."

Bester shrugged.

"Listen," the cop said to him. "You could help, here. I know Jem was attacking you. Louise is being stubborn, but *you* don't live around here. If you could swear out a complaint, I could get these guys off of the street. I think you were trying to help Louise, but if you really want to help—"

"I had no intention of helping her," Bester said. "I was just walking around, looking for a place to stay. This is a hotel, and I was looking at it. The gentleman in question simply mistook what I was interested in. You don't really think an old man like me thought he could handle those fellows, do you?"

The cop cocked his head skeptically. "You didn't look too worried to me."

"I don't worry much, anymore. I've discovered that the universe dumps on you when it wants to. Being upset about it doesn't help a bit."

The cop rolled his eyes in disgust, but Louise quirked a reluctant little smile.

"Have it your way, then," the officer said. "Louise, I'll see you later. Alive, I hope."

"Good-bye, Lucien."

Bester took that as his sign to leave as well, but he hadn't turned the corner when Louise's voice floated after him. "It's ten credits a night, or five a day if you plan to stay for more than a week."

He turned, slowly, really looked at the hotel for the first time. It had a small café—just a room with a few tables and chairs, it seemed—and three stories. The building looked nineteenth-century, maybe early twentieth.

"Does that include meals?" he asked.

"Meals are a credit extra, and you can't complain about what I make."

He walked a few steps toward her. He was, after all, feeling tired, and his juvenile buoyancy of an hour earlier had defiantly reversed itself.

The Alfred Bester hunters were combing the universe to find a man who liked the finest things. The apartments he had abandoned were spacious, capaciously furnished with art, provisioned with good wine and brandy. Who would ever think to look for him in a crumbling hotel in the Pigalle?

"May I see the room first?" he asked.

— chapter 3 —

Bester passed a forkful of chicken étouffée to his mouth and chewed. He sensed someone watching him, and glanced around.

It was the hotel owner, Louise. "Well?" she asked. "How is it?"

They were alone in the little dining room, though a young couple had been there when he arrived. Business did not seem brisk.

"I can't complain," he replied.

She nodded. "It's one of my better dishes."

"No—I mean I can't complain. You told me so this afternoon."

She folded her arms and looked down at him. "You don't like it?" she asked.

"I certainly didn't say that."

"What's wrong with it?"

He looked up at her with his "thinking cap" face. "Well—I'm not complaining, mind you—but for chicken I might have made the roux a shade or two lighter. And I would have chopped the onions much finer."

"I see."

"But I'm *not* complaining," he said, eating another bite.

She looked at him severely for a second or two. "You didn't tell me how long you're staying," she said at last.

"Oh, at least a week. Maybe more."

"Very well. But if you stay only six days, I will charge you the ten credits a night, you understand?"

"Perfectly," Al replied.

"Well . . . well," she finished, and went back into the kitchen. A second later, she popped back out. "And don't blame me if Jem and his gang come back and give you a beating. You saw what the situation is. You understand?"

"Yes," Bester replied again, wondering when she would leave him alone to finish his meal in peace.

"Good." This time she stayed in the kitchen. He could hear the pots and pans banging around as she did dishes. Did she really work here all alone?

Outside, the streets faded to purple, and then the lights came on, puddles of yellow in the dark.

What was he doing here? What was he going to do? Given medical technology and his own good health, he could easily live another thirty years—a small lifetime. He had planned to spend those years guiding the Corps toward its destiny, mentoring younger telepaths, righting all of the wrongs that had plagued his kind. He'd had a mission, and certainty, and had never considered retiring.

For the past several years, running had taken the place of his mission, but he could only run so long. If this worked—if he managed to hide here on Earth, indefinitely—he had to find something to do, or he'd go crazy. But what?

His papers said he was a businessman, a midlevel sales manager for an engine coolant manufacturer that had gone belly-up during the Drakh crisis. Pretty obscure, and he had been briefed about his fictional job, but seeking a similar position was out of the question. First, because he didn't want to be a salesman; second, because any check of his references was unacceptably risky.

So what to do?

He picked at the chicken. There was no hurry.

Sometimes Garibaldi thought his desk was too big. Any desk you could play regulation Ping-Pong on had to be too big, right? Especially on Mars, where every inch of space had to be paid for in oxygen, in power to heat it, in the cost of the dome that kept both of those in and the UV rays out.

Hell, his desk was bigger than the bedrooms in some low-rent housing.

Like many things, the desk had come with the office, a legacy of the late William Edgars. When Edgars had sat behind the desk, there had been almost nothing on it. It had been a stark reminder that he was a man with so much wealth, he could afford to pay for as much unutilized space as he cared to have.

Garibaldi could afford it, too, but he had grown up on Mars, taking one-minute showers and sleeping almost standing up. It irked him, that desk, but some perversity made him keep it, maybe as a reminder of where his power and wealth had come from, of what it could do to him if he wasn't careful. A bottle wasn't the only thing that could trap a soul. Of course, he had Lise to remind him of those things.

Lise, who had also come with the office.

Nope, he wasn't going there. That way lay, if not madness, at least stupidity. He'd behaved stupidly enough with Lise to lose five wives, and by some miracle she still loved him. Let *that* rover lie.

The desk. He had spent years filling it up with odds and ends. A bigger workstation, models of starships and motor-cycles, a Duck Dodgers helmet, a hologlobe of Mars. So now it was a big desk covered with junk, and whenever anyone he really wanted to talk to came in, he dragged himself out from behind it and sat on the front edge. He didn't like that distance between him and his friends, and he liked it even less between him and his opponents.

He wasn't sure which he was seeing today, but it didn't matter. He sat on the edge of the desk and watched him enter.

The fellow walked in—just a boy in EarthForce uniform, like so many Garibaldi had seen die. Except for the psi patch. That put everything out of kilter. A lot of things didn't work for him: mousse made out of fish, cats on a space station, zero-g synchronized tumbling, pink T-shirts—telepaths in EarthForce.

"Lieutenant Derrick Thompson, sir," the boy said.

"Don't call me sir," Garibaldi said. "This isn't the military, and I'm not in the chain of command."

"What should I call you then?" Thompson asked.

"Oh, Lord Zeus or Mr. Garibaldi will do. Have a seat."

Thompson did, looking distinctly uncomfortable.

"You're wondering why you suddenly find yourself in my office, aren't you?"

"The thought had crossed my mind. If you'll pardon me, Mr. Garibaldi, you say you aren't in the chain of command, but I sort of wonder about that."

Garibaldi smiled tightly. "Let's just say I have a lot of friends—or people who like to think they're my friends—and leave it at that, okay?"

Thompson nodded.

"Let's get something right out in the open, Thompson. I don't trust you. Not that I don't want to—from your record you seem like a good kid, hardworking, disciplined, dedicated. No one you've served under has anything bad to say about you, which is surprising, and no one who has served *under* you has anything bad to say about you either, which is impossible.

"Now, I'm not a trusting sort of guy, though under ordinary circumstances I might turn my back on you now and then, for a second or two. But—I don't trust you. Bester has been in your head, and that makes you a threat. And I think I can say with confidence that EarthForce sees it that way, too. You can stay in fifty years and you'll still be a lieutenant. They'll stick you behind a desk and quietly hope you go away."

Thompson's face went almost the color of his hair, brick red. "You think I don't know that, s—*Mr*. Garibaldi? You think I wanted this to happen to me?"

"I want to know why you didn't recognize Bester. You went to the academy, when you were a kid."

"Mr. Garibaldi, I went in when I manifested, when I was twelve. In those days there wasn't much of a choice. It was only three years later that the crisis changed things. I never met Mr. Bester during that time."

"You never saw a picture of him? You couldn't sense that he was a telepath?"

"Sure, I saw pictures of him—I even thought he was a little familiar looking when I met him. But he had a beard, and he wasn't in uniform, and—I just wasn't expecting to meet a war criminal on leave on Maui. It's a big universe, Mr. Garibaldi, and if you move around in it, you see people you think are other people, you know that. And he didn't *act* like a monster. He was funny. He seemed like a nice guy."

"Until he cored out your mind."

Thompson nodded miserably. "But he didn't do a perfect job. I started remembering, and the second I did, I authorized recovery scans. Those *hurt*, Mr. Garibaldi, especially when someone of Bester's power puts guards in against scans."

"Yeah, I'm sure it did hurt. But see, here's the part I can't figure out, the part maybe you can help me with. Bester is evil. No argument from me there. He's probably one of the five most evil sons of bitches in the last two centuries. He's cold, and manipulative, and he has no more soul than the Great Whoozits gave a piranha. But what he *isn't*, is sloppy. If he thought you were a threat he would have killed you, or burned your brain into a fraggin' pile of slag. He wouldn't have done the half-ass job he did on you unless he had a reason to."

"Maybe he didn't have time. Or maybe he's getting old. There were rumors he was nearly killed during the telepath crisis, that he lost the use of most of his power."

"Yeah? A rumor and two credits will get you a cup of coffee. I don't believe it—I know some of the things he's done since then. And I don't believe he screwed up on you. Now, I know you're awfully concerned about what I *do* think, aren't you?"

"Sure."

"I think that you are, *one*—" he held up his index finger "—a Trojan horse. Everyone thinks you're fine and then one day, blam, you kill Sheridan or somebody."

"Mr. Garibaldi . . ."

"Or, *two*—" he ticked off another finger "—you're a false

lead. After all, you had information that pointed toward his destination, right?"

"Yes, sir. Apparently I *did* fight him . . ."

"Uh-huh. Like I said, if he had the slightest worry that you could ever point a finger in his general direction, you'd be taking a dirt nap about now. See, I don't trust you, but I do trust Bester. He thinks things through. So why are you alive and functioning?"

"Are you accusing me of something, Mr. Garibaldi?"

"I dunno. Do you feel accused?"

"If you'll pardon me, Mr. Garibaldi, I don't think you have any damned idea what you're talking about. You don't know what I've gone through, and—"

"Don't I? Bester got in my head, screwed with my mind. Made me betray my best friend, almost ruined my life. After all these years I still don't trust *me*, Lieutenant."

Thompson's mouth dropped open, then closed. "I didn't know," he said.

"I don't advertise it," Garibaldi said. "But maybe you understand, now, why you're in my office."

"No, actually, I don't. You have a grudge against Bester. You think he let me live to deliver a lie, to lay a false trail. You seem pretty convinced of it, and you're even implying I may have cooperated in the whole thing. You seem to have all of the answers, Mr. Garibaldi. So what do you want with me?"

Garibaldi scooted back on the desk and put his hands on his thighs. "Well, I figure it this way. If you're on the up-and-up, you may have it in for Bester almost as much as I do. He messed with your head and ruined the life you'd picked out for yourself. In that case, I can use you.

"You were the last person known to have contact with him, and you're a telepath. You might recognize his psychic imprint or whatever. Did I mention I don't trust telepaths? I don't. Especially not the ones in the Metasensory Division, which you aren't, and that puts you a little ahead in my book. On the other hand, if you are one of Bester's pals, or if he's put some kinda sleeper program in you that the monitors didn't catch, I'd rather have you right here where I can watch you."

"Are you offering me a job, Mr. Garibaldi?"

"You catch on pretty fast, Thompson. I like that. Yeah, I want to offer you a job. And I want my own team to look you over—they won't dissect you or anything, but I want you examined."

Thompson shook his head, slowly. "You're a very confusing man, Mr. Garibaldi."

"I try to keep it that way," Garibaldi replied.

Bester watched his enemies gather, and smiled coldly to himself. This was where it ended, this ridiculous war. This was where he paid them back.

"Proud of yourself?"

Bester jerked out his PPG and spun toward the voice.

"Byron! You're—"

"Dead?" The younger man's eyes were contradictions. Sad, compassionate, but at the same time sharp and condemning. Bester hated them.

He noticed, as always, the ghostly flames licking up around his one-time student.

"Truth doesn't die, Bester."

But Bester's pounding heart was calming. "You aren't the truth," he said. "You're just the memory of a ghost, an imprint in my brain."

"Yes. When I died—"

"Killed yourself."

"When I died, you reached out to me, to try to stop me. It was touching, in death, to know how much you cared. And it allowed me to leave you this little gift, this piece of me, like an angel on your shoulder, like the conscience you never had."

"You always were self-important, Byron—but imagining yourself an angel? You started the war, set telepath to fighting telepath. You began the slaughter when you killed yourself, and neatly ducked out of responsibility at the same time. Coward."

"You could have given us what we wanted. Freedom. Our own Homeworld."

"Oh, yes, your little telepath's paradise, your imaginary Nirvana where you would all live in peace and harmony with your chanting and your candles. A place where the mundanes would *never* bother you, never become suspicious or worried about you. Your fantasy was the ultimate capitulation to the normals, Byron, the ultimate act of cowardice. Earth was our birthplace. It was always meant to be ours, one day. The normals have been trying to kill us from the beginning—from the first pogroms when our kind were discovered, to Edgars' scheme a few years ago. Do you think they'd like anything better than to have us all in one place? Do you think they could tolerate the idea of a planet full of telepaths?"

"This is what I think," Byron said. "I think you did such terrible things in your life, in the name of the Corps, that you couldn't see any other way without losing your mind. Now that I'm part of you, that's clearer than ever. What was the girl's name—Montoya? Your first love?"

"Leave her out of this."

"But you loved her. I can see it in you, the space where love was, the fossil of it. And you turned her in."

"She was going rogue. It was my duty. I'm not going to defend myself to you."

Byron laughed. "But I'm *not* me, am I? I'm you, or part of you. You said so yourself." He cocked his head. "Why didn't you ever have me removed? It would have been a simple matter."

"Shut up."

"Maybe you think you need me, since you have no heart of your own. To help you feel the guilt."

"I feel no guilt. I only did what I had to do. You were the one who divided us, who made me—" He broke off.

"Made you kill your own kind? The Corps is mother, the Corps is father. You always thought of us as your children. And yet you slaughtered telepaths, tortured them. You made the reeducation camps into killing fields . . ."

"You did that," Bester said. "Until you, I never understood how diseased the rogues had become. What you were planning would have destroyed us all. What you did accomplish *will* destroy us. It will be a slow death, by degrees. Psi Corps was always meant to be a tool for the normals, allowing them to control us.

"I fought to take that tool and turn it against them, to put the Corps in control of telepaths. I succeeded, finally, and you chose just that moment to make your grand play, your idiotic attempt to create paradise, just like every other self-deluded messiah with a mindless following. You could never see the big picture, the reality, that the normals are always waiting, waiting for us to relax, until our guard is down. They fear us as they fear no alien race, because we are them, only better. The next step in evolution. And you wrecked it all, gave it all back to them. They've won, thanks to you."

"Now who is a self-deluded messiah?"

"Do you know who backed your precious rebels after you died? Who funded them?"

"My love, Lyta."

"Lyta. For all her power, she was as much a fool as you were. A child given too big a gun. No, the man behind the rogues was a mundane—Garibaldi. A teep-hating bigot who got his fortune from another teep-hating bigot. To see us destroy ourselves must have given him terrible pleasure. You asked why I keep this little part of you alive? This is why. So you can see what you have wrought."

"So you can say I told you so."

"Yes."

"Petty."

"It's all that's left me. Everything I've ever worked for lies in ruins. A lifetime of accomplishment swept away. I always believed that if I had nothing else, I had my people, my telepaths. You took even that from me, Byron. Even that."

"So lie down and die, then."

"No. I'm not you. I am not a coward. I live with the consequences of my actions. And I *live*."

"Well, then, by all means—let's watch this."

"No. This is a dream. I can end it."

"No, you can't. You know that. Not until it's done."

"Let me go, Byron."

"I can be petty, too."

He tried to turn away, but the scene just followed him.

It would have been the masterstroke. It would have ended the rebellion, brought the rogues to their knees. Two hundred of his finest, his most loyal . . .

He could still hear their screams, still feel the terror of their obliteration, the awful snuffing of their lives, their very souls.

"You ran away," Byron said. "You found out, seconds before, and you ran away. You saved your own skin and let your men die."

"They were going to die anyway. There was nothing I could do."

"And you call *me* a coward."

"Shut up."

"Listen to them, Bester."

"Shut up!"

"Listen." Byron's eyes were holes, holes in a skull, and the flames were everywhere. Byron was Satan, surrounded by damned souls.

"Listen!" Byron was Bester, the cold face in the mirror, smiling without humor.

"Shut up!"

Then he awoke, with someone trying to kill him.

— chapter 4 —

Old instincts sent his hand darting for a PPG that wasn't
there, but even older ones collected a mental assault with
lightning speed. Sometimes the space between two breaths
meant life and death.

In this case, it was fortunate that between that first waking
gasp and the exhalation, he realized he wasn't under attack at
all, that it was Louise standing over him, a look of concern
fading from her face like Martian frost touched by first light.

"Monsieur Kaufman? Are you okay?"

For an instant he wondered who she was talking to, but
then everything snapped into focus. Claude Kaufman. That
was the name he had given.

"What are you doing in my room?" he asked.

"First of all, it is *my* room—you merely rent it. In the
second place, I heard you in here shouting as if you had seen a
Drakh. I thought you were in trouble—now I see it must have
merely been a bad dream."

"Yes," Bester confirmed. "A bad dream. I'm sorry, it was
just confusing, to wake and find you there, especially after
that nightmare."

"You have many nightmares?"

"I have my share."

"My father used to have nightmares," she said. "About the
war. The Earth-Minbari War."

"It's not the sort of thing you forget, war," Bester said,
dryly.

"No. I suppose it isn't." He noticed lances of pale gold

40

light shining through holes in the curtains, turning dust motes into tiny, furious suns. "What time is it?"

"Almost eleven o'clock."

"I've missed breakfast, then, haven't I?"

Her expression softened a bit. "I think I can find something for you, if you want to come down."

"I will, then. Thank you." He hesitated an instant. "Thank you for your concern."

"It is nothing," she replied. "Imagine the trouble I'd have if someone died in one of my rooms!"

"Ah, yes. Coroner's inquest, what to do with the body, cleaning up the mess. You have a way of making a man feel special, Ms. . . ."

"Bouet," she said, after a second's hesitation. He thought he caught another name, floating on her surface thoughts. Colis? A great deal of pain associated with that name. A name that was also a wound.

Much like his own.

"Where are you going?" Louise asked him after breakfast, as he made his way toward the front door.

"Just walking," he replied. "I haven't been in Paris for a long time. I'd like to see it again."

"How long?"

"More than twenty years."

"Oh. Does it seem to have changed, to you?"

"That's what I want to find out."

She hesitated. "Are you going anywhere in particular?" she asked.

"No. Why—do you need me to pick up something?"

"No, but I was going to the market this morning, and to a shop across town. I could use some help carrying things, if you have nothing better to do."

Bester studied her for a moment. Her face was neutral, but beneath he could sense that she felt sorry for him. She thought he was a lonely old man.

Well, so he was, but the pity galled him. Still, there was

also an undercurrent of truth. She wasn't lying, she could use help carrying groceries.

"Who will mind the hotel?"

"Francis—an employee of mine—will be by shortly, if you can wait."

"I'm in no hurry," Bester replied.

As promised, Francis—a gangly, teenaged boy with olive skin and black hair—arrived a few moments later, and Bester and Louise started out. She wore a checked blue-and-black skirt, ankle length, and a navy sweater over a white cotton shirt. He noticed, for the first time, that she was a little shorter than he.

He was at first distracted by the strained silence between them, but as they both became more comfortable with the fact that they weren't going to chat, he relaxed, and was surprised to find that, despite the events of the evening before and the ensuing dream, his sense of vitality had returned.

It didn't come so much from within as from without, from the bustling throngs they moved through. The removal of the Drakh plague had been a global reprieve from the gallows, and like a condemned man suddenly freed, humanity was full of joie de vivre, bursting with a sort of energy that he simply did not remember from his Earth-bound childhood or any subsequent visit.

And Louise was part of it. Oh, she was reserved, cautious, but as they walked along he felt the crackle of joy in her step, the pleasure she took in the air, the feel of the breeze, the scent wafting from a patisserie as they walked by. He tried not to listen, but her voice was as compelling as the city itself, not because it was simple, or pure, but because it was alloyed. It was the joy of someone who had known sorrow, but whose heart still worked.

They walked up the hill to the Sacré Coeur. As they reached the top, he noticed Louise was watching him, an odd expression on her face.

"A bit out of my way," Louise admitted, "but if you'd like to play the tourist . . ." She shrugged. He sensed that she felt she had been rude to him, and wanted to make it up. Pity, again.

"No need for that," Bester said. "We can just walk where you are going."

As they crossed the sightseer-packed square, a man—a street artist—practically leapt in front of him, sketchbook in hand.

"You have an interesting face," he said. "Surely you want a souvenir to remind you of your visit here." He was already sketching, his hand describing a series of arcs with his charcoal.

"Not today," Bester replied, and moved on.

"No, no, wait. You don't know how cheap this will be, practically nothing. And when you see how I have captured you . . ." He stopped, noticed Louise. "Oh, but of course— you would rather have a sketch of the lady?"

"No, of neither," Bester replied, still walking.

The man followed, his hand moving ceaselessly. "You'll thank me when I am done, monsieur, do not doubt it."

Bester wondered if he shouldn't give the fellow a little mental push. A sudden fear, nausea. He decided against it. Telepaths still had to be registered, and the last thing he wanted was to call that sort of attention to himself. He glanced at his naked hands ruefully. There had been a time when the mere sight of him and his gloves would spare him this sort of harassment.

"Look, he isn't going to pay you," Louise told the man. "We aren't tourists, and we know this game."

"Then I will keep it myself," the man said, defiantly.

Bester's heart skipped. He couldn't have *that*. There were plenty of other street artists on the square, and most of them displayed sample sketches. How many people walked through this square a day? Thousands? And of those thousands, how many *might* recognize Alfred Bester, with or without a beard?

So he was on the point of buying the drawing anyway. Strangely, however, Louise, who was still shooing the man, suddenly fell silent. She took the sketch from the fellow and looked at it for a moment. Then, still without speaking, she reached into a pocket and produced a credit.

"There," she said. "Now go away."

She took the picture and rolled it up. The artist walked off, a bit smugly. "I told you so," he called over his shoulder.

"Why did you do that?" Bester asked, as they continued on.

"I like the picture."

"I don't understand."

"I like to watch the sky," she said. "I like all sorts of skies. Pale, powdery blue, indigo near twilight, or laced up with clouds. But my favorite sky is one with black clouds, when— through the clouds, just for an instant—a crack of gold peeks through."

"I still—" But he got it before she explained. It was much the same thing he had been thinking about her, moments earlier.

"You have seen much, I think, and a little of it made you happy, yes? You are like a dark cloud. But there was an instant, a moment ago, just an instant, when your gold appeared. The first since I met you. And this fellow, this street artist caught it. In that, he showed genius of a sort. Enough to deserve a credit."

"May I see?"

"You may not laugh at me."

"I won't."

She handed him the paper, and he unrolled it. And stared. It wasn't him.

Oh, it looked like him. The man had put the same weary lines in his face, the proportions were right. But the eyes were young, touched by wonder.

It made him feel very peculiar, and a little guilty. What the man had seen on his face was him admiring Louise. It was her, reflected in him.

"What will you do with it?" he asked.

"It's yours," she replied. "You should hang it where your mirror is, to remind yourself you can look like that."

He didn't want it. On the other hand, if she kept it . . .

"Thank you," he said.

He bought a book.

The shop across town turned out to be a *librairie*, which

hadn't interested him at first. But there had been a time when he had loved to read. An old mentor of his, Sandoval Bey, had given him the taste for it, introducing him to classic and contemporary alike. Even after the old man was murdered, Bester had continued to read—a sort of tribute to Bey's memory.

But as he got older, the stories he read tasted more and more like the paper they were printed on. And one day he had stopped. Thinking about it, he couldn't even say when that was. Ten years ago? Twenty?

What were people reading these days?

He looked over the bestsellers. Memoirs were hot, especially those of the *Excalibur* crew and other explorers. One caught his eye in particular: *Freedom of Mind: Memoirs of a Telepath Mystic*.

He picked it up. He bought it.

The next afternoon he sat in a dim café called Le Cheval Heureux, hunched over the last few pages. Little Corinthian columns of cigarette smoke seemed to hold up the low ceiling, and the light from the various table lamps didn't reach far. Despite all of that, it seemed a popular place to read. Seven or eight other people were doing so.

"Insipid," he grunted, closing the book and making a face.

"Indeed?" A gaunt fellow, perhaps thirty, peered at him over old-fashioned wire-framed glasses. These were surely an affectation, given that any defect in eyesight could be corrected by a few seconds of inexpensive outpatient surgery. "I just read that and found it illuminating. How does it seem insipid to you? Or did you mean the coffee?"

"No, I meant the book," Bester replied.

"Well, then?"

"Rather presumptuous, don't you think, demanding an explanation? Perhaps I threaten your opinion, and thus threaten you?"

A hint of curve turned up the man's lips. "Perhaps. Shall I ask more politely? Or are you afraid you can't defend your opinion?"

"It isn't in need of defense." Bester turned away, then turned back. "But if you must know—I found the style gaudy, trite, and simplistic. The philosophy is rehashed twentieth-century quasi-Buddhist sentimentality, which was rehashed even then, with a healthy bit of theft from the Book of G'Quan. The first person, present tense is pretentious, and the stream of consciousness sequences would have made Faulkner reverse his lunch."

"I thought it was poetic and insightful."

"Well," Bester said, "you were wrong. Don't blame me."

The young man stuttered a little, contemptuous laugh. "Would you care to put that in writing?"

"What do you mean?"

"I edit a small literary journal. Paris is full of writers these days, and most think they are quite brilliant. Most aren't. I think some sorting needs to be done, and I need critics to do it."

"But we don't agree about this story."

"Agreement is beside the point. To read, to think, to express what you think—"

"—to sell your opinions to those who can't think for themselves?"

"Yes, *exactly*. Or, in a few cases, to those who will argue against you. Ninety-nine out of a hundred people, had I challenged them on their opinion, would have capitulated or turned away. Why bother, eh? It's only art, not worth arguing about—except that it *is*, because nothing is so pointless as undiscussed, uncriticized art, yes, and so—"

"What does this pay?"

"Oh. The inevitable crass question. It pays ten credits for every hundred words. You are interested, yes?"

Bester, to his own great surprise, heard himself answer, "Yes."

He returned to the hotel. It had rained, so his shoes broke pastel puddles, wet canvases left by the downpour and painted by the sunset. The silver-winged silhouettes of swallows spun in the lambent air, and for an instant he saw, not birds, but Black Omega Starfuries coursing across the universe-devouring face of Jupiter. *His* ships, *his* people, unstoppable. He trembled, with the thought of what he had been. He brought down governments, diverted rivers of destiny to fill new oceans. Without him, the Shadows would have won, destroyed all of humanity.

That never seemed to come up, at the hearing. He had never seen it once in any of the gory stories about him.

Sheridan knew. Sheridan the hero, the one honest man. He knew, but remained oddly silent. Garibaldi knew, too.

Of course Garibaldi wasn't a big-picture sort of man. Garibaldi only cared about Garibaldi—what Garibaldi liked or didn't like. What had given Garibaldi pleasure, what had hurt him. Especially what had hurt him. There was probably a wasp somewhere that had stung Garibaldi when he was five, that his operatives were still trying to track down . . .

His mind was wandering. Where was he? Ah, yes, the next street over.

He had commanded thousands, saved the world, saved his own people—whether they knew it or not, appreciated it or not.

Now he was going to write a column for a third-rate literary review?

Well, *that* certainly wasn't something Alfred Bester would do. Garibaldi and his Psi Corps lapdogs would be a long time searching before they started to check the literary reviews.

He turned the corner and found the street busy, confusingly so. There was a crowd, and police cycles, and a fire truck.

The excitement, the lust of the crowd struck him. They wanted to watch something burn down, to see Human forms come writhing out in flames. Just like the crowd at the hearing, screaming silently for *his* blood—

Wait. That was the Hotel Marceau, Louise's hotel. The place where he was staying.

He began pushing his way through.

The crowd was going to be disappointed. The blaze had been a small one, and it was nearly out. The front window had been shattered, and the small dining room blackened, but otherwise the hotel seemed to have survived.

Louise stood, watching the firemen work, her face blank with shock. As Bester arrived, the cop, Lucien, was talking to her, though she didn't seem to be listening.

"Nobody saw anything," he was saying. "Of course. Louise, you *must*—"

"Leave me alone," she said, distractedly. "Just . . . leave me be."

A swift anger passed across the policeman's face, but then he gave a little Gallic shrug and did what she asked. Bester stood for a moment, wondering if he ought to say anything.

She noticed him. "Monsieur Kaufman," she said, in a small voice, "I withdraw what I said earlier. I won't charge you extra for leaving early."

Bester nodded. He was about to tell her he would have his things out as soon as the fire died down. After all, he was trying to avoid attention, not court it. And there were bound to be reporters.

No. There was already one here, pushing forward, newstaper close behind.

He felt, suddenly, like a trapped animal, his heart picking up several beats per minute. If his face appeared, even on a local newscast . . .

He stepped quickly away, ducking into the crowd. He touched the reporter and found no image of himself in the man's surface thoughts. He hadn't been noticed, and he wouldn't be remembered. The camera, though—had *it* seen him?

If it had, it would probably be edited out.

Get ahold of yourself, Bester, he told himself. *No one noticed you.* But his heart was still beating too fast. How he hated this feeling, this helpless, watched feeling.

That's when he noticed Jem and his buddies, observing it all, wearing wide, bestial grins.

Suddenly his helplessness turned to cold anger—an old, comfortable friend. Here was something he could deal with.

Jem hadn't noticed him. Bester went up an alley, until he could just see the thug, and there he waited.

Soon night fell. Jem and his friends left, but they didn't leave alone. Bester followed them down the narrow streets, his step quiet and purposeful.

This was what he was, a hunter. Bester had been meant to chase prey, not run from predators. In the old days, a rogue knew his days were numbered when Alfred Bester was on his trail. He smiled thinly at the familiar rush.

He followed them to a set of apartments a few blocks away, which they entered, laughing and slapping one another on the back. Bester kept watching, waiting.

Hours passed, and an orange moon rose into the faintly hazy sky. Bester was patient—he knew more about waiting than perhaps anything else. He listened to Paris; he hummed old tunes to himself.

Finally, well after midnight, the gang members began to slip off. He counted them as they went, until he knew Jem was alone. Then he brushed his jacket with his hands, adjusted his collar, and walked up to the building.

It was an old building, but it had a fairly good security system. There were a series of contacts and a small vidscreen. To enter, he would either have to bypass the system, which he hadn't brought the tools to do, or get Jem to buzz him up. He could go back to his room, get the matrix chip that had allowed him to pass Earth security—but no, where was the challenge in that? He could make Jem open the door.

Closing his eyes, he tuned out the mind of Paris, bit by bit, as though through a sieve, running everything through it until finally only a faint something remained. *Very* faint.

Without line of sight, making contact with a normal was almost impossible, even for a P12. But Bester had been at this for a long time and found that the limits of his abilities were extended by his belief in them. He couldn't scan Jem from here, couldn't burst the blood vessels in his apelike brain. But he could touch him, just a little. He could suggest that one of Jem's friends had just buzzed . . .

Jem's mind was already confused. It was a rough sea, queasy to the touch, thickened and slowed by alcohol, salted with drugs of some sort. He was already hearing things that weren't there. If Bester had asked him to make himself more vulnerable, he could not have.

Still, it took fifteen minutes of terrific concentration before he heard the lock click. The outer door opened, revealing two more doors on either side and a stairway going up.

He felt Jem above, and so took the stairs. When he stood in front of what felt like the right door, he knocked softly.

An instant later it opened, and Bester found himself staring down the ugly hole of an automatic pistol.

— chapter 5 —

"Well," Jem grunted. He wore a black tank top and sweatpants. "If it ain't my old friend grandpa. Come in. Now." He extended the gun meaningfully, and Bester noticed it was an old Naga 12mm, probably with mercury-filled slugs that would leave an exit wound the size of a softball.

"Don't mind if I do," Bester said, calmly.

Jem watched him with bloodshot, small-pupiled eyes. The apartment was large, and furnished in moderately expensive but poor taste. Gaudy. A poor boy's idea of what having wealth was all about. Bester noticed a bottle of red wine and picked it up.

"Ah, the '67 Château le Ridoux," he said. "Not a bad year—a poor choice with pizza, however." He'd noticed the delivery boy coming in earlier, and the remains of the meal were scattered about on a large wooden table.

"It costs a hundred credits a bottle."

"Oh, well, then it must go with *anything*," Bester replied. He went to the wine rack, selected a glass, and poured himself a bit.

"What the hell do you think you're doing?"

"You know," Bester observed, "you were cheated. This is a cheap côte du rhône, rebottled. I would say you paid ninety-five credits too much."

"You've got about six seconds to live, old man."

"Oh, I don't think so." He took another sip of wine.

With a sort of animal growl, Jem jumped forward, swinging the gun at Bester's face like a club. Bester seized his voluntary nervous system and watched him go down, felt the

51

bright tinkle of pain, like the sound of glass breaking. Only it was Jem's nose that had broken, on the parquet floor. And several of his teeth.

"Yes, please, make yourself comfortable," Bester said. "We have a long night ahead of us. At the end of it you will be dead, but I intend to take my time about it. It's so rare I get to do this, these days." He took another sip of the wine, rubbed his good hand on his permanently clenched one. "Shall we begin?"

He had frozen Jem's vocal cords, so all the thug could make was a sort of clucking noise. But his brain—ah, that was filled with panic, with a beautiful sort of terror.

Just a bad trip, Jem was telling himself. *Not real . . .*

Bester inserted his thoughts like a scalpel into butter. *No, I'm afraid not. This is more real than you can imagine.*

And with the scalpel he began to cut, to whittle Jem away, piece by piece. He made sure that the thug felt himself die, watched what he had lost slip away. His wide eyes faded and misted, his throat pulsed with the urge to scream, but Bester wouldn't give him that.

And then he was dead, though his body was still working. Everything that had actually been Jem was cut away from him.

Bester took a break, sipping a little more wine while the breathing corpse stared at the ceiling. He moved away, since Jem's bowels and bladder had emptied themselves, opened a window for a bit of fresh air. He stretched, tried to work the crick out of his neck, flipped on the vid to see what, if anything, had been reported about the fire. It got a ten-second spot on the local update. The footage showed the hotel, Louise, the fire trucks, but he didn't see himself.

He went to the kitchen and made some coffee, then returned to where the body lay, specter-eyed. Then, with due consideration, he started putting Jem back together.

It was almost morning when he returned to the hotel. The broken window had been boarded up. He used his key to open the door and was greeted with a pungent, wet, burned smell.

A single lamp was on, on one of the unburnt tables. Louise

sat in its light, an empty bottle of wine in front of her. She looked up wearily.

"You've made other arrangements, I take it, and come to get your things?"

"No. I thought I would get some sleep, instead."

She shook her head. "The hotel is closed."

"Why? The damage is only cosmetic."

"There's nothing cosmetic about a firebomb tossed through the window."

"You don't want to close the hotel."

"Who are you to tell me what I want? You know *nothing* of me."

"I know the woman I first saw, defending what was hers. I know she would not give in so easily."

"There's nothing easy about it. About any of it. For five years I've tried to keep this place going. Five years, watching my savings dwindle. It's enough. I'm finished."

"You don't have the money to clean up a little fire damage?"

"What would be the point? They'll only do it again, or worse—unless I start paying them again, which I also can't afford."

"You might be surprised."

"What do you mean?"

"Just that you might be surprised, that's all. Things happen. Things change."

"Some things don't." She patted her hand slowly on the table. "You know, at first I thought you were hoping for something from me. To share my bed. Is that it? Is that why you persist?"

"No."

"What, then?"

"I need a place to stay, that's all. And I don't like bullies. I don't like being told what to do."

"I suppose you don't. You were in the war, weren't you?"

He froze, uncertain what to say. Which war did she mean? "Yes," he finally settled on.

"I thought so. You have a way about you. I think you have

already seen the worst thing you could ever see, and it ate all of the fear in you. And maybe more than your fear." She looked up at him, but he didn't think she was expecting an answer.

"Have you ever been in love, Mr. Kaufman?"

"Yes."

"What happened to her?"

"Nothing I want to talk about."

"I was in love, once. Crazy, stupid in love. Now all I have is a broken-down hotel." She picked at the table. "He left me. See, that is none of your business, but I tell you anyway. I don't know why—the wine, maybe. He left me with my debt, and my empty room, and he left me with no notions of love whatsoever. I no longer believe in it, I think. Is that what happened with you? Did you leave her? Are you hiding from your old life?"

Bester nearly echoed that it wasn't *her* business, but instead, he sighed. "No," he said, remembering Carolyn the last time he had seen her alive and conscious, wired and meshed with Shadow technology. Worse than dead. But he hadn't left her.

"No, I tried everything I could to be with her. I—went to great lengths." He smiled briefly. "It just didn't work out." He remembered what was left of Carolyn, after a rogue terrorist had bombed the facility. Remembered how angry he had been, because he had *promised* her that he would make things all right. But putting a shattered body back together was quite different from rebuilding a psyche.

Some promises shouldn't be made, because they couldn't be kept. "No," he repeated, softly, "it didn't work out."

Because of Byron. Because of Lyta. And most of all, because of Garibaldi, whose engineers had doubtless built the weapon that had killed his love.

"Yes, well, that's life, isn't it?" she said. "It doesn't work out. We grow old, we die. The universe doesn't care."

"You've had too much wine."

"I haven't had enough. Did you know I wanted to be a painter? I studied at the Paris Académie d'Art. I was very serious about it, but I gave it up. For love. For this." She swept her hands disgustedly around the room.

He sat silent, gripped by the unaccustomed feeling of not knowing what to say.

"You still paint?"

"Hmm. Yes. Walls and doors, mostly. This room most recently. Do you think it needs a new coat of black?" She indicated the film of carbon that coated the once-white walls.

"I think you should go to bed and think more clearly about it later. And I think I should do the same."

"I would prefer to sit here and feel sorry for myself for another day or so. Would you care to sit with me? You seem to feel at least as sorry for yourself as I do."

"What makes you say that?"

"Your every word and expression. The way you study things." She frowned. "Except the other day in the square, when that man drew you. You were different, then. What was different? What occurred to you?"

Again, he tried to think of something to say. Because he knew what the painter had seen in his eyes. He had seen Louise.

"I don't remember," he answered.

She shot him a skeptical glance, but didn't dispute him.

"I got a job," he offered.

"Really."

"Yes. As a literary critic."

"That's a strange job for someone who was in your line of work. Your papers say you were a salesman."

"A boyhood dream. I'm retired, and now it's time to live out my fantasies, I suppose. Live in Paris, write."

"Well, Mr. Kaufman. Welcome to your fantasy." She hesitated. "This writing job. Is it full time?"

"No."

"How would you like free rent for a while?"

"That depends, of course."

"Help me clean up this mess. I'll pay you a day an hour. It's a good deal."

"So you aren't throwing in the towel, after all."

"I suppose not."

He nodded.

She rose, steadying herself with the table. "I suppose I'll catch a few winks."

"Good night—or morning, rather."

"Yes. To you, too. And . . . thank you."

The words surprised him so much he didn't know what to say. That seemed to happen to him a lot, talking to Louise. What had he done to be thanked for? Had he been sympathetic? To a normal?

He went back over the conversation in his head and realized that he had. What had made him do that?

He would think about it later. Destroying and rebuilding Jem had taken a lot out of him. He would be more reasonable after a few hours' rest.

He woke with the remains of a headache, something like a hangover, but otherwise felt pretty well. He got up, splashed cold water on his face, and began to plan his day.

Well, he was a reviewer, now. So he needed something to review. And something to review it on—a desktop AI or something of the sort. His pocket computer could take dictation, but somehow he felt he ought to use an old-fashioned keyboard, if not pen and paper.

Over the years, writers had generally agreed that the disjunction created by the mediation of fingers between thoughts and the written word was necessary. Writing was a different form of communication than speaking, a different way of thinking—a more considered one.

It looked as if the day was going to be a warm one, and all he had was his leather jacket and black pants. Another thing he needed to do something about: he needed to acquire a wardrobe.

Louise was downstairs, already scrubbing the walls.

"Ah. Good morning," she said, taking in his outfit with an up-and-down glance. "I have some work clothes I think will fit you."

"Excuse me?"

"You are going to help me fix all of this, aren't you?"

"I distinctly remember that I did *not* agree to help you," he replied.

"And I distinctly remember you talking me into staying here, which makes you responsible. So. Are you going to help or not?"

He eyed the room distastefully. "I would rather not," he replied.

"Too bad. The clothes are on the counter over there."

"I have things to do."

"You can do them later."

"But . . ." Bester frowned.

Up went the brush, down went the brush. Bester watched the thick paint streak over the grey beneath. At this rate, it would take him all day to paint a single wall.

"You've never painted before," Louise said. It wasn't a question.

"No, as a matter of fact. Am I doing it right?"

"No. You use the brush to do the trim work, then roll the large sections."

"Trim work?"

"Here." She stepped over and took the brush from his hand, then knelt down next to him.

"See? I've put tape on the floor next to the baseboard. Now I paint the baseboard, like so."

Her hair, caught up in a kerchief, smelled clean, and faintly of lavender. Also of paint—she had managed to coat a few hairs with it, despite her headcover.

He realized that it had been a long time since he had been so close to a woman.

He hadn't had much luck with women. As a boy he'd had a crush on a girl—another telepath in his cadre. He had unexpectedly come upon her and another boy, kissing, and had the unpleasant experience of psionically sharing the pleasure they got from one another.

Later, as a cadet, he had truly fallen in love, with fiery Elizabeth Montoya, whose passion for him had nearly swept him away. But she hadn't loved *him* enough—not enough to stay in the Corps with him. She had tried to go Blip, to run away, and he had been forced to turn her in.

He had been so angry at her, for forcing him to do that. Now he felt nothing at all. He couldn't even remember her face.

The Corps had arranged a marriage, of course, a genetic match guaranteed to produce telepathic offspring. There had never been love there, though for a time he had thought there might be at least companionship. Until he had come home to find Alisha in the arms of another man.

He supposed he was married still, and his son—if indeed it was his son, which he much doubted—was a stranger.

No, probably during or after the telepath wars Alisha had sued for a divorce. Who would want to be married to the terrible criminal, Alfred Bester?

And Carolyn. He had loved her. She had proved to him that his heart wasn't as empty as he had thought. Which in the end only proved he could still be hurt. It wasn't worth the trade.

So why was he noticing the smell of Louise's hair, the way her fingers gripped the brush, the stray, white-coated hairs straggling across her face?

Ah. That would be because he was an idiot. She was less than half his age, still young and beautiful. His body was responding to her, that was all, a last gasp of hormones. Or maybe he liked the fact that she needed him, if only a little. He had once had thousands of people who depended upon him, and he had been without that for years. Empty nest syndrome? It was an elementary fact that you could make more friends by making them feel like you needed them than the other way around.

Yes, simple physiology and psychology. He wasn't really attracted to her. And she *certainly* was not attracted to him. Why was he wasting time with this?

Perhaps because, against his will, he was *painting* for the first time in his life.

There was a knock at the door. Her head jerked up, and her cheek brushed against his. He banged his head into the wall jerking away.

"You!" Louise shouted, her voice trembling with rage and fear.

Jem stood in the doorway.

Louise picked up a piece of charred chair leg from a pile of rubble. "Get out. Get away from here."

Jem's face spasmed with sudden pain. He looked confused. Bester frowned. Maybe he had been more tired than he thought. Maybe . . .

But then Jem cleared his throat. "Look, ah, madame, I'm—I went too far. I'm sorry. This isn't good business, this kind of thing, and I shouldn't have done it."

"What? Don't play with me. I'm sick of you. So help me . . ." She hefted the makeshift weapon.

Jem withdrew a card from his pocket and held it out. "There's eight thousand credits on that. If it doesn't cover the damage and the lost business, I'll transfer more. Okay?"

Louise just stared for a moment, utterly amazed. Then her expression took a turn back toward suspicion. "What are you up to, Jem? Are you going to snatch that away from me, maybe grab my hair, try to give me a good beating? If you do, you'd better kill me."

Jem set the credit chit carefully on the counter. "There it is," he murmured. "Check it out. It's real." His eyes flickered once to Bester, and his face spasmed again. Then he turned and left.

"What the . . ." She picked up the chit, looked it over, then went behind the check-in desk.

"Eight thousand credits, just like he said." Her tone was so unbelieving, Bester couldn't suppress a small grin.

She noticed it. "Did you—what did you do to him?"

"Me? Nothing."

"Last night, when you were telling me something might come along—you meant this! How did you know?"

"I spoke philosophically," Bester said. "It's just that I've been around long enough to know you can never guess what's really around the next corner."

"No. You knew. How?"

"I promise you, I didn't. Don't you think it more likely that your policeman friend got some of his buddies together, off duty? That they went and, ah, 'talked some sense' into Jem? Or maybe he really had a change of heart."

"No, not Jem. But Lucien—no, I don't believe that either. He's too upright, too respectful of the law."

"He likes you. Maybe this attack was just too much for him."

"Maybe. I don't believe it."

"Yes. He knows you don't like help, like to fend for yourself—"

"Oh, do I?" Her eyes narrowed again, but this time there was something playful about it.

"That's my impression."

"Gathered in only three days?"

"Maybe I'm wrong."

"No, you're right. I usually do. But whoever did whatever they did to Jem—has my thanks." She held his eyes for a moment, then went back to work.

Bester reflected that, if she actually knew the details of what he had done, she would probably take a very different attitude toward it.

Still, it felt good, her thanks.

Physiology and psychology. It was always good to feel needed—even when you didn't want to be.

— *chapter 6* —

Garibaldi walked carefully around the room, as if his feet were bare and the floor covered in broken glass.

"He was here," he muttered. "I can smell him."

He couldn't, of course, not literally. But sometimes he thought he had developed a sort of sense—not telepathy, of course, but something older, deeper, more primal. Animal, even.

"It's a good bet," Thompson drawled. "This house was registered to one Susan Taroa, but that was just an alias. We traced her back through several other fake names, until we came to Sophie Herndon. She was one of Bester's interns."

"And that's the woman they fished out of the drink a couple of weeks ago?"

"Yes. Someone sunk her in a fishing net. But a ship went down in the same area in a storm, and the search and recovery mission found her. When they did an ID check, irregularities popped up. Sheer luck."

"Not for her."

"No, I guess not."

"I want a full tracing team in here. DNA, everything."

"The local police already did a sweep."

"They didn't know what they were looking for. I want another one."

"Of course."

Garibaldi continued his survey of the monster's lair. The clues Bester had left with Thompson hadn't led anywhere— or more accurately, they'd led everywhere *except* to any trace of Bester. The man was a ghost when he wanted to be. He

61

could screw with people's heads, make them forget, make them remember things that had never happened.

Make them do things they never wanted to do.

Garibaldi had tried following the money. Bester had to have money, to keep moving like this, but even the considerable Edgars resources had failed him. Some banks really were tamperproof, unbribable, beyond his ability to influence, as perverse and unthinkable as that seemed.

So, what was left to follow? A trail of corpses? Bester was usually careful about that, too. Then again, it seemed as though he was starting to slip up. That was a hopeful sign.

"What are you looking for, Mr. Garibaldi?"

"I don't know. Something. Anything. How about you? Can you pick up any—I don't know—psychic signature?"

"No, nothing. Strong telepaths sometimes leave them, it's true, but they don't last long. Hours, maybe a day. There's nothing like that here."

"Damn." He went to the drawers of the polished coral dresser and started opening them. Nothing. Searched under the mattress. Nothing.

He reached to pat under the bed, and his fingers touched something small, cool, smooth.

"What's this?" He got a cloth from his pocket and reached again, came up with a small cylinder.

"This is an ampoule," he grunted. He stood and lifted it toward the light. "Some sort of pharmaceutical."

"That should be right up your alley."

"Or on my gravy train, anyway. Yeah, I've got a guy I want to see this. And Thompson, I don't want you talking to anyone about this—understand? Right now this is just our little secret."

"Got it."

Niles Drennan was a slight, stiff young man, the sort you could never really imagine cutting loose and having fun. Garibaldi didn't like him, but he was one of the best synthesizers in the business.

Technically, his job was to examine the herbal and folk

remedies from a thousand worlds and try to isolate their active ingredients. Lately he had worked more on the various biogenic materials turned up in the hunt for a cure for the Drakh plague.

In actual fact, he was a sort of alchemist-inquisitor, someone who could drag the secret out of any compound he was given, no matter how strange or complex. So Garibaldi didn't really care if the guy knew anything about living it up.

"It's choline ribosylase. It controls the production of certain irregular neurotransmitters."

"Which means what? In English? In *plain* English."

"How much do you know about neurons?"

"Sixth-grade stuff."

"Hmm . . . Well, nerves are often compared to wiring, or to some other linear, conductive system. It's a bad analogy, on any number of levels. The nervous system—the brain, the spinal cord, sensory and motor nerves—are all composed of specialized cells called neurons. But neurons, strictly speaking, don't act as conductors. They act as generators, in a sense, each one producing its own electrical pulses."

"So far I'm with you."

Drennan's face said *I should hope so*, but he held his tongue. "A neuron has a sort of branching tree of dendrites that *almost* connect it to other nerve cells—I'll get to that in a moment. Each one also has a longer appendage called an axon. When an electrical pulse is generated by the neuron, it flows down the axon until it comes to the next neuron—or, rather, to the gap separating it from the next neuron, the synapse."

"And the pulse jumps the gap or not, right?"

"Not exactly. The impulse itself doesn't cross the space. When the impulse reaches the end of the axon, it triggers small packets, telling them to release a combination of neurotransmitters. These are complex chemical compounds that float across the intervening space and tell the neuron next door what to do—whether to generate its own electrical pulse or not. There are upwards of fifty kinds of neurotransmitters in most people. They're triggered by different sorts of impulses, and in turn cause neighboring neurons to react in different ways. When these neurotransmitters malfunction, especially when they are underproduced, they cause neurological problems. Alzheimer's, for instance, involves among other things the underproduction of a neurotransmitter.

"Certain kinds of messages can't be carried from one neuron to another because there is no messenger that will do so. Most psychotropic drugs mimic neurotransmitters in some way, causing neurons to react to stimuli that don't really exist."

"So these are irregular neurotransmitters?"

"There's a long list of them, but I imagine you're interested in the case at hand. There is a rare condition involving a viruslike organism that mimics glial cells—the cells that maintain the biochemical functions of the brain. Imagine them also as the packing pellets that support the fibrous, fragile neurons. Given time, these mutant cells can subvert and replace all of the brain's natural glial cells. What's interesting is that in most cases, this process is harmless, as the invasive cells perfectly mimic those they replace. They have latent genetic machinery that makes them different, but it isn't ever activated. In a minority of cases, however, they stimulate the production of certain neurotransmitters that don't occur naturally in the human body. This scenario is limited to telepathic individuals, and—"

"Hold it right there. Telepaths?"

"Yes."

"Why?"

"We don't know. We still don't know exactly how telepathy works. Telepaths have quirky glial cells anyway, and we've never quite hammered out the link."

"Okay. So this is a disease, right? A virus?"

"Not exactly a virus, but it's not a bad analogy either."

"Natural?"

"Good question. We don't really think so. The imitative cells are too, um, well-designed, so to speak."

"What does it do, this disease?"

"At first, nothing. There actually seems to be some enhancement of telepathic abilities—or more specifically, of the processing of telepathic information and impulses. It speeds it up. But inevitably, the neurotransmitter starts over-producing, triggering functions without threshold electrical potential—"

"It short-circuits?"

"Put crudely, yes."

"And only telepaths get this. I bet they were all Corps telepaths, weren't they?"

"I can check."

"Yeah. The Corps had dozens of black-box experiments de-signed to make telepaths stronger, or make them telekinetic. Five will get you ten this was the result of one of them."

"They experimented on themselves?"

"Man, have you been asleep all your life? Those guys in Psi Corps did experiments on people that would have made Josef Mengele lose his lunch. What do you think all of those trials were about a few years ago?"

"I don't pay much attention to the news."

Yeah, I'll bet you don't, Garibaldi thought to himself. Not important.

"Still, I can't imagine *this* guy volunteering to be a guinea pig." He scratched his chin. "Of course, he had enemies in the Corps, or if the insertion was done with a virus, like you said, he may have gotten contaminated accidentally." He smiled suddenly, clapped Drennan on the back, and indicated the choline ribosylase diagram on the notebook. "Doesn't matter. What happens if he doesn't take this?"

"Oh—first euphoria, heightened senses, faster cognition. Like being on a stim. That's followed by hallucinations and seizures, and finally the collapse of the nervous system."

"Any other treatment?"

"Not that I know of. The mutant cells are resistant to gene tampering. You can insert a replacement sequence to try and normalize them, but within weeks they return to the state they started in. We think they somehow code their genetic infor-mation in non-DNA form in the neural net itself—another good indication that they are engineered. In fact, in that way, they resemble the Drakh plague. You can't kill them all and replace them with normal cells, either, because in the meantime the neurons they keep alive, functioning, and supporting would die. Besides, there aren't enough people who have this to make the research worthwhile, and it doesn't seem to be communicable."

"But if the man using this inhibitor takes this medication every—how often?"

"Once a month."

"Once a month, he's okay?"

"Yes. The drug is a hundred percent effective, when used on schedule."

"Yes!" Garibaldi said. "That's great. Thanks, Drennan."

The fellow nodded, but he'd turned away. Apparently the whole conversation had already been forgotten in favor of whatever he was working on.

Garibaldi left the lab whistling.

"One of your own damn bugs bit you, Bester. Serves you right. And now I've found your little trail of breadcrumbs. When I find you, you're gonna wish the wicked witch had just eaten you."

But at that a thought dampened his spirits, if only a little. Bester was sick. What if he couldn't get the treatment? What if he was dying?

No. Nothing could beat him to the punch—nothing. Garibaldi took comfort in knowing something about his enemy, and that included one very important fact: Bester wanted to live. And nobody and nothing got between Bester and what he wanted.

In that one way, he and Bester were alike.

Here was something he could trace, something Bester had to have. At last he had a real lead.

— *chapter 7* —

"Always dark clothes," Louise said, her voice somehow laughing and complaining at the same time.

"I'm a winter," Bester replied, checking the price tag on a gabardine suit.

"Even in winter it isn't always nighttime. What about this?" She held up a deep burgundy jacket with a flaring collar. Big collars had come back in style while he had been gone, apparently.

"Not me," he replied.

"So you ask me to come shopping with you, and now you disregard all of my advice."

"I didn't ask you to come shopping with me," Bester replied, mildly.

"Well, you should have. You have terrible taste. You dress like a gangster."

"Maybe I am a gangster."

She put her chin between her fingers. "Yes. That would explain why Jem has been so nice to me for the last several weeks. You put the squeeze on him, as they say."

Bester shrugged. "Maybe he was just intimidated by my massive physical presence."

"And your black clothes. Come, just let me select one outfit for you."

He cocked his head and looked over at her. "Okay. On one condition."

"No more painting?"

"That's not it."

"What then?"

"You let me pick one outfit for you. And pay for it."

Her mouth dropped open as she realized that she had been trapped.

"Pick it, yes, though I warn you I won't wear black. Pay for it—I can't."

"Yes you can. You haven't bought anything new since I met you. I insist."

She looked as if she were preparing another objection, but then she arched one eyebrow. "I pick out *any* outfit for you, and you will wear it?"

Uh-oh. "Within reason. And given my conditions."

"Done," she said, grabbed him by the hand, and started pulling.

It was his bad hand, the clenched one. She had never mentioned it, never asked about it, never touched it—until now.

He actually felt a blush coming on. In the Corps, you always wore gloves, except when you were alone—or intimate.

He had a sudden flash of Elizabeth Montoya, the first woman he had slept with. Another telepath. They had just passed a field test, and they were drunk, and they had started kissing. When they got to the hotel room, she had stripped off his gloves and kissed each finger, digging her tongue between them to the soft junctures, sucking insistently on the tips . . .

It was such a powerfully erotic memory that for a moment nothing existed but the remembered sensations and the warmth of Louise's fingers on his crippled hand. It had been that hand, too, that Liz had kissed, long before the accident that had robbed him of its use.

He shook himself out of it, and worried. Had he actually gone into a fugue state? Had he missed a dose of his medication?

No, he had taken his last shot less than two weeks ago. He was fine. It was just the hand. The hand . . .

Normals made fun of it. He had seen vid comedies lampooning telepaths and their "hand fetish." But then, they always made fun of what they didn't understand, and what they could never, never have. They could never know what it meant to feel both sides of pleasure.

Louise wasn't like that. She didn't judge. Sometimes he

thought he could tell her who he was, tell her everything, and she would somehow make a place for it.

He didn't think that very often, because he knew it wasn't true. No matter how much better she was than the average normal, no matter how understanding, no one could ever understand him, or the things he had done. No one.

He blinked. They were standing in front of a rack of clothes. Very bright clothes. Shimmering clothes.

"Within reason," he reminded her.

Moments later, he was looking dubiously at himself in the mirror. The slacks were okay—a sort of dark chocolate, some material from Centauri Prime that resembled shantung silk. The jacket—wasn't a jacket. It was a sort of dressing gown, loose, flowing, with wide sleeves, and it hung halfway down his calves. It was a smoky brown, but almost-paisley curls of subdued gold and rust shimmered and vanished in the light.

"See? Not so bad."

"I—where would I wear this?"

"You're a writer now! It's all the rage. Voltaire had a coat almost exactly like this."

"That was five hundred years ago."

"It's back in style. It's the literati uniform. Surely you've noticed."

In fact, he had. Young men dressed like this in the coffee-houses, and the look had somehow irritated him. It seemed pretentious.

But part of him had to admit that on him, it didn't look half bad.

"Well . . . I suppose I could wear it around the hotel. It looks like something you would wear to breakfast."

"You'll see. It will grow on you."

"Okay," he said. "Okay, you win. And now it's my turn."

Louise went through the women's section rather noncha-lantly. "This is nice," she said, fingering a practical denim jumper. "And this," a modest suit. Bester nodded at each. She was trying to fool him into buying her something cheap and practical.

Her thoughts betrayed her, however. He wasn't scanning her, of course, but people leaked feelings, and when she saw the evening gown, he felt a sudden surge of desire from her.

For an evening gown of the times, it was modestly cut, but the fabric was Centauri tersk, a material once reserved only for Centauri women of noble birth. The Centaurum had fallen on hard times, however, and they were, in many ways, a practical people.

Tersk was as thin and iridescent as a film of oil. It was affected by body heat and chemistry, so it never looked the same on any two women.

And it was expensive.

He chose the nicest of the things she pointed to, a navy blue dress.

"Thank you," she told him when they were done. "I can wear it to the opera next week."

"A bargain is a bargain," he replied.

"Do you want to get something to eat? There's a nice bistro around the corner."

"No, I'm afraid I have business to attend to. I'm meeting with my editor in half an hour."

"Very well, then. See you this evening. I'm making the étouffée again—perhaps I can manage to get the roux right, this time."

"Well . . ." he said dubiously, ". . . good luck."

She hit him lightly over the head with her wallet. "That, for you, monsieur connoisseur."

"See you this evening."

Jean-Pierre barked a little laugh. " *'The plot staggers like an epileptic in shock'*? Don't you think that's a bit much?"

"Not at all," Bester replied, sipping his espresso.

"Well, far be it for me to censor my most popular critic."

"Me?"

"Well, you certainly draw the most response from our readers. Half of them think you're a genius, the other half hate you with a raging passion. A good balance for a critic."

"I aim to please."

Jean-Pierre took a drag on his clove cigarette and exhaled grey plumes from his nose, a fragrant Chinese dragon. "This isn't a criticism, just an observation—I've noticed you never review anything favorably. Don't you like anything?"

"Sure I do. *Hymns for the Damned* was one of the best books I've read in ten years."

"But you didn't review *Hymns for the Damned*."

"Exactly. Why should I review something I liked? What's the use in that?"

"You're an odd man, Kaufman. Are you certain you weren't born in Paris?"

"As certain as I can be of something I don't remember, I suppose."

Jean-Pierre nodded absently and stubbed out his smoke in a small jade ashtray. "I have some good news, of sorts. We're increasing our circulation. The magazine is selling better than we hoped. I have to admit, I am of two minds about it. We've begun to attract attention."

"I'm sure that's what you wanted."

"Yes, but we are beginning to get . . . offers."

"Of what sort?"

"Publishers are asking us to review certain books."

"Ah. And to take a certain stance in those reviews."

"An insidious business, yes? But I started this magazine to tell the truth, not to pander to commercial interests."

"Good for you," Bester said, dryly.

"Still, it might be worth it to—compromise a bit, if it means we can expand our readership."

"Not to me," Bester said. "I like doing this. I don't *have* to do this, and I won't if I can't do it my way."

"Yes, of course, I agree with you completely. Completely. I would never ask you to give a favorable review to a book you didn't feel deserved it. But if you were to be presented with a book and *liked* it—"

"No. I've just explained that to you. The object of the critique is to improve literature. Nothing was ever improved by applause."

"What do you mean?"

"Fear of failure, fear of criticism, fear of rejection—those are the only things that writers are accountable to. Praise makes people weak. Why improve if you think you are doing things right?"

"You've never heard of positive reinforcement?"

"I've heard of it. I've also heard of unicorns and minotaurs. Do you think any sort of evolution works by positive reinforcement? It is the *eliminative* process of natural selection that makes biological evolution work—positive traits are only positive in the sense that they aren't negative. The same is true in literature. We can cut away the chaff, but we can't improve the quality of genius in good writers simply by feeding their egos. Nothing works like that. It's a simple fact."

"Well. Magazines don't get printed without money. That is another simple fact."

Bester shrugged. "Whether or not the magazine is printed is your problem, not mine."

"You've had other offers?"

"A few. I won't take them unless you force me to."

Jean-Pierre pulled out another cigarette and lit it with a Narn touch-wand. "I give up. I suppose a critic must be incorruptible."

Bester smiled. "I'm not incorruptible. I'm so corrupt nothing you can offer me is tempting."

"Well, it works out the same, yes? Very well. There are others who will write the sort of review we need."

"I'll take them to task."

Jean-Pierre frowned. "This is not *your* magazine, Mr. Kaufman. I still decide what gets printed and what doesn't."

"I'm sure you do. And I know you'll make the right decisions." He smiled in such a way as to cast doubt upon that.

He made a stop on the way home. When he arrived, the hotel's little café was full. Business had been good since Jem and his boys had moderated their behavior.

The étouffée *was* better this time, and the wine Louise brought out was almost exquisite. He suspected special treatment—it looked like the house wine on the rest of the tables.

He finished his meal and went to work on his next review, there in the café. There was something about the place, something that felt more like home than anyplace had since he had fled his apartments on Mars. Perhaps it was the fact that he had helped restore the dining room. The personal investment.

It was late before dinner was done. Louise came out of the kitchen, brushing her hands on her apron.

"May I join you?"

"Of course." He pushed his AI back.

Louise poured herself a glass of red wine and sat down with a sigh. "Ah, it feels good to be off of my feet."

"Long day?"

"A madhouse. All of the rooms are full!"

"Well, that's good, isn't it?"

"Very good." She frowned. "I left your new outfit in your room. I thought you said you would wear it around the hotel."

"Oh, I just went up long enough to get my AI. I'll wear it tomorrow, I promise."

"Well, I'll let it pass this once. Anything interesting happen to you today?"

He told her about the conversation with Jean-Pierre, and she nodded. "I had no notion that you were so idealistic," she said.

"It has nothing to do with idealism," Bester replied. "I don't have it in me to write that sort of thing. It would be like a monkey trying to do ballet, or a horse singing opera."

"Speaking of opera," she said, taking another sip of the wine, "I think I mentioned I'm going next week. I'll wear the dress you bought me. I was wondering if you liked that sort of thing."

"Dresses? They don't look so good on me. My calves are a little thick."

"Opera, you idiot."

"Ah. Unfortunately, I have things to do that night. I can't go."

"Oh."

"But, I did remember you mentioning it. And it occurred to me that the dress I got you today was no good for the opera."

"It's perfect."

Bester shook his head and reached into the sack by his chair. "No," he said. "*This* is perfect." He set the box on the table. Louise looked at it, then back up at him.

"What's this?"

"Open it."

She put her wineglass down and took the wrapping from the box, then removed the lid, then gasped.

"I saw you looking at it," he explained.

It was the gown of Centauri tersk, glimmering faintly in the candlelight.

"Mr. Kaufman, I can't—"

"You can and will. You can't return it—I made certain of that. And I won't."

"But . . . no, it's too extravagant. When will I wear it?"

"At the opera."

"Yes, but I go only once a year!"

"Well, perhaps you should go more often."

She stared at the material, touching it lightly with her fingers, watching it change colors.

"I don't—I . . ." A tear slipped from one of her eyes, a small ruby in firelight.

Bester cleared his throat. "Anyway. I think it's time I turned in. I've had a long day, too."

"No one has ever given me anything like this," she said.

"Well, someone should have," he said, quietly. "Good night."

"Good night, Mr. Kaufman," she said, very softly. "And thank you."

It didn't sound right. It sounded like she was thanking someone else. He suddenly, powerfully wanted to hear her say *his* name. Bester. Al. Alfie . . .

"What's wrong?" she asked.

He smiled. "Nothing. I was just reminded of an—old friend of mine."

"You seemed sad."

"My friend has passed on. He would have liked to have

seen you in that dress. It would have made him happy. He liked beauty."

"It will not look as good on me as it looks by itself. It's fantastic."

He hovered for an instant, thinking to correct her, to explain that it was picturing her in it that led him to buy it. He decided against it, and left her there.

It took him a long time to fall asleep.

Once, he had lost his soul—not figuratively, but literally. He had been much younger, and had volunteered to perform deathbed scans. These were often necessary in the case of a victim of a violent crime, who might know the face of his killer, or of a mortally wounded rogue who could reveal where his comrades were hiding out. It was hard and dangerous, following someone into death. Most telepaths could only stand to do it once. A few had done as many as four.

He had done eight.

Eight times, and each time a part of him had died with them. Finally, when he slipped beyond the final doorway they all passed through, he had looked into his own heart and had seen nothing there. Nothing.

But then, decades later, there had been Carolyn, and now . . .

So he lay there, listening as Louise came up the stairs, as the door to her room closed softly. Lay there wondering; if a man lived long enough, could he grow a new soul?

— chapter 8 —

"Michael, what the hell is this?" Lise Hampton-Garibaldi demanded.

"Shhh. I just got her to sleep!"

"Oh." Lise dropped her voice to near inaudibility. "I thought she would be in bed by now."

"I tried to get her to go, but she wanted to see the end of the flick. Not that she made it, anyway. Here, help me put her to bed."

Lise nodded, closed the front door of the apartment carefully.

Mary had fallen asleep with her head in his lap, her mouth slightly open. He eased his arms under her and lifted her off of the couch.

She stirred, and one eye came open. "I wanna watch the rest of the movie," she said, sleepily.

"You did," he said. "You made it, champ. Now me and mom are going to put you in bed."

"Mom?"

"Right here, sweetie." Lise bent and planted a kiss on her four-year-old forehead. "Did you have a good day?"

"Yeah. We played baseball. And then we went for a walk outside."

"Oh, you *did*?" Lise's voice edged back toward the danger zone.

"Heh," Garibaldi said. "Wasn't that going to be our little secret, sport?"

"Oh—yeah."

"C'mon, let's put you to bed." He carried her into the next room, her room, with its Red Sox posters; her mobile of *jeuf*,

76

an airborne sort of lava lamp that was a Minbari thing—a present from Delenn, probably meant for meditation rather than to amuse a child; stuffed animals; model starships; a scattering of clickbricks on the floor. She was already in her pajamas, so he eased her into the bed and under the covers.

"Good night," he said, giving her a kiss on the forehead.

"Tell me a story."

"I need to talk to mom right now."

"Just a short one."

"Ah, well. Okay. Once upon a time, there was this little girl named—umm, Mary. She lived in Olympus Mons, and one day her mom sent her down to the market with three credits to buy some swedish meatballs for dinner—"

"Yuck!"

"And you know, even though swedish meatballs are considered one of the most perfect foods in the known universe, that's exactly what the little girl said. And so while she was going to the swedish-meatball vendor's stall, this weird-looking alien came up to her. He was all covered with black feathers, and had an orange bill—"

"—like Daffy Duck."

"Yeah, a lot like that. Only with big ferlarls."

"What's that?"

"Don't interrupt daddy. And he said, 'Hey kid, I've got something a lot better than swedish meatballs.' And so the little girl said, 'Like what? And I've only got three credits.'

" 'Well, by coincidence, that's exactly what it costs,' the guy said. 'It's a boom-boo seed, from all the way out on the Rim.' And he held out this big, black seed.

" 'What's it do?' she asked.

" 'Well, you just plant it outside, and it'll bring you fame and fortune.' Well, the little girl liked the sound of that, so she paid him the three credits. Her mom was pretty mad when she didn't bring home the meatballs, 'cause that's how moms get when—"

Lise cleared her throat behind him.

"—Of course her dad got mad, too," he added quickly. "Because little girls are supposed to do what their parents say. They sent her to bed without supper, because that's what they did back then. Well, she snuck out the air lock and planted the seed, and the next morning there was this huge plant, a boom-boo, growing so high in the sky it went all the way up to Phobos . . ."

He had barely gotten the little girl to the garden of the giant sloth-man when Mary's breathing evened out. Once he was sure she was asleep, he stopped, kissed her on the forehead again. Lise bent over and kissed her, too.

"Isn't she beautiful, Lise?" he breathed. "I never imagined . . ."

"Yes. And you're good with her. *I* never imagined."

They stood there, looking silently at their child for a moment, before she tugged on his hand. "C'mon. We need to talk."

"First of all, I thought we agreed on no more trips outside, not till she's older."

"But Lise, she wanted to. She begged all day. And this is Mars—kids need to learn how to handle themselves outside early. What if the dome ruptures?"

"A suit rupture is a thousand times more likely." She made a face. "I know you're right. But it's so dangerous."

"I'm careful. You know I wouldn't ever let anything happen to her."

She nodded and reached to squeeze his hand.

"Okay. We'll talk about that later. Right now I want to talk about this." She tapped her notepad, held it up so he could see the display.

"Oh, yeah. I was going to tell you about that."

"It would have been better if you had told me *before*. We're supposed to make decisions like this together."

"Yeah, Lise, I know, but—"

"I mean, I don't get it. There are fewer than two hundred prescriptions written for this stuff. It costs four times as much to produce it as consumers pay for it, even with the subsidy. It lost money for Tao-Johnson—they wouldn't have produced it if it wasn't mandatory, and they hadn't had the bad luck to develop it. Now we own it, so *we* take the loss. Do you know something I don't? Is there about to be an outbreak, or something?"

"No. But believe me, it's worth the investment. To me, it is. And I'm sorry I didn't bring it up with you, because—"

"This has something to do with Bester, doesn't it? A medicine for telepaths. That has Bester written all over it."

"Yep. You got it. That's one of the things I love about you, Lise, always on the ball."

"Never mind the flattery. I'm vaccinated. Explain."

"It's a medicine he needs to live. Only a few people in the whole universe take it—and I still can't find him. Somewhere out there, someone is being supplied with this, but they don't need it. They send it to somebody, and they send it to somebody, who sends it to a Swiss bank, or something. I don't know how he gets it. But it's the only lead I have, and it wasn't taking me anywhere."

"So you bought the monopoly rights to produce it."

"Yes."

"How does that help?"

"I own the supply. I can cut it off."

"Michael! What about the rest of the people who have to have it to live? You wouldn't kill all of them just to get Bester! I know you! I know you're obsessed with this man, but—"

"No, Lise, calm down. I'm not gonna let anyone die. But I can claim that our people have discovered possible side effects and insist that anyone who uses the stuff submit to an examination before their next dose. Then somebody shows up, we test 'em, find they don't have the disease, and we know he's our link to Bester."

"Michael, I thought this was over. I mean, after the war, and all of the death, the hearings—"

"It's not over until Bester is someplace he can't hurt anyone, ever again. I owe it to Sheridan, to Lyta, to the thousands he destroyed. Have you ever seen footage of the reeducation camps, Lise? Have you? I owe my daughter a world without him in it. And yeah, I owe it to *me*."

"Michael, I love you. I'm on your side. But Bester's your new bottle, your new addiction. It's not healthy."

"Lise, I've let most of what was bad about my past go. My life is here, now, with you and Mary. Except for this one thing.

"I can't get past him, I can't get around him. Not if he's still out there, still free, laughing at all of us. I can't. The only way out is dead straight *through* him."

She stared at him for a long, hard moment, before her face finally softened. Her shoulders relaxed, and she put her arms around him and leaned into his neck. "I know," she breathed. "Just be careful. I've lost you too many times. I can't bear the thought of losing you again—not to the real Bester, not to your obsession with him. And I don't want you hiding things from me, like you used to try to hide your empties when you'd been on a bender. If you do this, *we* do this. Understand?"

"Aye, aye."

"Fine." She kissed him, first tenderly, then playfully, then with awakening passion. He kissed her back, trying to force the leering face of Bester out of his mind.

— *chapter 9* —

Bester wiggled his fingers slightly, so that the point of his épée described a small circle. His opponent, a much younger man whose name he had forgotten, rapped at his bell guard. Bester took two quick retreats, then beat sharply and feinted toward the foot. As he had expected, the boy parried instead of retreating. Of course—he was fencing an old man, wasn't he? He was sure to be quicker.

But it's better to be right than quick, Bester mused. In fencing, precision is everything. Bester put the defending blade in a bind and drove the point into the fellow's shoulder. His jacket flashed a bright green.

"Rats!" the fellow shouted. It sounded like American English.

Bester took off his mask. "Nice bout, Mr.—"

"Nary. Thanks."

"I'm guessing you normally fence foil."

"Yeah."

Bester shook his head. "A young man's sport. All of that jumping and lunging." They shook hands.

Bester wiped a little sweat from his brow. When he had been in the Corps, he had followed a fairly strict exercise regime. Sure, a good Psi Cop wasn't often called on to possess physical dexterity, other than marksmanship, but he had learned early that when those times did come, it was usually a matter of life and death. So he had practiced various martial arts, run a few miles every day.

His years in exile had softened him in that way, as they had toughened him in others. It just hadn't seemed worth the trouble. Now, though, he was suddenly conscious of those few extra pounds and wanted the harder muscles of youth back. He had tried his old routine, but found it depressed him. His new life needed a new regimen.

He had fenced in the academy and been quite good. Fencing other telepaths had been useful for developing strategies of mental blocking, sending false signals, and so forth—but after the academy he had thought of it as a sport, with no practical application.

Well, that was his life now—a life without practical application. He wrote literary critiques, he bought young women dresses, he fenced. He was in Paris—why not?

And fencing normals was satisfying. Years as a Psi Cop had taught him to read body and facial language without scanning, but if he really needed to, he could pick up their strategies without them noticing. He didn't feel bad about it—men with long arms didn't feel bad about having more reach, after all. But he was careful. Though he hadn't met any other telepaths who used the salle, you never knew when one might come in. Another P12 might just notice him using his abilities, even at a very low level.

He was done for the day, he decided. He said good-bye to the maître d'armes, a knotty old man named Hibnes, and hit the showers, where he enjoyed the feel of hot water on his abused muscles. They were tightening up, he noticed with pleasure. He was leaner and felt years younger than when he had arrived on Earth. Paris almost seemed to be aging him backward. Yes, it had been right to come here. Perfect. That became more obvious with each passing day.

He took a roundabout way back to the hotel. He never followed the same route twice—having a routine an enemy could pick up on was a bad idea, and some habits shouldn't die. After all, it wasn't paranoia when people really were out to get you. And there was a whole universe of people out to get Alfred Bester, all of whom would give anything to know where he was at the moment.

Today his walk took him through the Bois de Boulogne, finally bringing him to the Metro station at Boulogne–Pont de St.-Cloud. He stood waiting for the train as the platform filled up.

He remembered Louise in the dress, how it clung to her contours. She looked embarrassed, but her surface thoughts told a different story. She *knew* she looked good in it.

That had been last night. He hadn't seen her this morning, and he wondered idly if she had met someone at the opera and gone home with him. Or maybe Lucien, the cop, had finally talked her into going out with him.

He found he didn't like that thought much. Maybe he *should* have gone with her. But he didn't want to be obvious, a pathetic old man chasing a younger woman.

Of course, he *could* just read her mind, find out what she did think of him. But with Louise, that seemed somehow wrong, a violation.

No, he said to himself. *That's not it. You're just afraid of what you'll find. That she likes you and pities you, but has no interest in you as a man.*

He felt a sudden anger. That was the ghost of Byron, taunting in his head. What made him even more angry was that it was probably true.

A train arrived, but it wasn't his. He stood there, frowning, some of his good mood dissipated.

And he caught someone watching him, felt a telepathic touch.

He jerked his head around, and a face jumped out of the crowd. An older face, pale, snub-nosed, weak-chinned. He recognized it in an instant—he had always had a good memory for faces.

A telepath. What was his name? Askern? Ackeron? Ackerman. He had worked at one of the reeducation camps . . .

The fellow looked away. Bester managed a light scan, one he knew would be undetectable to a telepath of Ackerman's feeble abilities. Bester looked familiar to Ackerman, but the fellow hadn't placed him. The beard made a big difference.

Bester started pushing through the crowd, but the man was boarding the train. By the time Bester got there, the doors had shut.

Ackerman hadn't recognized him, he was sure. He hadn't.
He suddenly realized his hands were shaking.

"What's wrong?" Louise asked. "You look like a ghost."
Bester settled wearily into his chair. "Maybe I am," he said,
bleakly.
"Well, if you want to talk about something—"
"How was the opera?" he cut in. "It must have been a long
one. I never heard you come in."
Her face darkened. "You were here, eh? I thought you had
something to do last night. I thought that's why you couldn't
come with me."
"I lied. I hate opera."
"You're still lying. I've heard you playing it in your room."
"Louise—"
Her face softened. "I'm sorry," she said, with an odd
abruptness. "It's none of my business, and I'm sorry. Just as
it's none of your business that I came in late, yes?"
"Yes," Bester replied, nodding, feeling somehow relieved.
She stood for a long moment, unspeaking. It should have
been uncomfortable, but it wasn't.
"Will you come with me? I want to show you something."
"Of course." He stood, his legs feeling a little light. His
medication was a day late, but it couldn't be that—he still had
a week before he would become symptomatic. He wasn't
worried about that.
Maybe just old age.
He followed Louise from the café and up a flight of stairs,
all the way to the upper loft of the building. Bester had asked
about it once, about why she never rented that space out, but
she had tersely changed the subject.
She unlocked the door with one of the old-fashioned keys
on her ring, revealing a spacious room with high ceilings and
tall panels of windows. Lavish afternoon sunlight draped
golden on the polished wooden floors. Other than that, the
room was empty, except for an easel with a canvas on it, a
wooden paint box and pallet, and a chair.
"This is where I lived with my husband," she explained.

"After he left, I couldn't stand to even come up here. I hadn't opened that door in five years. This morning I did."

"You're taking up painting again?"

"Yes."

"Well, I'm glad."

"Are you? Good. Then you shall agree to model for me."

"What? No, I couldn't do that."

"And why not? You've used up the free rent you earned helping me clean and paint. Here's your chance to make a bit more."

"No."

She dropped her bantering mood and laid her fingers on his arm. "Please? I want a chance to capture what that street-scribbler did. I want a chance to paint something difficult, hidden, and true. I think, once, I could have done that. I want to see if I still can."

The sincerity in her voice got to him.

"Very well," he said. "I suppose it can't hurt. But you won't get me out of my clothes, young lady."

"No? Then you will wear the outfit I picked for you, yes?"

He shrugged. "Why not?"

They stood there for a moment, until she said, "Well?"

"Well, what?"

"Go change."

"Don't fidget. There, like that."

"Can I breathe?"

"Breathe, talk, whatever you want, just hold that position, more or less."

"I'll try," he said, dryly. In his peripheral vision, he saw her regard him, then the canvas, then tentatively lift her brush.

"I've never painted portraits before, you know?" she said, after a few moments. "It was considered passé when I was in school. Minbari dialectic perspective was all the rage."

"Minbari what? You're making that up."

"No, sorry to say, I'm not. It was a key philosophy in the nouveau post-ante-postmodern tradition."

"You're making that up, too."

She laughed, a musical trill, the first such laugh he had ever heard from her. A child's laugh.

"Somebody made it up. It wasn't me. I've read your literary columns, you know. Don't play the epistemological innocent with me."

"You read my column?"

"Yes, now and then. You have a most apt way with insults."

"Is that a compliment?"

She chuckled again, this time in her more accustomed, more cynical voice. "What good is a compliment? No one ever gained anything from praise."

"Ah. So you *have* read my column."

"Yes. If you don't mind me saying so, Mr. Kaufman, I don't really approve of it."

"Criticism of criticism? Now you try to improve me?"

"It's easy to take a house apart. It's harder to build one."

"Meaning?"

"Meaning you have a way with language, and you ought to use it in a positive way. Write something of your own."

"So that it, in turn, might be criticized?"

"That's what stops you, then? Fear?"

Bester considered that. "No. To be honest, it actually never occurred to me to write anything."

"You seem like a man with a lot to say. Isn't there anything you want people to understand, something you think the Human race has missed, somehow?"

From the place in his mind where he kept Byron, he heard a sardonic chuckle. *Yes, Mr. Bester. Wouldn't you like to make them understand? Understand why you made me slaughter defenseless mundanes? Why you murdered your own kind? Why the gutters of the reeducation camps ran with tears and blood? Tears and Blood—now there's a title for you.*

"Maybe you're right," Bester said, trying to ignore Byron. "I'll have to think about it."

For whatever reason, his medication hadn't shown up in his secure postbox. The one thing he really needed from what remained of his network, and it hadn't come. It was three days late now. What could have happened? The people involved simply couldn't betray him—he had too much on them, and in some cases, *in* them.

In another week, things would start to get bad. He would start leaking, telepathically. Louise, if no one else, would find out what he was. She might even be able to handle it, but would she be able to handle it when he lost his mind and began the agonizing process of dying? Would she be able to handle having to spoon-feed him like a baby, change his pants?

He wouldn't put her through that, no matter what, not that she would do it anyway. No, he would end up in the hospital, where eventually a routine DNA check would slip past his insiders in the Metasensory Division of the EABI. Then the hunters would come. But of course they wouldn't find much, would they?

It was just a delay, nothing more. The ampoules would arrive tomorrow, and everything would be fine.

When two more days passed with no sign of his medication, he did something he did not want to do. He went to a pay phone and dialed a certain number. That connected him to an AI in Sweden, which in turn uplinked him to Mars, and finally to the off-world colony of Crenshaw's World. Supposedly, at each node there was only a two-percent chance of being traced either way, and through three transfers he should be safe no matter what.

The call took a long time to connect. Finally, someone answered the phone.

"Hello."

He stood stock-still. He didn't answer. He knew the voice well enough, but it wasn't the one he had expected.

"Bester? Is that you? You know who this is, don't you?"

It was Garibaldi.

"I'm coming for you, Bester. I'm coming for you, you son of a bitch."

Bester hung up.

* * *

Jem made a stuttering sound when he opened the door to find Bester standing there. It took him several seconds to compose himself enough to invite Bester in.

"I haven't been giving Louise a hard time," he rushed to say. "In fact, I've been keeping trouble away from her and givin' the other hotels in the neighborhood *more* trouble so she'd get more customers. Just like you said."

"I know, Jem, and I'm very pleased. That's not what I came here for."

"No?"

"No. I need some help with something, something right up your alley."

"Oh. Uh—sit down, won'tcha?"

"I don't mind if I do," Bester replied, taking a seat in an overstuffed armchair.

"Mind if I get a drink?"

"Not at all."

"You want one?"

"It's a little early in the day for me."

Jem poured himself a tumbler of scotch, then sat on the couch, rolling the glass between his palms. "What's the deal?" he asked.

"It's pretty simple, really—a little breaking and entering."

"Where, what, and when?" Jem's voice was smoothing out now, growing more confident now that they were talking about something he knew how to deal with.

"A pharmacy downtown, the big one on the Boulevard St.-Germain."

"I know the place. It's pretty tough. During the plague there was a rumor that they had a cure, but only the rich were getting it. After a few break-ins they screwed security down good. What do you need? I can probably get it on the black market."

"Not this. And it's the only place in Paris that has what I want."

There were four people in Paris besides himself who suffered from his condition—he'd checked that before coming. He had even acquired their names and addresses, against just this sort of eventuality. His original contingency plan had been to simply go to their houses and take their doses if he needed them. That was before Garibaldi got involved. The drug was made by a rival company, but Garibaldi must have discovered Bester's condition somehow and tracked down Bester's supplier.

That complicated matters considerably. The number of people who needed the inhibitor were few enough that a man with Garibaldi's resources could have tracked them all down. If one of them turned up dead, or had to apply for another dose, it would attract attention. So far, Garibaldi didn't—couldn't—know where he was. His contact on Crenshaw's World couldn't have given up his location because he didn't know it.

But if he took the serum from one of the other telepaths in Paris, Garibaldi would know where he was, probably within days, certainly in under a month.

Hitting the pharmacy itself was safer, more oblique. Pharmacies got robbed all the time. The trick was simply to make certain no one could tell *why* it had been hit.

"I need you to torch it, too."

"Why?"

"That's on a need-to-know basis, Jem, and you don't need to know. How about it?"

"Sure thing, Mr. Kaufman. I'll do it."

"Actually, *we'll* do it. I need to be there."

Jem absorbed that with clear surprise, but didn't say anything. He took another gulp of his drink and stared down into the amber fluid. "What did you do to me, Mr. Kaufman?" he asked, in a small voice. "I tried . . . I tried to tell my buddies, but I couldn't. Sometimes I try to think about killing you, too—" he winced, suddenly "—but I can't even think about it. And the dreams I have . . . I keep dreaming I'm dead, that I'm just this walking hole in the air.

"I haven't asked please in my whole life. Never, not even to my old man. But I'm asking now. Please. *Je vous en prie.* I'll do whatever you say. Anything. But just—can't you make the dreams stop?"

Bester tilted his head. "You'll do anything I say, no matter what, or it'll get worse, and worse, and worse, until you can't stand to even blink. You know that. I don't have to do anything for your obedience. As far as you are concerned, I am God, the only thing in the universe that really matters."

"Please." He was weeping.

Bester reached over and patted Jem's shoulder. The big man flinched. "I'll consider it, after this job. Consider it, mind you."

"Okay," Jem said, and finished his drink. His eyes didn't seem to hold much hope.

"Now, why don't you be a good little boy and go check out the pharmacy? Everything—floor plan, guards, security equipment. I'll give you two days to get all of that together, then I'll meet you back here and we'll make our plans. Okay?"

"Okay. I'm right on it."

"Good boy. I'll see you in two days."

— chapter 10 —

Bester's skin itched, and the light played games with his eyes. He found it more difficult than ever to sit still, and Byron's voice was louder in his head. So were strange voices, floating in from the street like unpleasant and unwanted fumes.

He told himself it would be okay. Tonight he would speak to Jem again, and in a few days he'd have the inhibitor. If not—if not, he would do what he had to. Find one of the other teeps, take their dose, and leave Paris.

The thought of being on the run again, beneath cold and unfamiliar stars, hurt more than he thought it would. For a terrible instant, he actually thought he would weep. He was losing control of his emotions, not a good sign.

"You seem sad today," Louise observed, from her place at the easel.

The sound of her voice soothed him, but it also highlighted his dilemma. Soon he would start leaking, telepathically. Soon she would know what he was, maybe even *who* he was. Would she hate him then? Probably.

Definitely, Byron mocked.

"I'm just feeling sorry for myself. A common failing in the old."

"You aren't *that* old—but I must say, you do seem rather alone in the world, Mr. Kaufman. Don't you have any family, any friends?"

The Corps is mother, the Corps is father. We are the children of the Corps, Byron interjected, in a snide tone.

91

"Not anymore," Bester said wearily. "What about you? Don't you have family?"

"I had a pretty big family," Louise said. "Three brothers and three sisters. I was the middle child."

"Where is this big family of yours?"

"Well, it's not so big now. Dad suffered a heart attack six years ago. My youngest brother, Pierre, was on the *Victory* when the Drakh took her out. Jean and Francois immigrated to Beta Colony years ago. Mom is remarried and lives in Melbourne; we talk on the phone but it's been two years since I saw her. One of my sisters, Anne, fought with Sheridan against Clark, and my oldest sister was in Clark's personal guard. They haven't spoken since, and after one attempt at making peace between them, I haven't spoken much to them, either."

"That leaves a sister."

"Ah. I stole her boyfriend and made him my husband."

"Oops."

"Yes. I keep hoping she'll forgive me—you'd think she'd see by now that I did her a favor. But I'm not going to beg."

"I'm sorry to hear all of this."

"Don't be. I still love them, and I think they all still love me. You never really lose family—you just misplace them now and then. But I've learned that it isn't smart to count on them, either. A lot of people from big families never really learn to be independent. I did, and I'm glad. The rest will work out, eventually."

"And now *you* seem sad."

"Sad, yes. Depressed, no. And you dodged my question, I think. About your family."

"I had a big family, too," Bester said, and to his surprise he realized it wasn't exactly a lie. "I had a brother—Brett. We were always rivals, I guess, always trying to one-up each other. In a way, I think I was closest to him, of all my siblings." He watched the clouds in the sky beyond the window. He thought he could see faces in them, Milla, Azmun, and yes, Brett. The kids from his cadre, the ones he had grown up with. What were they, if not siblings?

"Brett's been dead for many years. I still miss him, even though it sometimes feels like he's looking over my shoulder. Our parents—" *The Corps is mother, the Corps is father* "—our parents were tough, but fair. Pretty old school."

He smiled, but behind his eyes a memory flashed so vividly that for a moment he didn't see Louise, or the clouds, or anything else. Instead he saw fire and smoke, a rogue stronghold on Mars almost half a century ago.

The leader of the rebel telepaths was dying at his feet. A man who claimed to have held Bester as a baby, to have known his real parents. Matthew and Fiona Dexter, the kingpins of the underground until they were killed in 2189, the year he had been born.

He shot the rogue for saying that, shot him until the fist holding the gun clenched permanently, into a useless, dead—

"Claude? What is it? What's wrong?"

He blinked. Louise was watching him with a look of concern in her face.

"Nothing. I . . . just a memory."

"Must have been some memory. Are you sure you're okay?"

"I . . . yes. Don't worry about me. You just keep painting."

"I can't. I'm not seeing what I want to—that thing in you I wanted to capture. I think it's never been farther from your face."

"I'm sorry to disappoint you."

"I'm disappointed in myself, not in you. But I'll find it eventually."

"May I see the painting?"

"Not until it's done. Old tradition. Still, we're done for the day, I think."

"Now *I'm* disappointed," he blurted, and was instantly sorry he had done so.

She didn't answer, though he thought he felt a mental blush from her. The air seemed to dance, and not in a good way.

He was getting worse. He had to see Jem.

* * *

"I'm not sure we can do it," Jem explained.

"Why?"

"They went the whole nine yards and made it a smart building. Anybody goes in there gets detected by motion, sniffers, and sound. Sends an alarm to the security company and the cops. The response time was only six minutes last time somebody tried to get in, and it could be even quicker.

"The whole thing is run by an AI, so there's no way to fool it. It's wireless and has its own power supply, so there are no lines to cut. Plus, there's a live guard. Even if we get the job done fast enough, it'll take records of us—the damn thing is lousy with eyes and sniffers, and most of 'em are probably hidden."

"I think I can solve that problem," Bester said.

"How?"

"With this." He held out a small black chip, about the size of a book of matches.

"What's that?"

Bester tumbled the object between his fingers. It was one of the things that had gotten him to Earth through the tight security and quarantine. A bit of Shadow technology that Psi Corps had been able to copy and make use of.

"Have you ever read Descartes?"

"Uh, no."

"You should broaden your mind, Jem. It's good for you. He said, 'I think, therefore I am.' "

"Yeah, I've heard that."

"You understand it?"

"I guess so."

"It was part of a larger point Descartes was making. I know I exist, but how do I know anyone or anything else does? Can I really trust the information I receive from my senses? Maybe not. It could all be an illusion, or a delusion. I might be imagining all of it."

"I know the feelin'," Jem said. "What's this got to do with the security system?"

"Just this. The building is an artificial intelligence that examines the information provided by its sensors, decides what it has seen, heard, smelled, and then acts upon that data. *This* device—" he held up the black chip "—can map the AI's system, then impose its own logic. In effect, it will make the AI unable to act upon the data it receives—because the AI won't 'believe' it."

"You're going to screw with the computer's head."

"Exactly."

"I've heard of that kind of thing. Usually it doesn't work—the computer recognizes it as a virus or whatever."

"This isn't a virus. It can perfectly mimic the AI, which won't recognize that any foreign intervention is involved. The internal alarms won't go off, and the 'OK' signals will go out just as before."

"I guess I'll take your word for it."

Bester smiled. "As in so many things, Jem, you don't have a choice."

The street was quiet enough at two in the morning, but Paris was never truly quiet. In the distance, groundcar horns blared, voices rose in protest, anger, and joy, adding to the background noise that was building in his head.

The April rain was a godsend. Oh, it was miserable and cold, winter having its last say, but it drew a beaded curtain across the world. In the rain, people put their heads down and hurried to wherever they were going. People missed things, in the rain.

Bester found that he liked it. Years—maybe decades, now that he thought about it—had passed in his life without him ever feeling a drop on his cheek. The closest thing to rain that Mars ever got was a subtle condensation, a frost. Nothing like this, this smell of wet pavement, of the air itself being washed clean.

Jem seemed less happy. He hunkered against the downpour. He was probably one of those people who tried to calculate whether he would get wet faster running or walking. As if it mattered, Bester mused. As if a tiny bit more or less wet could make a difference.

A car passed, and the rain became gems, falling in slow motion, white-hot metal, dripping . . .

Get a grip, Bester, he thought. *Just a little longer, and this particular problem will be solved.*

What then? Byron asked. *Will you go somewhere else and pretend not to be a monster?*

"Shut up," he muttered.

"Eh?" Jem asked.

"Nothing."

"Well, we're here. This is the back door I was telling you about."

"Oh." He fumbled the black chip out of his pocket, touched one of the contacts. Almost immediately, a green light flicked on.

"That's got it," Al said. "You can open the door now."

Jem opened his heavy black bag and pulled out a bulkhead drill. He stuck it against the lock and turned it on, pulsing bursts of coherent X rays in rapid cycles.

Rain began to hiss against the door as the metal heated up. A few moments later, Jem pushed it open. It went with a sigh, the loudest sound either of them had made so far.

Al pulled a Colt 9 mm from his coat pocket and made sure the silencer was in place. Not the PPG he was used to, but those were hard to come by on Earth. In space they were great, because the phased helium plasma they fired could wreak terrific havoc on flesh and bone without punching a hole through a bulkhead. But PPGs were expensive, generally limited to security and military personnel, and in the end no better for killing quickly than a slug thrower. Less so, in fact, in many ways.

As they ghosted into the building, Bester concentrated and probed for the guard, but came up with nothing. That was odd. His senses should be heightened by his condition, not dulled.

Maybe that was the problem. The city was practically shouting at him. The gentle murmur and cadence of minds—which had once so intrigued him—had, in the past few days, become a loathsome racket. What was that line from Poe?

"Above all was the sense of hearing acute. I heard all things in the heaven and in the earth. I heard many things in hell. How, then, am I mad?"

Yes, if he didn't get the serum soon, he would end as the protagonist of that story, screaming madly about some imaginary telltale heart . . .

He shook his head to clear it, and scanned again. This was no time for slip-ups.

Still nothing. Maybe the guard had the night off.

Jem could move with admirable grace when he wanted to, like some sort of big cat. And Bester, of course, had the benefit of long years of practice, from that first time he had gone after Blips, on his own, when he was only fifteen. That had been in Paris, too . . .

He caught it, then, the sudden feeling that someone was walking on his grave. And the almost forgotten sensation of brushing across someone's blocks.

Blocks. *Blocks.*

The guard was a telepath. Of course. Telepaths could do almost anything these days, couldn't they? The possibility had never occurred to him.

"Hold it. Hold it right there."

No. It had never occurred to him, and as a consequence, the telepath guard was right behind them.

"Don't make it worse on yourselves. So far it's just breaking and entering, not theft or possession. The police are already on their way. I know one of you is a teep, but don't think you can get away with any funny stuff. I'm a P10, and I'm well-trained for psi combat."

Bester suddenly felt absolutely absurd. Caught napping by a P10.

Kill him, Jem, he sent.

Jem dropped and spun, pulling two pistols, like a cowboy from some ancient vid. Muzzle flashes lit the scene. Bester got a glimpse of the teep ducking behind a row of shelves, letting one round go as he did so.

As Bester jumped up and ran the other way, Jem came back

to his feet, firing into the shelving, obviously hoping a blind
bullet would punch through and hit his target.

Bester ducked low and scuttled down the row.

He must have been leaking and not known it. The teep had
been on to them from the beginning. He had called the cops,
which meant they had a few minutes, at best.

Behind him, the firefight continued. The guard's gun
wasn't silenced—it cracked, loud and brassy. Jem's weapons
were almost inaudible—the thunk and whine of his bullets,
whizzing into and through things, had a ghostly quality.

Bester reached the vault. The choline ribosylase would
have to be stored there. How many minutes left?

He needed the drill. Jem had it.

Not for the first time he cursed the Corps gene-whizzes, the
scientists who had created his damnable condition. They'd
been too technology-happy, in those days. Enhancements—
dust, for God's sake! Whose bright idea had it been to give
normals the gift of telepathy?

Not his. He had fought tooth and nail against it, but that
was before . . .

Concentrate. Byron was laughing at him. *Ignore it.*
Concentrate.

He slipped back though the aisles, searching for the guard,
but his pistol had stopped firing. So had Jem's. Was it over?
He reached out, felt Jem. The big man was radiating pain. He
was probably hit. But the guard . . .

Behind him again.

Bester didn't drop, or roll, or dodge. He just turned around
and fired, as thunder exploded a few feet from him. He felt
something hot graze his face, but he didn't flinch. Why
should he flinch? Who could dodge a bullet? Might as well
try to avoid getting wet in the rain.

Then the teep was squirming on the ground. He'd been hit
in the chest, probably not a mortal wound. For a moment,
Bester felt a sudden pang. This was one of his own, one of his
family. A telepath.

Then he remembered Byron, and the war, and the hearing.

He shot the man in the head, twice. The body twitched grotesquely and stopped moving.

Jem was hit. Bester couldn't tell how bad.

"Jesus, it hurts," the big man grunted.

"I know. We'll get it looked at, soon. But first we have to get what we came for. Can you walk?"

"Yeah." He came jerkily to his feet. They found the satchel and went back to the vault. Outside, Bester could hear the weird sound of Parisian police cars, that undulating call that hadn't changed much in centuries.

The vault took a tad longer than the door, and once they were inside, it took Bester a few minutes to locate the serum. Meanwhile, as instructed, Jem stuffed his bag with the drugs that had street value.

"Got it," Bester said. His fingers were shaking. There were four ampoules. He took them and slipped four similar ampoules filled with water in their place. "I'm going now, Jem," he said. "Take care."

"Okay," Jem replied. He sounded unsure, his voice shaking. "What's happening? What am I doing?"

"It's okay, Jem. You'll be okay. And you won't have any more nightmares, just like you asked. Okay?"

"Okay."

Bester left him then, back out the door they had come in. Cars were everywhere. Most were out front—he had seen their lights through the window. But there was one here, in the side alley. Two uniforms held guns pointed at him, shielded by their car.

"Don't move," one of them said.

"I'm unarmed," Bester replied.

"Put your hands where I can see them."

"Okay, okay—just don't shoot." He walked slowly toward the car.

"I said stand there!" the cop commanded.

Bester continued to sidle away from the door.

One of the cops got up and came forward, his gun unwavering. "Down on the ground. Hands behind your head."

"As you say, Officer."

It wasn't a loud explosion—but it was a bright one, and very hot. Six grams of Kerikan X in Jem's bag. The doorway into the building might as well have been a tunnel into the sun. Bester had his eyes closed and was facing the ground, and he still saw the light, felt the heat lick across his back.

The cops weren't so lucky. Still, they would have had a slightly better than even chance of recovering their sight if he hadn't carefully placed a bullet in the brain of each before he walked off into the night.

He wasn't followed—there were no other cops on this side of the building, and the ones out front had their own worries to occupy them.

"No more nightmares, Jem," he murmured, feeling the ampoules in his pocket. "No more."

— chapter 11 —

"You're sitting well today, Mr. Kaufman," Louise said.

"Thank you," Bester replied. "I feel better today than I have in a while. I think I had a touch of something."

"I thought so, too. I was starting to get worried about you." She dabbed at her palette, scrunching her face and twisting her nose to one side. Bester found himself watching her, not for the first time.

Yes, he felt a hell of a lot better, as a matter of fact. His symptoms had faded entirely, leaving him only with a slightly jumbled memory of what he and Jem had done, two nights before.

Looking back on it, he was amazed he hadn't been caught, so close had he been to the edge of reality. Still, his instincts had pulled him through, if not his intellect. He knew about trails, had been following them all his life, and so he knew how not to leave them.

There were three possible complications, of course. Someone might have seen him and might be able to describe him. That was the one he was least worried about, given the rain and the general mayhem that had been involved. His second was that when they began to investigate Jem—if they ever managed to figure out who he had been—it could bring inspectors around who might recognize him.

The third—and the one that most worried him—was that Garibaldi would somehow notice the caper. True, when they found what remained of the ampoules where they ought to be, and a drug dealer's body in the shop, they would have no reason at all to check for traces of the serum among the melted glass.

But they *might*.

He really should leave. Leave Paris, leave Earth. The vacation had been fun, but there was no reason to take chances.

"You were out awfully late the other night," Louise said. "Did you have a hot date?"

"You might say that," Bester replied.

"Really? Anyone I know?"

"No, I was kidding. I was just out, walking and thinking. About what you said—about writing a book of some sort."

"Memoirs?"

"No, that would be too close to home. A novel, perhaps. Something that would allow me to approach things more obliquely."

"I think novelists are cowards, sometimes."

"I thought *I* was the literary critic here."

"You are. I would have assumed you thought the same. Novelists put the things they'd like to say themselves in the mouths of fictional characters. It distances them from it. They can always claim it was just the character saying those things, that they were simply portraying an opinion rather than expressing one."

"Sometimes they are."

"Yes. An effective smokescreen, I think, for their real thoughts."

"So you think I should write memoirs."

"I didn't say that. I don't know enough about your life to know if it would be interesting without making things up. But I bet it is." She put down her brush and looked squarely at him. "Who are you, Mr. Kaufman? What are you?"

A little chill walked up his spine. She sounded almost— angry. Where had *that* come from? Had he let something slip, while he was sick? He wished he had a clearer memory of those days.

"I don't understand."

"The other day. After the opera, when you wondered where

I had been. You thought I was with someone, didn't you? A man?"

"I didn't give it a thought. Besides, didn't you just ask me something similar?"

"Very good," Louise said. "In the same breath you say 'no I didn't, but if I *did*—' et cetera. Be honest. You thought I was with someone, and you didn't like it."

He didn't answer that, just tried to look at her as if she had gone crazy.

She shook her head and walked toward him.

"No. You know where I was that night? Walking. Thinking. Trying to make some sort of *sense* out of a man who would give me a dress fit for an empress, then wiggle out of taking me anywhere in it. A stranger who appeared in the worst hour of my life and was *there* for me, like no one else has ever been. And for no good reason. Or no reason he will admit."

"What do you mean?"

"You know what I mean. You either know it or you are stupid. I've thought a lot about this. And these past few days—the whole of last week—you seemed . . . unguarded somehow. I saw things on your face, obvious things. But they're gone now. Why?"

"I don't have the slightest idea what you're talking about," Bester said, trying to sound irritated, rather than as he felt—at sea, almost panicky.

"Must I be blunt? I think you have fallen in love with me. Have you?"

For a second his head rang as if he'd just fended off an attack by two P12s. And try as he might, he couldn't tear his gaze from the floor, couldn't confront her eyes.

"Yes." He sighed.

She abruptly turned her back to him and paced a few steps. Then she came back, closer and closer, until she stood over him, her arms folded defensively in front of her. He could feel her staring at the top of his head, but he had no sense of what she was thinking at all. None. It was as if he had been given sleepers, as if his psi were turned off.

"You stupid man," she said. Then she took his chin in her

fingers and tilted it up. She bent and kissed him, softly, on the lips. She took his head in her hands and kissed him more firmly, but finally, finally he understood what was going on, and his lips remembered what to do.

He got his feet under him, and his arms around her, and he was shocked by the warmth, the solidity of her in his arms. Startled by the shape of her back, by the close scent of her, by how different her face looked, this near his own.

He felt like a comet, a million years in the void beyond Pluto, finally approaching the Sun, ice turning to vapor . . .

Her room was neat, and tidy, and mostly blue, and not something he paid much attention to when they finally reached it. Not when he had her hair, and her sky-bright eyes, and eventually the delicious feel of warm flesh, the tangle and sliding of limb against limb, face against belly, kisses that had long since gone from precious to hungry. He felt like a boy, like a man. He felt nothing at all like any Alfred Bester he had ever known.

He cheated a little—he could feel what she felt, which made him a fast learner. He slightly stimulated certain brain centers at the appropriate time, too—he wanted to give her everything he could. He wished she were a telepath, so she could feel what he did, know what he had just found in his heart. But then she might see how otherwise empty he was, too, and the things he had done, and be afraid.

They didn't speak afterward, either, as night crept into the streets outside, but curled together and fell slowly asleep, as if both understood that words were pointless. He didn't sleep long, though. It had been a very long time since he had shared a bed, and he wasn't used to it. He watched her face in the pale illumination of the small lamp on the dresser.

He got up quietly, to turn the light off, but paused at the window. He moved the curtain aside and glanced down on the empty street.

In his reflection on the dark glass he saw Byron's face, Byron's sardonic smile.

You don't deserve her. You don't deserve anyone, Byron said.

"Deserving has nothing to do with it," Bester whispered. "I have another chance. A real chance. I've never been happy, never in my life. I've never known how to be."

He closed his eyes. "I don't need you anymore, Byron. You are a part of what I was. You're a part of what I couldn't let go. It's like I fell in a fast-moving river, and for years did nothing more than hang onto the rocks, my arms aching, trying to tear from their sockets. I might have died, holding onto that rock. Instead, I'm going to see where the river goes. I'm turning loose."

That's not you, Byron said. *That's never been you. You have to have control. Always control.*

"Good-bye, Byron."

And Byron was gone, unraveled. His haunting was over.

Then Bester lay against Louise, and she made a happy sound. He fell asleep, and he did not dream.

Garibaldi woke up with the sweats, wondering where he was.

There was a certain kind of dream, the kind when you think you've done something horrible, irrevocable. There were mild versions—the dream that you had an exam coming up for a class you never attended, for instance. There were darker ones, too—the kind where you've committed a terrible crime, which you could try to hide. But not forever, never forever . . .

In his dream, he'd betrayed the best man he had ever known to the worst people he had ever known, on purpose, with malice aforethought.

The thing about dreams like that, usually, was that you could wake up from them and realize that it *had* been a dream. No exam, no manslaughter, no betrayal.

But for Garibaldi, waking only made it worse, because then he remembered it was true. He'd really done it, and no dream could capture the depth of the harm he had wrought.

And while he would never get over the feeling that some of the blame was his to shoulder, he inevitably came back to one fact. Bester had been the cause. It wasn't an excuse, nor the old "devil made me do it" line, but the literal truth. Garibaldi had been programmed, like some kind of wet-brained robot.

That's the alcoholic in you, he thought. Alcoholics always had excuses explaining why they weren't responsible for what they did. It was one of the things that had caused him to drink, back when he had done so. It gave him a license to screw up.

Well, he'd kicked the bottle. So maybe Lise was right. Maybe Bester *was* his new addiction. Maybe it was time to kick the Bester habit, too.

He lay there for a while, listening to Lise's gentle breathing, trying to shut down his mind, to get some sleep.

After half an hour, he gave up. He went into the next room, switched on his AI, and stared sleepily at the screen. He called up his choline ribosylase hotlist.

No bites. Everyone who had been tested, except the guy on Crenshaw's World, really had the condition, and no one had applied for an extra dose. Nor had any been stolen.

Wait . . . Four people in Paris had put in for prescription refills, only hours ago. What was up with that?

Within moments, he had the story. An attempted robbery had gone bad, a drug-crazed mobster had blown himself up when he got caught.

It didn't look like any of the inhibitor had been taken. There was a rundown of everything his company needed to replace, and all four doses of the stuff were accounted for in the drugstore safe. Destroyed, but accounted for.

Still . . .

He ran down the dead crook's record. Jemelah Perdue, thirty-two years of age, with a police record that accounted for twenty-three of them. No surprises there. No visible ties to Psi Corps.

What about the teeps? He ran them down, too, and they all looked clean, but you could never tell.

He shook his head and looked at the clock. Three in the morning. What the hell was he doing?

Lise *was* right. How many drugstores had been robbed that

night? A quick inquiry brought that up, too. Six hundred thirty-three robberies or attempted robberies of drugstores reported. That meant, in all of Human space, there were at least that many again that hadn't been reported yet, or he hadn't gotten the record for.

"Say good night, Mike," he grunted, flipping off the screen.

Garibaldi had a life to live, and Bester had already taken too much of it. No more. The hell with him.

He went to bed.

part ii

Reckoning

— chapter 1 —

Paris in summer. For Bester the days were molds filled each morning with golden heat, ordinary and extraordinary intimacies, flowers, and candlelight.

"I've never fallen in love like this," he told Louise one morning, in a little restaurant called Isabelle, tucked in a corner of the new market off the Rue de Martin.

"Like what?" she asked.

"Like this. Quiet evenings, and moonlit walks, and breakfasts in bed."

"No? How did you fall in love before?"

"In the war. On the go. Shells falling all around—that sort of thing. Or earlier, in school, when I wasn't supposed to."

"Ah. Forbidden romances. The sort they write books about. How does this compare?"

He took her hand, marveling, still, that her fingers gripped him back. "It doesn't," he said. "Before, there was always something I wanted more than a relationship. I was in love with my goals, my work. And love, however pleasant, was just . . . in the way.

"It isn't like that now. If I had known you fifty years ago, or even twenty . . ."

"If this were twenty years ago, you would be arrested for pedophilia, at the very least."

"There is that," Bester replied. "I still don't know what you see in an old man like me."

"Age doesn't matter much to me," she said.

"So I see."

"No, I don't think you do. I think it worries you."

He shrugged. "Okay—yes. Maybe not for exactly the reasons that you think. When I was in the military, I held a position of some authority. It attracted young women to me, in search, I think, of the father they had always wanted. One of those psychological things."

"Electra complex. Woman seeks man like her father because she's subconsciously in love with her father and knows she can't have him."

"That's it."

"Would it help if I told you, you are nothing like my father?"

"I'm sure it would."

"You're nothing like my father."

"Well, if you say it, I believe it."

"Credulity. I like that in a man. What else shall I ask you to accept without question?" She paused, as if to think about it, then looked him levelly in the eye. "How about this? You are the very best thing that has happened to me in a very long time. I don't know what brought you to my hotel, but I'm glad it did."

"I wouldn't question that," Bester said, a bit stiffly. "I might doubt it, but I couldn't question it. You make me . . ." He searched, but everything sounded so trite, so awkward. "You make me happier, I think, than I've ever been."

"Well," she said, her eyes flashing, "now that we've got the mutual appreciation out of the way, how shall we spend the rest of our day off?"

"Hmm. What's the one sick, secret thing you've always wanted to do in Paris, the one thing no real Parisian would ever be caught dead doing?"

"Oh, that's easy. The Eiffel Tower."

"The Eiffel Tower it is, then."

"Eh. We have to go disguised as tourists, then."

"Yes, of course. Cameras."

"Shorts and knee socks for you."

"An 'I love Paris' T-shirt for *you*."

"And ugly shoes for the both of us. Fine. A perfect idea. And you have to ask directions."

"But I *know* the way to the Eiffel Tower."

She mussed his hair. "If we are going to play tourist, we have to play it all the way. I don't want anyone recognizing me. Oh, and sunglasses for the both of us, yes? Big ones."

"You look hideous," Louise observed, an hour or so later, when they were dressed much as they had discussed. "The Hawaiian shirt is a particularly awful touch."

"Thank you, my dear. You look my perfect match."

"I say we're ready to go, then. Are you sure you're up to it?"

"From here on out, I speak no French at all," Bester replied.

They pretended to be Ugly Americans and gape-jawed Marsies. They asked for "real" ketchup in restaurants and demanded ice in their drinks. When they couldn't make themselves understood in English, they spoke English very loudly and very slowly. They were utterly obnoxious, and Bester found he was enjoying himself more than he had in a long, long time.

They took a tour down the Seine, wandered around the Louvre, then went to the top of the Eiffel Tower, where they stood with a mixed group of mostly Japanese and Narn tourists and watched the sun touch the horizon.

"I came up here once, as a little girl," Louise told him. "I haven't been here since. It's a shame, really." She squeezed his hand. "I've had a wonderful day. It's been a long time since I felt like being silly."

"Is that what this is?" Bester replied. "I'm not even sure I know the definition of the word."

"Probably you don't. You take life pretty seriously. Too seriously, I think."

"This was *my* idea."

"I know. But it's funny—I've wanted to do something like this for a long time. It's almost as if you read my mind."

"Hah. I wish I could. I never know what you're thinking." But of course, he had. Why should he feel guilty about that? But he did, somehow. It felt like cheating.

"Oh, I think you do, sometimes." She squeezed his hand again, and they were silent for a few moments.

And in the midst of a glowing, quirky contentment, he felt someone try to scan him.

His smile froze on his face, and he looked around slowly, searching the crowd. After a moment he found him. It was Ackerman, the same fellow he had seen on the train platform.

And Ackerman was thinking *ohmygodohmygodohmygod* . . .

"Louise, dear," Bester said, "I'm getting tired. Would you mind terribly if we got a bite to eat and went home?"

"Home sounds good," she replied. "I can fix us a sandwich."

Bester tried to hide his agitation. Ackerman had recognized him this time, of that he was perfectly certain. As he went by, Bester lifted his surface thoughts. He probed just a little deeper and found an address.

Home sounds good. Louise's thoughts rang in his head, but with a bitter edge. Alfred Bester, it seemed, was never to have a home.

— chapter 2 —

"Going somewhere, Justin?" Bester asked softly.

The bent figure froze, stopped shoving things into a suitcase, and straightened slowly.

So it is you, he 'cast.

"Shh. Talk to me, Justin. How long has it been? Seven years?"

The old man turned, slowly, to face him. "About that long. I'm surprised you remember me, Mr. Bester."

"You were a good man. Loyal to the Corps. Believe me, I noticed people like you." He looked back down at the half-packed suitcase. "You look like you're in a hurry. Can I help?"

"You followed me?"

"Yesterday you practically 'cast where you were staying. I didn't think you'd mind an old friend paying you a visit."

"N-no, of course not. Can I—ah—offer you something to drink?"

"Water would be nice," Bester replied. "Just a tall glass of cool water."

"Sure." Ackerman went off to the kitchen. Bester quietly closed the door behind him and went and stood in the window. The hotel overlooked the Bois de Vincennes, a large public park. A group of children in school uniforms were playing soccer on the lawn, supervised by a couple of nuns.

Ackerman returned with the water. "There you go, sir."

"No need for the 'sir' anymore, Justin. I'm a civilian now, just like you. Trying to live a quiet life, just like you."

"Yes, s—Mr. Bester. That's all I want."

"Are you on the run?"

"No, sir. I served two years in prison, and then they let me out on parole. I've been out for almost a year."

"I'm sorry that happened, Justin, but at least it's behind you now, isn't it? I wish I could say the same." He looked up and smiled. "But I imagine they would give me more than two years, don't you?"

"I . . . think so, Mr. Bester," Ackerman said, very carefully. He was still holding the water out. Bester took it and drank a little.

"It was a terrible thing, the war. Not something I ever thought would really happen. I never believed I would see our people divided like that, turning on each other like a pack of starving dogs. And even later, in the hearings—some of my oldest and dearest friends sold me out, testified against me. Made deals to spare themselves. Tell me, you personally oversaw the execution of at least five of our prisoners of war. How did you manage to get only two years?"

"Mr. Bester, please—"

Bester raised an eyebrow. "Come, now. I'm just curious. I'm not accusing you of anything."

"I—I know."

"Relax, Justin. I didn't come here to hurt you. Just to talk. To see what your intentions are."

"What do you mean?"

"A lot of people would like to know what you know at this moment. A lot of people would pay very well for the information only you possess. You've just been released from prison. You must be a little down on your luck. You must be tempted—just a little—to do what so many of my colleagues have already done."

"No," Justin said, emphatically. "I just want to forget it— forget all of it. No offense, Mr. Bester. I always admired you, even when the others started talking against you. I always thought you had it right, about the normals, about the rogues— about all of it. Whatever you may think, I didn't witness against you. Okay, I gave some people up, but not you. You can look at the court records."

"I'm not interested in revenge," Bester told him. "Even if they did coerce you into some sort of betrayal, I wouldn't really blame you. I haven't tried to take revenge against anyone who betrayed me. I understand their choice. I don't agree with it. I think it stinks, really, but I understand it. Let it be on *their* consciences. I'm done with it. What I'm concerned about is the future, not the past."

"Me, too," Ackerman said. "Me, too, Mr. Bester. Like I said, I just want to forget it all—you included. And I want the world to forget me."

"Well, we're the same, then, Justin. So what can we do about it? How can I give myself peace of mind, where you're concerned?"

"I swear to you, Mr. Bester, I won't tell. I won't tell anyone."

"I believe you mean that. But don't they check up on you? Isn't that part of the new process, they monitor your activities to make sure you haven't been 'abusing' your abilities? Make sure you've been good and not evil little telepath boys and girls?"

"Ah—yes."

"And so what if they find me in there, in your head when they start digging? Good intentions or not, the end result might be the same for me."

"They won't. I won't let them."

"Again, I think you believe that. But I can't depend on it. You wouldn't, if you were in my shoes, would you?"

"I guess not."

"See? I knew you were reasonable."

"Please don't hurt me. I'll go someplace no one can find me. I'll—"

"All I want to do," Bester said, "is make a few alterations in your memory. Take *me* out of there. You know my reputation— you know I'm a pro. You won't feel a thing, and you won't miss it when it's gone." He paused. "It's not the *only* solution I can think of, but it's the best one for both of us. Think about yourself. If they found out you have been hiding *me*, just how long do you think your parole would last?"

Ackerman sat down on the stiff-backed chair and put his head in his hands. "I'll do it," he said. "I'll do anything you say. I want to help."

Bester put his hand on Ackerman's shoulders. "You're one of the good ones, Justin. I knew I could count on you. And I appreciate it."

He took his time, carefully cleaning any memory of himself from Ackerman's mind. Then he put the other telepath into a sound sleep and carefully wiped everything that might leave fingerprints or significant traces of DNA. Then he departed, his head pounding from the exertion.

He bought Louise some roses on the way home.

That afternoon, he sat for her again. The painting was nearer completion.

"Are you seeing what you want, now?" he asked, as she dabbed and made little satisfied sounds.

"Yes."

"You knew what it was all along, didn't you? That what you saw in me was me seeing *you*."

She blushed. "No. Not at first."

"You were so—alive. So vital. It woke me up, made me alive, too."

"I can't believe you were ever otherwise."

"I was. My life has had its disappointments, Louise. I was tired of feeling—feeling anything. Because you can't feel joy without opening to the possibility of pain. It's hard to risk that, when you've had a . . . disappointing life. Wake to your feelings, that is."

She came over and kissed him. "Well. I'm glad you did."

"Can I see it yet?"

"Not quite. There's a little more to do. But soon. And promise me you won't peek while I'm gone."

"Gone? Where are you going?"

"Oh, I thought I told you. I'm going to Melbourne to see my mother, and my sister, Helen. That's the one I stole the husband from. I think it's time I finally set things right between us."

"What brought this on?"

"You. Us. I want to move on with my life, Claude, and I want to do so with you. I've had some disappointments, too, and there are too many things I've left tangled up. I want to unsnarl a few. I think—I think it will be better for us. You deserve someone whole."

"You *are* whole." He wanted to tell her that she didn't *need* her family, not when she had him. That it would only make things harder. One of her sisters had been in Clark's guard. Odds were good that she'd seen Alfred Bester, at least once or twice.

But he couldn't say that to her, because he knew she was right. Reconciling with her sister was best for her, and he wanted what was best for her, even if it opened a little hollow place in him. After all, he was used to hollow places. He could bear it.

"I'd ask you to go with me, but it would just complicate things. I hope you don't mind." She must have seen something in his face, then. "I'm not being presumptuous, am I? I mean, I know we haven't known each other for that long, but I think we're—I mean, I think we have some sort of a future."

A future. Would she follow him from planet to planet, if he had to run again? Could he ask her to?

But that was what he wanted. He wanted it, the brass ring he had never even been able to see before, never imagined existed. The chance to really be happy, before the end.

He deserved it.

He took her hand. "I'm glad for you," he said. "Go see your sister, get this off your chest. And we'll go forward from there."

She kissed him, sweetly, on the lips. "Thank you, Claude. I knew you would understand."

"Well, I must congratulate you, Mr. Kaufman."

Jean-Pierre stood over him, adjusting his fashionably pointless eyeglasses.

"I'm sure you must," Bester replied, sipping his coffee. He hadn't noticed Jean-Pierre enter Le Cheval Heureux. The normally sleepy café was full today, nearly bursting with tourists—an unusual but occasional event. "But is there any particular compulsion to do so, this time? Or is it just your general admiration for me overflowing?"

"Don't play coy with me. You know *Le Parisien* has started running your column."

"Believe me, Jean-Pierre, my interest in playing coy with you could not be observed even at the quantum scale. I haven't heard anything about this."

"No? Well, it's true." He dropped a paper in front of Bester. "They ran this today."

"This is my review of *Farther Clouds.*"

"Yes, so it is. The one we published only a few days ago."

"I never gave them permission to run that."

"Well, *I* certainly didn't," the younger man said, icily.

Louise had left the day before, and Bester had been feeling more and more uneasy ever since. Now his disquiet took a sharp dig at the inside of his ribs. *Le Parisien* had a circulation of six million, not just in Paris, but in Quebec, Algeria—on Mars.

It could have been worse. They could have run his picture beside the column. Of course, they didn't have one to run . . .

"We'll see about this," he said. "Where are their offices?"

Simon de Grun was a round man made of round parts, and even in an impeccably tailored suit he looked like an over-dressed balloon. He smiled at Bester and offered him a black cigarette tipped with gold.

"No, thank you," Bester said. "I would much rather discuss plagiarism."

"Got your attention, didn't it?" de Grun said, lighting his own smoke and taking a satisfied drag. "I've been trying to contact you, you know. Your present publisher wouldn't supply me with an address or a phone number."

"He doesn't have them. I value my privacy."

"But I take it he also did not pass my messages along to you."

"No, I don't believe that he did."

"It's very simple, Mr. Kaufman. I like your column. Paris likes your column." He opened a desk drawer, removed an envelope, and passed it to Bester.

"There's a chit with two thousand credits in there. You'll get one of those each and every time I publish one of your reviews—and I plan to publish one every time you write one. I daresay that's a better deal than you have with that pretentious little rag you've been working for. Not to mention the fact that many of our readers buy their issues on *real* paper. Think of it, Mr. Kaufman—to see your name in *ink*, like Faulkner or Liu."

Bester stared at the envelope. "You're kidding."

"No, I'm not. You have bite, Mr. Kaufman. You have style, and a vicious streak a mile wide. The response to your first column in our publication was astonishing, even better than I expected."

"I don't know what to say." He felt totally disarmed. As a child, there was nothing he had wanted more or worked harder for than the admiration of his peers. In time, he had gotten beyond that, and the work itself had become more important than the praise. Yet the praise had continued. There was a time when every young Psi Cop wanted nothing more than to *be* Alfred Bester. He had become comfortable with his accomplishment, with excellence.

It was only after the sea of respect he floated on had vanished that he'd understood just how much it had buoyed him up, how much weight it had taken off his feet.

Now, for the first time in years, he felt some of that lightness again. And the funny thing was how wholly unexpected it was. He hadn't sought praise—it had found him of its own accord. Of course, they didn't know who he really was, but that made it all the more delicious.

And dangerous. How could he risk it? He had taken too many risks already.

He was about to push the envelope back toward de Grun

when an equally unexpected flash of anger hit him. Why *shouldn't* he do this? Had he become so timid that all he could think of was hiding, making himself smaller and smaller, until he just vanished? That was what his enemies wanted, wasn't it?

"Three thousand," he said.

De Grun didn't blink. "Twenty-five."

"You have a deal," Bester told him. "But only on my terms. I review what I want, the way I want to."

"I can live with that."

"Well, then. Good day, Monsieur de Grun."

"Wait. How can I contact you?"

"Don't worry. I'll contact you. I still value my privacy, all the more if my audience is going to increase."

"We'd like to run a picture of you with your column."

"Out of the question. I'm very shy."

De Grun burbled a laugh. "You don't seem shy to me."

Bester looked him dead level in the eyes. "I'm shy," he repeated. "If you run a picture of me, or even take one, I'll sue you."

"What, are you some sort of war criminal?"

"Yes, of course," Bester said, sarcastically. "I'm the secret leader of the Drakh."

De Grun shrugged jovially. "You could be, for all I care. Fine. No picture. Anything else?"

"Nothing else. You'll have your next review tomorrow."

But he didn't start on the review right away. Instead he went back to his room, and he savored a small glass of Pernod. And for the first time, he started to see a coherent road before him.

From the day he was born, the path stretching in front of him had been as straight and sure as the arrow of entropy. He had never doubted where he was going, though the trail had often been narrow, no more than a tightrope.

Then came the war, the aftermath, and flight. Suddenly there were no roads before him at all—or rather, all rocky paths leading nowhere good. Then Paris, where he discovered that he might do almost anything, be almost anything. Where he first understood the concept of freedom.

But even freedom needed direction, a path, a plan. And here it was forming, from chaos and joy. It was so wonderful, so *delightful*, that he was afraid of thinking about it, of making plans, of stepping out of the moment.

But if he just kept depending on fortune, he was bound to get into trouble. Life had taught him that God *did* play dice with the universe. And any game of dice went, not to the man with the lucky rabbit's foot, but to the man who knew how to toss the dice just so. Or to switch them for the weighted ones in his cuff.

He stared at the blank sheet in front of him, and thought about the book Louise wanted him to write. He thought about the cosmic crap game, and began fooling with titles. *Loading the Dice: A Telepath's Story.* No, that wouldn't do.

He sipped his drink. The dice were already loaded in favor of telepaths, if they knew how to throw. Normals knew that. That's why normals had always tried to keep them out of the game, kill them, lock them away, or tame them as pets. Telepaths were the next step in evolution, as pivotal as that first primate ancestor who had been born with one finger that curled differently, that opposed the others.

That was it. He cleared the screen.

The Third Thumb, he wrote.

It wasn't his story he wanted to tell, but the story of his people. Of all of his people, even those who had betrayed him, and worse, betrayed their own kind.

He would do it. But first, he had something else to do.

Justin Ackerman looked at him without comprehension for a few seconds, then recognition dawned.

"Mr. Bester?" he asked.

Bester scanned him lightly, nodding in satisfaction. "Well, I did do a good job on you after all. You don't remember me, do you?"

"Yes, sir—of course I do. We worked together in the Brazilian camp."

"Yes, yes, I meant—oh, never mind."

Ackerman glanced around nervously. "Would you, ah, like to come in, sir?" He turned slightly, gesturing into the room, his gaze retreating from Bester.

"No, Justin. But I do need you to come with me."

"Why?"

"You've known me for a long time, Justin. Did you ever question me before? It's important."

"But sir, I was just going to bed. It's late, and I—"

"Please. I'm asking as an old friend, not as an old commander."

Ackerman hesitated for another second. Bester could taste his fear and curiosity.

"Let me get my coat."

The doorman wasn't on duty. Bester had suggested that he take a nap, something he'd been close to doing anyway.

The air was warm as they walked through the midnight city, until finally they came to the quay along the Seine. Far to the left, the Eiffel Tower thrust its ancient silhouette against the city-lit underbellies of the clouds. They looked, Bester thought, like the sulfurous clouds of Herig 3, heavy and poisonous.

"Sit with me here," Bester said, letting himself down onto the quay. It was quiet, far from the heart of the city.

Ackerman did, tentatively. "I can't believe you're on Earth, sir," he ventured. "It's dangerous for you here." He paused, looking at Bester's hands. "Especially if you keep wearing those gloves. We don't wear them anymore."

Bester smiled thinly. "It's dangerous for me everywhere," he said, watching a small boat move almost soundlessly up the black glass surface of the Seine. "I tried almost everywhere. Little colony worlds. Non-Human worlds. I spent almost a year in one of my old asteroid bases, going stir-crazy. They always found me. Maybe they'll find me here, maybe they won't.

"When I decided to come here, I thought Earth was my best chance. I still do. But I'm going to ask you, Justin, do you know of a place? Somewhere I can go where they will never think to look, where I can live out my life in peace?"

Justin shook his head.

"Think carefully, Justin. This is very important to me."

"No, sir. They want you bad. I can't think of any place."

"Well. I had to try. There was a small chance that you had thought of something I hadn't. And I owed you that chance."

"Mr. Bester, please—" Ackerman started to raise his eyes toward Bester, but his gaze never reached him. Bester had already placed the muzzle of the pistol against Ackerman's head and squeezed off the first round. The weapon sighed, sighed again. Ackerman did, too, as the small-caliber bullets ricocheted around inside his skull, shredding his brain but leaving no exit wounds, no ugly spatters of blood.

Ackerman swayed, then began to slump. Bester caught him and held him upright, then took a plastic bag and a rubber band from his coat pocket, and fastened the bag around Ackerman's head. That would keep what little blood there was from getting on anything.

The plastic sucked up to Ackerman's nostrils, and his chest heaved uselessly for another minute or so. Bester kept himself tightly blocked—he didn't want to feel Ackerman's death. He had done that too often in his life—once he had thought it had cost him his soul.

He had his soul back, and he wasn't about to risk it again, not now.

When he was sure Ackerman was dead, he removed the bag. Then, almost gently, he pushed him into the river. The body sank as the current took him away. He would surface again, of course, but as in any large city on Earth, people were murdered in Paris every day, every night. He would become another statistic, nothing more. There was nothing to connect him to Alfred Bester, much less to Claude Kaufman.

On the way back to his room, he began outlining the first chapter of his book in his head. It helped. By the time he got there, his sadness had faded to melancholy.

— chapter 3 —

Bester paused typing in midsentence, a smile creasing his face.

Louise was home. He could feel her blowing through the front door, a zephyr, a breeze with scents of honeysuckle and paint. He closed what he was working on and hurried down the stairs. When he reached the café, Louise was indeed there, just setting down her luggage.

"Claude!" Her smile seemed to explode across her face, and an instant later he had her in his arms. Tensions melted away as he felt the solid warmth of her, doubts eased back into his subconscious. This was worth anything.

She kissed him briefly but warmly on the lips. "Are you ready?" she asked.

"Ready for what?"

"Just hold my hand and tell me you love me."

"I love you. What . . ."

"So *you* must be Claude."

He turned toward the source of the slightly disapproving female voice.

"Yes, this is him," Louise said, brightly. "Claude, meet Major Genevieve Bouet, my sister."

Bester smiled at the tall brunette with all of the false charm he could muster. Louise needn't have bothered giving her rank—it was plain enough on her EarthForce uniform. He saw a bit of Louise in her serious, no-nonsense face, but he would have never guessed they were sisters.

"Enchanté," he murmured, taking her hand. Her grip was firm, and the thoughts that flooded his mind as they touched

were ordered and clear. The disapproval was real, but came mostly from concern for Louise—the major didn't want to see her sister hurt again. To his vast relief, he sensed no hint of recognition.

"Likewise," the major said. "I must say, Mr. Kaufman, you have a lot to live up to. Louise has been rattling on about you like a schoolgirl, something she never does."

"Well, I'll do my best," he replied. "If ever I had expectations worth living up to, Louise would provide them. She didn't tell me your rank. I'm quite impressed."

"You needn't be. The last ten years have taken their toll on officers, and promotions have come cheap."

"From what Louise has told me, I think you're being modest. You were in Clark's personal guard, weren't you?"

She nodded at that, and there was an uncomfortable moment of silence. Bester filled it.

"So when did you two hook up?" he asked Louise. "I thought you were going to see your other sister—the one in Melbourne."

"I did," Louise replied. "That didn't go so well as I hoped—but by good luck Genny was there on leave, and I managed to talk her into a visit. I wanted to show off my new boyfriend."

"Well, I'm hardly a boy, as your sister has noticed."

He was rewarded by a slight feeling of shame from the major.

"I wouldn't care if you were two hundred," she said, "so long as you make my sister happy." That was half a lie, but Bester accepted it in the spirit with which she meant it, nodding graciously.

"We're starving," Louise said. "Why don't you two chat while I fix us something?"

"Nonsense," Bester replied. "I'll cook, you two sit and have a glass of wine. I'm sure the flight must have taken a lot out of you."

"Claude doesn't think much of my cooking," Louise said, playfully. "He doesn't realize it's all a ploy to get him to wait on me hand and foot."

"Well, I do now," Bester said. "But really, I just bought a bottle of chateau neuf. Let me get it. Give you two a chance to compare notes on the boyfriend."

"I won't refuse *that*." The major smiled. Bester grinned back, not at her words, but at the grudging feeling behind them. This was going well.

"Well, no man who can cook like that can be all bad," the major said, laying down her fork next to the remnants of soufflé. "Some of these older models run pretty well, it seems."

"No need to tell me," Louise beamed.

Bester raised his glass. "To family reunions," he said.

"To *some* family reunions," Louise corrected, but she toasted anyway.

"Oh, yes. So things didn't go so well with Helen?"

"She'll come around," Genevieve said. "Helen is good at holding grudges. She puts a lot of energy into it. But it was a good start. At least she spoke."

"At least," Louise allowed. "Of course, she comes by that trait honestly."

A cynical smile flitted across the major's face. "Let's not bore Mr. Kaufman with our family squabbles. At least the two of us are friendly again. Like I said, a good start."

"I'm not in the least bored," Bester said. "I could never be so complacent about something that concerns Louise so much."

The major sighed. "Be careful what you wish," she said. "You might get it. Another glass of wine or two, and we might get into it, and we'll be here all night." Her steely gaze settled on her sister. "For the record, Louise, I think you're right. I've been trying to get in touch with Anne. After all, it's been almost ten years. If EarthForce can be reconciled, the two of us can, too." She turned back to Bester. "The problem, you see, is that our family tends to be a passionate one, often at the expense of common sense." She swirled her wine around. "No, enough. Mr. Kaufman, I understand you were in the military?"

"I was, sort of. Hush-hush stuff. Fortunately, I was a private citizen when Clark took office, so I wasn't involved in the civil conflict. The choice you had to make wasn't one I would have wanted, but I respect it."

The major shrugged. "For me, at the time, there was no choice. It's the job of the senate and the courts—and ultimately the voters—to determine the legitimacy of a president and his decisions. It is emphatically *not* the task of officers in the military to do so. If that precedent held, where would we be? Privately, I question the worthiness of every single instance that puts my soldiers in danger. But publicly, no military can function without an unquestioning chain of command."

She shrugged. "My sister didn't see it that way. I imagine she still doesn't. Looking back on it, in some absolute scheme of things, I believe she was right. But put in the same situation, I would make the same choice. But you know what? One gets older, and as certain parts get stiffer, others loosen up, *n'est-ce pas?* I'm tired of having this between me and Anne."

"To loosening up," Bester said, raising his glass again.

"I'll drink to that," Louise said. And they all did.

"She likes you," Louise told him, that night in bed.

"She's dubious of me," Bester replied. "She thinks I'm a cradle robber."

"She's cautious, that's all. But she's my sister, and she loves me. She wants what's best for me, and anyone around you for half an hour can see that what's best for me is you."

He rolled over so he could see her face. Her eyes glistened faintly in the dim light that filtered in from the street outside. "You make me humble," he said. "You give me memories I've never had and dreams I've never imagined." He paused. "I started writing a book yesterday."

"Really?"

"Yes."

"When can I read it?"

He chuckled. "When can I see the painting?"

"When it's done."

"Well, then you know my answer, too." He felt a prickle of

fear. One day she would read the book, and then she would have to know, at the very least, that he was a telepath. She would know that he had been lying to her, in a sense—the lie of omission. But at the moment it was impossible for him to believe she wouldn't understand, wouldn't forgive. He had never in his life been this close to a human being, not even to Carolyn. It was the most frightening and the most wonderful feeling he had ever known.

"How long is she staying, your sister?"

"A few days, maybe a week. You don't mind, do you?"

"No. You need this." That was a lie, too, but not a big one. His fear that the major would recognize him seemed to be groundless. There hadn't even been a hint of it, the whole evening, not even a subconscious reflex. And he had been watching, carefully. This roll of the dice had come out in his favor.

"Thank you, Claude. It's all because of you, you know. You made me understand that it was worth the risk, to love again, to repair fences. You gave me that."

"I understand perfectly," he breathed. "Perfectly."

She kissed him, and kissed him again, and the night dissolved into soft sighs and touches, nothing urgent about it, but sweet, comfortable, happy.

Afterward, drifting to sleep, he thought of Justin, of his body sinking slowly into the river. He thought of what Louise would say, if she knew, and he felt an odd little catch, an explosion of grief so strong it nearly choked him. Faces passed across the darkness behind his eyelids. Byron, Handel, Ferrino, people whose names he couldn't remember.

This was the end of it. This was the end of him. It occurred to him that when Louise had said his name earlier—*Claude*—he hadn't flinched, as he once had. Hadn't wished she could call him Alfred. Alfred Bester didn't deserve Louise, wasn't worthy of her. But Claude—well, perhaps Claude wasn't either, but he *could* be. If he worked at it, if he always reminded himself he could be better.

I'm sorry, Justin, he thought. *I had to do it, but I'm sorry.*

You are the last man Alfred Bester will ever kill. Because Alfred Bester is dead.

"Claude?"

"Yes?"

"Are you crying?"

"I—" He was. He hadn't recognized the sensation, but his face was wet.

"Why?"

"Because I'm happy," he replied. "Because I'm so very happy."

— *chapter 4* —

"He was dead before he hit the water," the examiner said, adjusting his gloves. "Not a drop of water in his lungs." He touched a contact on the edge of the examining table. A ribbon of blue light appeared on the toes of the naked corpse and moved slowly toward his head. "Let's see what the toxicology shows us," the doctor murmured.

Inspector Girard nodded wearily. He had just pulled four shifts back-to-back, and was having a hard time concentrating on what the examiner was saying. That was bad, but it was better than going home, where his wife would either start screaming at him or just sulk, sullenly, burning him with her eyes. And going to Marie, now, was out of the question.

He was a detective, yes? He should know better. The mistake every criminal made was in thinking that *they* were smarter than every other criminal, that *they* were the ones who wouldn't be caught. He, an inspector with almost twenty years behind him, and he had thought he could keep his affair with Marie a secret?

He supposed he might have, *if Marie hadn't become pregnant,* or if . . .

Bah. No ifs. He had been stupid.

He shook his head, trying to clear the amorphous fish-things trying to obscure his vision.

"Another tourist?"

"I don't think so," the examiner said, prodding the head to one side as the blue strip of light finished its journey. "Lamp, high," he said. Harsh white light suddenly filled the room.

The corpse was an old fellow. Rigor mortis had come and

gone, and his blue-tinted face was composed, almost serene.
*What did you try to get away with, my friend? What business
has this ended for you? Was death a relief, in the end? A well-
deserved peace?* He shook his head again when he realized
he had missed what the doctor had just said.

"I'm sorry. What?"

"I said it looks pretty professional. Small-caliber slugs, so
there are no exit wounds. I think the killer put a bag over his
head, too—there is a faint ring of capillary damage around
the throat, here." He pointed to what, for Girard, was an invisible line, but if the examiner said it was there, it was. The
man was a necromancer, a wizard of the dead, and Girard had
come to respect him deeply.

"The muzzle was placed right against the skull, too, so the
killer was close."

"Was he bound?"

"No sign of it. No abrasions of any sort on the hands or
feet, no odd muscle positions."

Girard had a sudden flash. *Two men talk to one another,
like old friends. One casually pulls a pistol, as though he's
taking out a cigarette lighter. The other doesn't notice, until
the steel touches his head, and now he's puzzled. His puzzlement deepens as he feels a thump, and everything goes
strange, as if he is very drunk, and he forgets where he is,
what he's doing, and there is another thump, and another . . .*

Girard had these flashes. He had wondered, often, if he
might not be some sort of telepath, but all the tests came back
negative. No, he was merely damned to have that sort of
imagination that put things together without consulting his
intellect, a brain that dreamed while it was awake. It made
him a good detective, but he didn't like it. Sometimes, when
he was wrong, when his flashes proved incorrect, he was actually more relieved than when he was right.

It didn't happen often that he was wrong.

"Have you identified him yet?"

"That's the puzzling part. Considering how professional
the execution was, you would think the killer would have

tried harder to get rid of the body. Dissolve it in acid, or some-such. Cut off the fingertips, knock out the teeth."

"The killer was working alone," Girard said. "If this were a syndicate hit of some sort, there would have been no body, as you say. And I'm guessing that not only is this poor fellow's DNA registered someplace, but the killer knew it. So. Since he didn't have the means, or the time, to entirely destroy the body, he did the next best thing. He disposed of it in an en-tirely conventional way, hoping we wouldn't notice him in the piles of bodies we fish from the river every day."

"Or perhaps it really was just a robbery-murder, by some-one with a professional technique."

"Perhaps." He paced around the corpse. His personal troubles began to fade, overwhelmed by the puzzle. "His DNA *was* on file, yes?"

The examiner tapped a small display. "Let's see. Yes, you're right. He—"

"No, don't tell me who he was, yet."

"As you wish, Inspector."

"The killer killed him near the water, so he wouldn't have to carry the body."

"That could be. He soiled himself when he died, but the pattern of absorption by his clothes suggests he was im-mersed almost immediately."

He tried to picture it another way. A tourist out for a stroll, an out-of-luck, unemployed hitman looking for his next meal. He walks up, asks for a match or something, and when his victim looks down, kisses his head with the end of his pistol.

No. Why the bag? The killer had wanted his victim dead, fast and certainly. And the way the victim was dressed in no way suggested a rich man. This was never a robbery. He couldn't make that scene come alive in his head.

"If his DNA was on file, he was probably either a convicted felon, in the military, or a telepath. Which one?"

"A telepath."

Well, that opened up a lot of possibilities. A hate crime? A lot of people hated telepaths for a lot of reasons. That might explain the execution-style slaying. The killer saw himself as a cleansing force, out to make the world safe for those without unholy powers.

Or it might have been an old grudge, yes? There must be plenty of grudges after the telepath war. Two telepaths, once friends, on opposite sides of the conflict. A pretense of reconciliation—that would explain why the victim wouldn't notice murder coming up to him, didn't even flinch as his bloody-minded companion drew his weapon with cold, certain intent.

Except it couldn't have been *that* cold. There were mistakes here, and a lack of planning that suggested panic . . .

No, wait—where had he gotten panic? A panicked man didn't calmly place a gun against someone's head and pull the trigger, then produce a plastic bag.

Ah, but people didn't always know they were panicking, did they? When Marie told him of her pregnancy, he had believed himself to still be in control. He had fooled himself, suppressed the fear, told himself that all he needed to do was act calmly and everything would be all right.

But there was nothing logical about adultery, about ruining a marriage of thirty years, the humiliation of his own children realizing what he had done to their mother. No, he hadn't acknowledged his panic. He had swallowed it, and it had poisoned him. It had made him stupid even as he convinced himself he was clever.

The mind worked like that. This wasn't the first time he had seen it.

So what did he have? Someone who wanted to kill a telepath, probably a telepath himself. Someone who thought he was doing the murder for all the right reasons and with all the proper precautions, while at the same time he was frightened at the most fundamental level possible.

Maybe the victim had learned something he shouldn't have, yes? Telepaths had a way of doing that. Maybe the meeting was at the victim's behest, an overture to blackmail. And the killer saw, with terrible lucidity, that the way out of the trap was to destroy the trap itself.

Enough. "Who was he?"

The examiner, who had become busy examining the man's stomach contents, didn't bother looking at the vid display. The faint gleam on the narrow goggles he wore suggested the information was scrolling there. "Justin Ackerman. Born in North America, in Toronto. Sixty-three years of age. He was a telepath, a P7. A war criminal, as a matter of fact. He had just finished serving his sentence and was out on parole. Applied for a work visa two months ago, rented an apartment near the Rue de Paris. He worked part time as a night guard at the club Pugeot."

"Have you informed Psi Corps yet?"

"No, Inspector. But we're supposed to inform them within twenty-four hours."

"We still have ten, then, yes?" He walked toward the door, snagged his jacket from the skeleton-coatrack that held it on an outstretched arm. "Hold off as long as you can. I want to talk to his landlord and his employer, before the EABI shows up and takes this one away from me."

Though why he should care, he couldn't say. Wouldn't he be better off without one more case? But he had a long-standing dislike for the Metasensory Division of the EABI. In the old days when they had been MetaPol, they had swept in like birds of prey, arrogant, dismissive, heavy-handed. He didn't like having them in his city. Oh, they were better on the surface now, but the arrogance remained. And perhaps he was envious of their abilities—sure, they claimed not to use them, but he knew better. Who wouldn't? He had never been able to escape the feeling that it was unfair, cops who could read minds, as often as he wondered if he himself didn't have a touch of their power.

No, this was his city, not theirs. His murder, his murderer.

And, he thought cynically, another thing to keep his mind off how his life was slowly disintegrating around him.

"He didn't *have* any friends. At least none that I saw."

Margarite de Cheney might have been attractive once, before life had scrubbed her face red and bruised her eyes with disappointments. Girard wondered, looking at her, if she ever felt joy in anything anymore.

He wondered if she could kill. If one's own life was gone, it was easier to take another's, yes?

He wondered wryly if that meant murder was next on his agenda. Would his life be easier if he had killed Marie? No, because he would have been caught. Everyone got caught, sooner or later.

Besides, he did love her, in his way. And the thought of another child, while immensely complicating, was not without appeal.

"No one came or went?"

"You'd have to ask the doorman. I never saw anyone, but then I don't spy on my guests. Is he in some kind of trouble?"

"He's dead."

He watched her reaction—this was the moment when a lot of them blew it. They always imagined they should act surprised, shocked. Real reactions were slower than that. Death was something people spent their whole lives pretending couldn't be real. When confronted with it, there was usually a comprehension gap, a moment searching through the words they had just heard, trying to see if there was some other way to interpret them.

"Dead? You mean . . ."

"Dead," he repeated, disappointed. But then, he hadn't really thought she was guilty. "Murdered."

"Here?" *That* scared her.

"Maybe," he lied. "We found his body in the river, but he could have been killed anywhere. Which is why it's so important that you recall everything you can."

"There are two doormen, one for night, the other for day. I'll give you their names and addresses, but Etienne is here already. You want to talk to him?"

"Of course. But first, I would like to see Mr. Ackerman's room."

"Oh, yes. This way."

They went upstairs to room 12. De Cheney exhaled into the cheap chemical lock and the door sighed open. There wasn't much to the place. A couch and two chairs that looked like they belonged there. Some clothes in the closet, a night guard's uniform and one new suit, undoubtedly the one he had received on release from prison.

The forensic team would be here soon, and he was loath to spend much time inside, for fear of contaminating the place, of erasing the trace elements and bits of hair, the physical clues that sometimes led nowhere and sometimes everywhere.

He just wanted to see it, to picture where the man had spent his last days. If Justin Ackerman had been killed for being Justin Ackerman, then knowing the victim would help him know the killer. If he had been killed simply because he was in the wrong place at the wrong time, well, it wouldn't help much at all. But it couldn't hurt.

"Was he noisy? Did anyone complain about him?"

"Not that I know of."

"The rooms next to his—are they occupied?"

"That one is. A Mademoiselle Carter." She pointed to the door on the right.

Girard knocked. After a few moments, a young woman answered. She was blond, perhaps twenty years old, a bit disheveled looking, pale but not unattractive.

"Oui?" she said. Her accent was terrible. An American.

"Mademoiselle Carter, my name is Raphael Girard," he said in English. "I'm a police inspector. I wonder if I can have a few words with you about your next-door neighbor?"

"Sure." She stood in the door frame and folded her arms, her eyes suddenly lively, interested.

"You've lived here for how long?"

"About a month, since the school year started. I'm studying antiquities at the Sorbonne."

"A graduate student?"

"Yes."

"I've always been fascinated by history. What period do you specialize in?"

"The early Roman period in Gaul, actually."

"Oh. Asterix, eh?"

She smiled, openly and genuinely. "Very good," she said. "I rarely meet anyone who has even heard of Asterix."

"My father was a professor of twentieth-century literature. He was responsible for the reprinting in the sixties."

"Well, thank him for me," she said. "I collected those, as a child." She smiled again. "Now that you've put me at ease, Inspector, what did you want to know about my neighbor? I'm afraid I can't tell you much."

"Well, did he ever have visitors? A girlfriend, anything like that?"

"No, not usually. Though somebody came by a couple of nights ago. I remember noticing it just because he never had visitors. I was studying, and someone knocked on his door. I could hear them talking, but not what they said. I was sort of surprised, y'know?" She scrunched up her face. "I think they left. I wasn't really paying attention. Something happened to him, didn't it?"

"We found him murdered."

"Oh."

"You don't sound surprised."

"I am—that he was murdered. I think . . . I think I expected him to die, though. When you asked me about him just now, I thought you had found him dead—in there." She gestured toward the room next door.

"Suicide, you mean?"

"Yes."

"Why?"

"He just seemed . . . sad. Worn out, or something. He spoke to me once, in the hall. You know that way that people act, when you speak to them, and you can tell they don't do it very often? The way they want to keep talking, even though all you meant to do was say hello? But I was pretty busy, and I was suddenly anxious. I need this place to study, and if I suddenly had this needy friend next door, always coming over—" She broke off and frowned. "So I sort of ignored him, after that, or just nodded at him and acted like I was in a hurry. I felt guilty about it, and I sort of worried—Well, but when he had a visitor, I remember thinking 'Oh, good, he has a friend.' "

"But you didn't see this friend."

"No. It was a man, though, I'm sure of that, from his voice. They spoke English, I'm pretty sure."

"And this was about what time?"

"Oh, midnight, maybe."

Another flash. *The same two men talk, but Ackerman knows how it's going to end. So there's no surprise when the gun touches his head. He knows running is useless. Maybe he doesn't care. Thump* . . .

Girard blinked rapidly. The girl was looking at him funny. "Does that help?" she asked, her tone suggesting that she was repeating herself.

"Yes. That's very near the time of death."

"Oh, my God. I heard the killer."

"Yes."

"Do you think I—"

"I don't think you are in danger, but you should be careful. Take normal precautions. Don't answer the door unless you know who it is—that sort of thing. Let me give you my card . . ." He produced a slip that had his name and address written on it. "It has my phone code in it, prepaid. All you have to do is swipe it through a payment slot. If you need anything, I'm at your service. And I'll come by to check on you, if you want."

She smiled, timidly. "That would be nice. But that isn't what I was going to say. I was wondering if there might have been anything I could have done, if I might have stopped him."

Ah. Young Americans. They always imagined the world would be a better place if *they,* personally, took an interest in it. "Don't worry about that," he told her. "There was no way for you to know. Besides, if you had tried, I would be asking these questions about you, I fear, and that would be a most unpleasant task. I much prefer having met you this way." He started to say more, but stopped. Was he flirting again? This was how he had met Marie.

"Once more, thank you, and good day," he said, and backed out, quickly.

The doorman didn't remember anyone, and looked uncomfortable about it.

"Well, *someone* came in," Margarite said, a little shrilly. "What do I pay you for?"

"Maybe it was another tenant," Etienne mumbled. "He might have just gone down the hall, for all we know."

"That's true. But let us suppose, for a moment, that you were distracted—" *say, by the inside of your eyelids* "—or were away from your post, maybe in the toilet. Couldn't someone have come in and out without you knowing it?"

"No, Inspector. The door records everyone who goes in and out, anyway. You're welcome to view the record, if you wish."

"Let's see it."

They searched for three hours either side of midnight, but found no trace of anyone other than tenants coming in or out.

"Monsieur Ackerman went out," Girard said. "Of that, there is simply no question. And yet, I do not see him here. How can that be? Is there another way?"

"No."

"A window?"

"The windows are sealed," Margarite said. "The building is environment-controlled, and open windows muck that up."

"We should check them, anyway. What is sealed can be unsealed. What about the recording device? Could it have been tampered with?"

"I don't see how. It's AI-controlled. Nothing I could do to it, if you're implying that," Etienne said, defensively.

"I'm not," Girard replied, suddenly recalling something. Hadn't there been something recently, in another part of town? Yes, an attempted robbery of a pharmacy, and even though one of the perpetrators had been found dead in the building, he hadn't shown up on the surveillance. The security company in question had claimed that the clumsy recovery techniques used by the police had badly damaged the circuits, but the experts he knew in the department had flatly denied the possibility. Still, nobody could figure out how the device might have been fooled, either. And since a guard and three policemen had died in the incident, there had been considerable effort in that direction.

Wait a minute. Hadn't the guard at the pharmacy been a telepath?

Could telepaths influence AIs? He had never heard of such a thing, but then, if they could do it, it might be a pretty closely guarded secret. Hadn't there been some rumor that telepaths had been able to do something to alien ships, back during the Shadow War?

And a telepath could easily have erased the doorman's memory, or fogged his mind, or whatever. Ackerman could have done it himself, for that matter.

This was getting interesting. Very interesting. Something *was* going on here, something to do with telepaths, he could feel it in his bones. Which meant he had better use the hours remaining to him very wisely, before Metasensory showed up. Otherwise, he might never know what had happened here. When any division of the EABI showed up, cases sometimes just vanished, as if they had never been.

His city. His murder.

— chapter 5 —

Girard sipped his vile coffee and glanced through the paper. He flipped to the arts section and read the book review. It was the new reviewer, and Girard enjoyed his acerbic sense of humor.

The plot of the book seems to be revealed only on a need-to-know basis—and apparently the author feels the reader doesn't need to know, he read, and chuckled.

Behind him, Louis Timothee, his deputy assistant, gave a sudden soft exclamation.

"Look at this," Timothee said.

"What is it?"

"Maybe we shouldn't feel so sorry for Ackerman after all. Did you realize that he worked in the Psi Corps reeducation camp at Amiento?"

"Yes."

"Really? I just found that. It was past one of the security curtains . . ."

"Yes, he was acquitted of most charges and served his time, so of course they make it difficult to access that part of his past. It's in keeping with the forgiveness statutes passed after the Civil War. We can get to them, we just have to work bloody hard."

"Acquitted?" Timothee said, incredulously.

Girard turned, and found his assistant staring at an image. It showed a heap of dead bodies. He clicked, and another scene came up—a group of men, women, and children, emaciated but alive, stared blank-eyed at the picture taker.

"He rolled over on some of his superiors, of course. The

age-old cry of the footman butcher, you know? 'I was only following orders.' "

"Well, what do we care this son of a bitch is dead, then?"

"We care because it's our job," Girard replied. "Furthermore—listen, give me your best guess. Who killed Ackerman?"

Timothee gestured at the screen. "One of them. Or the brother or sister or son of one of the dead ones. He oversaw the systematic torture, mutilation, and murder of thousands. Just because he was acquitted doesn't mean he's forgiven. *I* would have tracked him down, if one of mine had been in that camp."

"That's a good guess. Statistically, it makes the most sense. And you're right, in a way. I don't condone vigilantes. We can't. But maybe I wouldn't look far beyond the obvious, if I jumped to the conclusion you have. Maybe I would figure the killer was justified, and let it go at that."

"Damn straight."

"But that's why I keep my conclusions tentative. That's why I formulate alternate hypotheses. And if the one I've come up with is correct, I think you'll agree we should keep this investigation open."

"I don't see any alternative hypothesis."

"Well, you've blinded yourself then—not a good way to start an investigation. It's just like science, you know. You form various hypotheses and then you start testing them, or at least seeing which one best fits the facts you know."

"If you have a better fit for the data, what is it?"

"Maybe not a *better* fit, but I have *another* fit. There is another sort of man who might want to kill Ackerman, a sort with a motive other than revenge."

Timothee paused for a moment.

"Turn off the screen. It's distracting you. All you can think of is what you would do to a man involved in *that*."

Reluctantly, Timothee did so. He continued staring at the blank space where the picture had been.

"Well?" Girard asked, after a few moments.

"Holy shit."

"See?"

"You think it was someone else who *worked* at the camp? One of the war criminals who got away. Fernandez, or Hilo, or—" he paused "—*Bester*."

"Eh. La."

"Holy shit," he repeated. "One of the real mindfraggers, here in Paris? I thought they all were supposed to be off-world."

"Where would *you* hide? On a space station with a few hundred thousand, a colony world with a few million at best, or on Earth, hidden in a crowd of more than ten billion souls?"

Timothee sat open-mouthed for a few heartbeats, then lunged for his computer.

"We can cross-reference," he said, "find out who worked there, who was caught, who is dead, who—"

"—got away," Girard finished for him. "Only one, and you've already said his name."

But Timothee had it, now.

"Bester," he murmured. He might as well have been speaking the name of the Devil. "Alfred Bester. My God, if he's here in Paris—hey!" His screen went blank. He started working furiously to try to get it back.

Alarmed, Girard turned back to his own AI unit and found it similarly blank. It was still working, but when he tried to return to the screen with Bester on it, he got an icon that read "information not found."

"Uh-oh," he murmured.

"What happened?"

"I have no idea," Girard responded. "But I want to find out. We're supposed to have clear access to that database, and no one has the authority to cut us out of it. Not the EABI, nobody. When—"

At that moment, the com on his desk burred for attention. Girard stopped in midsentence, frowning. "Answer," he said.

"Picture?" the wall asked.

"Sure."

The screen came on, revealing a balding man of middle years. There was something very familiar about him, and when he spoke, recognition came. Girard had seen his face half a hundred times on ISN broadcasts.

"Hi," the face said—in English. "My name is Michael Garibaldi. And you would be Inspector Gerard?"

"Girard," Girard corrected.

"Whoops. Well, I guess that high-school French was a total waste, huh? Except there was this pretty blond thing who liked it an awful lot when I called her Ma'moiselle." He smiled. "But that's neither here nor there, is it? Look, it's come to my attention that you've been poking around in the law enforcement database that relates to one Alfred Bester."

"You're spying on me."

"Nooo, I'm spying on Alfred Bester's file. And keeping tabs on who looks at his file. That isn't strictly illegal, either. I checked."

"Yes? Well, neither is my viewing it."

"Of course not. But I think you oughta stop."

"It would seem I have no choice."

"Yeah, well, it looks like—by coincidence—there's been some sort of disruption in the system. Probably turn out to be solar flares, something like that, y'know? In an hour or so, you can probably access it again. That's how long it usually takes to get this sort of thing fixed."

"You sound like an authority on the matter."

"Authority? Me? Nah. Just an interested citizen who's seen his share of equipment breakdowns. Used to happen all the time on the station. All I'm sayin' is, when it comes back on line, I wouldn't look at Bester's file again, unless you want to be hip deep in feds from the EABI on down, that's all. And if you're like most locals I know—myself included, when I was a security officer—you don't want that."

"I'm not a security officer, Mr. Garibaldi. I'm an *agent de la police* of the city of Paris. I *have* to report this matter to the EABI—in a few hours, anyway."

"Maybe so, maybe not," Garibaldi said, though a brief look of approval flashed across his face. "I might be able to help with that, if there's reason. Why did you call up his file?"

"That's really not your business, Mr. Garibaldi."

"Look, I don't like to throw my weight around, but I'm making it my business. I can do it officially, which will make your life very hard—but what do I care? I *hate* Paris. It's not like you'll get a chance to spoil one of my vacations, or something. On the other hand, you and I can come to a friendly understanding, and help each other."

"I don't like being threatened."

"I wouldn't either, if I were in your shoes. But right now your choice is between me and some Metasensory squad from EA—and me. What's it gonna be?"

Girard let out an angry breath and tapped his desk for a few moments. Marsies. Worse than Americans.

"There's been a murder, an ex-convict named Ackerman. Professional job, but under odd circumstances. Ackerman was a telepath—he worked in the reeducation camp near Brasilia. I was just checking to see who his higher-ups might have been."

"Huh. You think someone did a 'see no evil, hear no evil' job on him, then. Bester?"

"A remote possibility."

"This telepath, do you know if he had a prescription for choline ribosylase?"

"I do not."

"Might want to check that—wait, I'll do it." There was a very brief pause, during which Garibaldi looked down at something. "Nope. Oh, well."

"Would that be significant?"

"You know it."

"Why?"

"Aha. Now you're getting interested in what I might have to say, right? I can be a big help to you, if I want to be. And I'll give you this for free—it's not a bad bet that Bester is in Paris. It's worth checking out."

"I assure you, I'm doing so."

"I believe you, but Bester has slipped through my hands one time too many. This is the first thing like a real lead I've had in a long time. And I'll tell you this, if Bester really is involved, you can't trust Metasensory people from the EA or anywhere else. He still has people inside. If the EABI knows you're looking at this, Bester will know an hour later, and an hour after that he'll be so long-gone, he might as well be a passenger pigeon."

"If he did this, I'm thinking he's gone already."

"Maybe. But maybe not. He may be overconfident. There was another incident, a few weeks ago—"

"The attempted robbery of a pharmacy?"

Garibaldi's eyes widened. "Hey. I'm starting to like you. This could be the beginning of a beautiful friendship. You tell me why you link the two, and I'll share what I've got."

"In that case and in this one, some sort of device was used to override AI security devices. Not much of a link, really."

Then he listened intently as Garibaldi outlined his connection—the drug for a condition only telepaths contracted.

"That's very interesting," he allowed.

"It's more than interesting," Garibaldi said. "I think he was there. I think he's *still* there."

"And I still have to report it to Metasensory."

"No, you don't. I have friends in some pretty high places. Listen, you want this guy, right?"

"Of course."

"So do I. Only thing is, *I* don't care if I get credit for it. I just want to see it happen. I want to be there, if it's possible. So just hold off. You'll get confirmation in an hour or so from EarthGov, guaranteeing that you won't get in trouble for holding out on the psifeds. Some government guys will come in to oversee, but ones I trust, and I promise you they'll just fade away after the collar. It'll be all you, a local bust by the local man."

"And what do you get out of this?"

"Satisfaction. The satisfaction of finally seeing that bastard put where he belongs, in a cave so deep he'll have to look up to see hell. Take everything you've heard about Bester, leave out the stuff that's merely heinous, and raise the rest to the sixth power. Then you've just begun to understand what he's capable of."

"I sense a personal grudge."

"You have a problem with that?"

"Not if you don't. This is my city. If you come here with some idea of taking personal vengeance, I'll lock you up myself—I don't care *who* your friends are. Is that clear?"

"Clear as vacuum. I'm on my way. I'll be there in four days."

"And if I catch him before that?"

"You won't."

"You seem pretty sure of that."

"I am. See ya."

The contact broke.

Girard gave another sigh, but then shrugged his shoulders. One more thing to keep his mind off the unsolvable problems, anyway.

He turned to find Timothee staring with eyes like saucers.

"Do you know who that *was*?"

"Of course."

"He's friends with Sheridan himself."

"So I hear. Things will become very interesting in a few days, if we don't have our man. I intend to prove Mr. Garibaldi wrong. I intend to catch Bester before he arrives. So let's not waste any time. If you were a war criminal and in Paris, where would you hide?"

Timothee snorted. "In the government. Where else?"

For the first time in days, Girard felt a genuine smile crease his face.

Garibaldi made his flight arrangements, then kicked back and gazed at the ceiling.

Lise was going to kill him.

Boy, what a schmo he'd been, convincing himself he didn't give a damn about Bester anymore. Of *course* he did, and anyone in his position would feel the same.

But his was a position that allowed him—no, *obligated* him—to do something about it.

Still, Lise would kill him. Maybe he should come up with a little white lie, in case none of this panned out. Tell her there was some emergency situation he had to attend to, right away. At least that way she wouldn't worry about him.

Probably Bester was gone already, anyway. He was too smart to hang around after a murder. Even the cleanest murder was a mess, right?

But something deeper—that monster-sniffing animal in him—didn't believe it. Something had happened. Something had changed in Bester's pattern. The bastard had some reason for hanging in Paris long after it wasn't smart to do so. He didn't know what, but he knew it, knew it in his ever-more-creaky bones.

This time Bester wasn't getting away without a fight. This time it was Bester, or him.

And he knew who *he* was betting on.

— chapter 6 —

Bester returned from Le Cheval Heureux, mulling over what he was going to do for the next day's column. He found himself in the unfortunate position of having liked the book he had just read. Not just liked a few things about it, but truly enjoyed it from start to finish.

Which, by his own criteria, didn't make it worth reviewing. Oh, he could nitpick about the strand of slightly disingenuous naiveté that ran through the work, except that, in context, it *worked*. He could point out that the demiplot was cribbed from Shakespeare's *Tempest,* except that it had clearly been a deliberate and charming homage, with nods to other liftings from the immortal bard—most amusingly, *Forbidden Planet.*

So what was he to do? He was in a critic's hell. He had no choice but to lie or not do a column, since his deadline was only hours away.

He could tell the truth and say he liked it, but who would want to hear that? His readers would assume he had sold out, was turning into another saccharine-spewing lapdog for the publishing industry.

The thought brought a small grin to his face. Was this the worst of his troubles? It seemed so. Almost a week had passed since he had silenced Justin, and the murder hadn't so much as made the papers. He was back in touch with his contact inside Metasensory, and they had heard nothing. Fortunately, this contact was one he knew he could trust.

Ford is in his tower and all is right with the world, he thought.

Now *there* was a book he hated. Why couldn't he have

picked one of the thousands of insipid dystopian allegories that crammed the shelves these days, to read and trash?

He supposed it was because he couldn't bear to read another. Ah, well.

He reached the hotel just in time to almost bump into Lucien d'Alambert. Bester's grin widened at as he caught the cop's disgruntled surface thoughts—surely he had come to see Louise, *not* Bester.

Lucien surprised him, however. "Ah, Mr. Kaufman. Just the man I wanted to talk to."

"Good afternoon to you, too, Officer," Bester replied. "I hope you've had a good day."

"Could have been better, could have been worse," Lucien replied.

"Well, that's the best most of us can ask for, I suppose," Bester said, brightly.

"Hmm. That's not what you said about *The Fugitive Paragon*."

"You read my column?"

"I suppose I do," the officer replied.

"Well, it's always nice to meet a fan."

Lucien quirked his mouth. "I wouldn't exactly call myself a fan. You're much too harsh, in my opinion."

"People are more interested in reading things they disagree with than things they don't, I've found. It's the nature of the beast. But what can I do for you, Officer d'Alambert?"

"You can tell me about Jem."

"Jem. Jem. You mean the street thug I met my first day here?"

"I'm sure you remember him. He was about to *dis*member you?"

"Yes, of course. I never forget a threat. What about him?"

"You may have read that he was killed trying to break into a pharmacy downtown, some weeks ago."

"Louise mentioned it, yes. I can't say I was surprised. Were you?"

"Actually, I was, for a couple of reasons. Jem had his fingers in a lot of things, but he rarely put himself deliberately

at risk, especially these last few years. He didn't have to—
he had lackeys for that.

"And his lackeys, I think, were genuinely puzzled by the
whole business. None of them seems to have been in on the
robbery, even though we know a man escaped."

Bester frowned. "Well, that's very interesting, I suppose, if
you are a police officer investigating the man—but I'm not.
This Jem was a bother to Louise, and I'm just as glad he's
gone."

"That's the other thing. He stopped bothering Louise right
after you came along."

Bester raised his eyebrows. "Did you know that upward of
ninety-nine percent of the people who contract cancer wear
shoes?"

"What's that supposed to mean?"

"I mean a simple correlation doesn't show cause and effect. Do you honestly think I had something to do with Jem's
change of heart? Louise thought perhaps *you* did something,
after the fire. I supposed the same thing, since you were
clearly interested in her. In fact, I wonder if that doesn't moti-
vate a lot of things you do."

"I'm not in love with her. I care about her, and I don't want
to see her mixed up with the wrong sort of people, that's all."

"Like Jem."

"For one."

"And me, for another? Is there something wrong with me,
other than the fact that I'm not *you*?"

The policeman's face clenched. "Look, this has nothing to
do with how I do or don't feel about Louise. It's got to do with
a police investigation in this neighborhood. In fact, I hate to
admit it, but you seem to be good for Louise—*seem* to be.
But I'll be frank, Mr. Kaufman—there's something not quite
right about you. Your record is clean, too clean, really. And
nothing in it explains why a man of your background and
means would come here, live in a small hotel, and start
writing a newspaper column."

"I thought this wasn't about me?"

"I didn't say that, Mr. Kaufman. I said it wasn't about my

feelings toward Louise. You may be right—Jem's peculiar behavior and your arrival might be sheer coincidence, but I only
resort to coincidence as a means of explaining something I
can't explain in any other way. You can help me eliminate
some possibilities by clearing up why you came here and why
you stay here."

Bester cocked his head. "I thought you were a street cop,
not a detective."

Lucien was silent for a few seconds, then he sighed. "Yes. I
am. What I'm doing now is . . . outside the job. There *is* an investigation. A detective downtown, and some feds of some
sort. They've gotten interested in Jem all over again. They're
searching through his old place, interviewing his cronies.
They talked to me, of course, since this neighborhood is my
beat. Here's the thing, Mr. Kaufman—I *always* thought you
had something to do with what happened to Jem. A friend in
the mob, an old black-ops contact, *something*. I didn't care,
really. The neighborhood is a lot better off without him, and
the investigation didn't get very far when they found out who
he was and what sort of fellow he was.

"But now, they're digging deeper. Now, Louise is in love
with you—yes, everyone knows that. I don't want to see her
hurt, and I don't want her implicated. I'm certain she can't be
tied up in this, because I know her, have known her for years.
But this detective from downtown, he *doesn't* know her. And
when he finds out all of the facts, he's going to be suspicious
of you, just as I am. And he's going to be suspicious of Louise
because she benefited from it. If you go down for this, Mr.
Kaufman, it *will* hurt Louise—"

"But you'll be right there to pick up the pieces, won't you?"

"It will hurt her," Lucien continued, stubbornly, "and she
has already been hurt enough. But worse, she might also end
up paying for your crime."

"What crime?" Bester snapped. "This is all in your head."

"Then why won't you answer my questions?"

"Because they're *personal*."

Lucien said nothing, but looked skeptical.

"Look," Bester said. "You may not understand this, but

I'm eighty-two years old. That's a bad age to realize you've been on the wrong track all of your life. How much longer will I live? Ten years? Twenty? Thirty or forty, if I'm lucky. I want to live the life I missed, Officer D'Alambert. I want to laugh, and do work I enjoy, and sit in the sun. I've seen a hundred planets, and I want to forget them all.

"I first came to Paris when I was fifteen. *Fifteen.* Do you remember how much potential you had when you were fifteen? How many things you had in you, how many buds just waiting to bloom if the right kind of rain came along? I fell in love with this city then. What did I do about it? Nothing. I went on to waste everything important that was in me, squander it, sacrifice it to the gods of success, while everyone I loved and cared for died.

"That happens to everyone, I suppose, but most people fill those gaps in their lives, make new friends, take new lovers. I didn't. If I had made a deliberate plan to become a heartsick, lonely old man I couldn't have done it better. Then one day, I saw it. I faced the truth, and I came back here, and I walked until I saw something interesting. Here. I didn't know it, but I fell in love with Louise the instant she spoke to me. How could I know? I had forgotten what love was. I couldn't even conceive of it. Now . . ." He broke off, folding his face into what he was sure was a convincing simulacrum of on-the-verge-of-tears.

He looked back up at the officer, who stood silently. Bester knew why. When Bester met people, he mentally profiled them, sorting clues from surface thoughts, from actions, from the congruence and incongruence of word, thought, and expression. He had chosen his words carefully, almost scientifically. He knew d'Alambert shared many of these feelings, knew the man couldn't help but sympathize. Just then, the officer was seeing himself in forty years or so, lonely, in search of elusive truth, of love.

"Look, I won't say I didn't wish Jem harm," Bester said, softly. "I won't say I'm sorry about what happened to him. But if you don't want Louise hurt, imagine how *I* feel. She's the first human being I've loved since before you were born.

That's a special kind of love, Officer d'Alambert, one I sincerely hope you never have the opportunity to appreciate. But if you do, I can only hope it is with someone as precious as Louise."

The two men stood there on the street, facing each other. Then the cop nodded slowly. "I've a suspicious mind," d'Alambert finally said. "I can't help it. And you're right, I did—do—have feelings for Louise. I'm also smart enough to know she won't ever return them." He met Bester's gaze, squarely. "I won't help them, won't point them here, but they'll come. Maybe I believe you—about not having anything to do with Jem. But they'll still come, turning over rocks. When you turn over rocks, you usually find something unpleasant underneath. I hope you're ready for that, and I hope Louise is."

"I've got a clear conscience," Bester replied. "They can ask anything they want."

"I'm relieved to hear it. Well, good day, Mr. Kaufman." He held out his hand.

Bester shook it and smiled. "I hope one day you'll trust me, and be happy for me."

"So do I," the policeman replied. "It would make me a better man."

Bester's breath quickened as he started up the stairs to his room. It had nothing to do with the stairs. For once, he was glad Louise wasn't around. She and her sister had taken a day trip into the country and wouldn't return until late that night.

Why were they investigating again? Could they link him to Jem somehow? What if someone had seen him coming and going from the thug's apartment?

When he got upstairs, he poured half a glass of port to calm his nerves, but he kept hearing Garibaldi's voice, on the phone.

I'm coming for you.

He threw the glass against the wall, suppressing the urge to scream. It shattered, and wine ran down the wall like thin blood.

Oh, wonderful. Louise will notice that.

He went to the bathroom, soaked a rag in cold water, and tried to wipe the wall clean. But of course it wouldn't come clean. The color faded to pink, but anyone walking into the room would still see it, still—

—and now the wallpaper was starting to tear.

What had he done wrong?

But that was a stupid question. He had done everything wrong. Coming to Earth, falling in love—yes, falling in love.

If he had just kept walking, let Jem go on with what he was doing, he wouldn't be in this mess. If he hadn't been playing tourist like some silly boy, he would never have gone to the Eiffel Tower and seen Justin again. Or even if he had, he would just have mindwiped him and left town, left the damned planet, headed back out where it was safe . . .

His heart was hammering, too hard for an old man. He sat on the bed, put his face into his good hand, ground the balled, white-knuckled hand into his knee.

"Did you do this to me, Byron? Are you still in there? Did you do this to me?"

It made a certain amount of sense. It was as if a part of him had been planning this all along, planning to back himself into a corner, painting big bright arrows on the universe with notes screaming *Look here for Alfred Bester! Look here!*

"Byron?"

But Byron wasn't there, hadn't been there since the night he had let him go.

So the problem was with him, Alfred Bester.

No, the problem was with the world. How could a world— a *race* he had served so well, despite their hatred for him— think of this as just? Part of him must have refused to believe it. Part of him had somehow imagined that it would all go away, if he pretended hard enough.

But they wouldn't go away. They hadn't gone away, leaving his first mentor, Sandoval Bey, in peace. They had killed him, the best man Bester had ever known. And they had killed Brett. Oh, yes, Brett pulled the trigger himself, but there was never any doubt in Bester's mind as to who had really killed him. Or Carolyn—they had gotten her, too. And how many times had they tried to get Alfred Bester?

Well, they wouldn't. If he accomplished nothing else in what remained of his life, it would be denying them all the satisfaction. Garibaldi and his cronies, Metasensory—all of the faces that *they* now wore. He was old, but he was smarter than them, better than them. He always had been.

Maybe he had done all of this just to prove that to himself. Subconsciously he had needed a real challenge. He remembered reading about certain head-hunting tribes who considered it more prestigious to return from war with the head of a woman or a child than with that of another warrior, because that meant that they must have gone into the heart of the enemy's territory, entered the village itself, killed, and escaped carrying the unwieldy trophy.

Was that what he was doing, in essence? Letting them get near enough almost to taste him, then dancing forever out of their reach?

Why was he having to second-guess himself? Was he finally losing his mind?

He realized he was weeping. *Stupid old man. You think you love her, but it's all been a part of your game . . .*

Liar.

For an instant he thought that was Byron again, but it wasn't.

He sat there, taking deep breaths, growing calmer. His mind stopped darting about like a trapped rat, and began to work rationally again.

I'm Alfred Bester. Bester. Alfred Bester. Remember who you are!

They didn't have him yet. This all might still slide right past him. The reinvestigation of Jem might have nothing to do with him after all. Panicking. Yes, that was what he was doing, panicking like some green Blip with a bloodhound squad after him. He could afford to wait a bit. Be careful, but wait. Stay the course, not let on that anything was wrong. He could do that, and watch, and wait.

But he might as well be prepared. When the time came, he might have to go on a minute's notice.

So he thumbed on his pocket tel-phone, dialed a number he had hoped never to dial, and spoke to someone he hoped never to speak to again. He was smooth again, composed. He cajoled, he threatened, and within five minutes, a new identity began taking shape. A new *him*, somewhere safe.

Then he called his contact in EABI Metasensory. She still hadn't heard anything. He still trusted her, too. She couldn't deceive him, in that most precious meaning of the word *couldn't*—the literal one. He told her to take extra care, watch extra hard.

Then he lay on the bed, doing relaxation exercises. When he felt Louise come home, hours later, he put on his best smile and went down to see her, to ask how her day had been, to make small talk.

— chapter 7 —

Rain made Michael Garibaldi nervous, more nervous than the hard, invisible sleet of radiation from a solar flare or the remorseless, terrible arrival of a Martian sandstorm—though intellectually he knew it shouldn't.

But there were just certain things water ought not to do. It ought not to collect in pools miles deep and thousands of miles wide. It ought not to form grinding, juggernaut mountains. And damn it, it ought not to fall out of the sky.

He was explaining this to Derrick Thompson as they made their way down a Parisian street, shoved by crowds of rude people with umbrellas. "I mean, water is dangerous stuff. It corrodes metals. It's a conductor. It carries all sorts of diseases and parasites—"

"Rain doesn't carry disease," Thompson disagreed, reasonably.

"Yeah? I'm not so sure. Every time I get caught in this stuff I come down with a cold."

"I enjoy the rain," Thompson said. "Not so much like this; I enjoy the sound and the smell of a good thunderstorm."

"Oh, yeah, perfect. Uncontrolled gigavolts of electricity jumping down from the sky. Wonderful."

"I've had other Marsies tell me rain was a real revelation when they first felt it—brought them back into contact with their ancient Human roots."

"I don't believe it. They're making it up. The only roots I've ever discovered in the rain are the ones that try to grow out of my toes. And the only thing I want to get in touch with is a healthy—" He stopped short, appalled. He had almost said "shot of scotch." *Damn,* he could almost taste it. "—cup of coffee," he finished.

"Coffee is a tropical plant. Doesn't grow so well without rain," Thompson pointed out.

"Coffee grows in little bags labeled 'coffee,' as far as I'm concerned," Garibaldi said. "Here, this looks like as good a place as any."

They ducked into a café-looking place. It was crowded—some Parisians, at least, shared his feelings about the unnatural thing the sky was doing—but they managed to find a table. He took his duster off and slung it over the back of a rickety wooden chair, brushed droplets from his stubbly scalp, and looked around for service.

"Don't hold your breath," Thompson told him.

"Oh, right. Paris." His face showed what he thought of Parisian service. "So, what do you have to report?"

"Two possible sightings at the airport. One witness gave me permission to scan, and yes, I think it was him."

"Happy birthday to me," Garibaldi said. "What name was he going under?"

"*That* we couldn't recover, but he's probably changed it already anyway. That's his pattern—travel under one name, then trade it once he lands someplace."

"Right. But sometimes people break patterns. He's broken his here, I'm pretty sure. The question is, why?"

"Could he have family here?"

"Family? You know better than that. Bester wasn't just raised by the Corps, they gave *birth* to him. There are absolutely no records linking him to any other human being."

"I noticed that. That's weird, even for the old Psi Corps. Keeping track of genealogies, notably for breeding purposes, was everything, especially back then."

"*Especially* back then?" Garibaldi echoed, suspiciously.

Thompson colored. "Well, uh, of course teep marriages aren't arranged, like they used to be."

"But you guys still like to marry each other."

"Sure. It's hard enough making a marriage work between

any two people, but if one's a teep and the other is a mun—uh, *not* a teep, it's even harder."

"Uh-huh. People used to say that about mixed-race marriages."

"They still do, on Earth, some places. You don't think racism is a thing of the past, do you?"

"I don't think we've lost *any* of our old baggage," Garibaldi said, "just put it in prettier bags."

"No offense, but I find it odd to hear you say that, considering your attitude toward teeps."

"What do you mean?"

"You wouldn't marry one, would you?"

"Nope. I wouldn't want a wife who knew my every thought."

"That's not how we operate. One of the first things we learn is to respect the privacy of others."

"Sure. Just like one of the first things I learned was that it's not polite to eavesdrop, but that doesn't mean I didn't catch my parents fighting, sometimes, hear them saying things they never meant me to hear. And I sure as hell knew I shouldn't peep on my buddy Devin's older sister when she was in the shower, but I did that, too." He hunched forward, lacing his fingers together. "When I was first assigned to Babylon 5, I was buddies with a Centauri named Londo—"

"Mollari? *The* Emperor Londo? You were *friends* with him?"

"Things were different then. *He* was different then. In a way, I think I'm still his friend. Anyway, that's beside the point. At the time, the Centaurum was in bad shape. The Narn had just invaded one of their colonies, and some relative of Londo's was there. The telepath on the station, Talia Winters, was probably one of the most scrupulous, law-abiding people I've ever known. Well, until—" he looked down at the table "—nope, that's a different story. Anyway, she just chanced to bump into Londo as he came out of a lift. Damn good thing, as it turned out, because she accidentally picked up on the fact that Londo was on his way to assassinate the Narn ambassador. She told me, and I managed to stop him without any fuss or muss."

"And this wasn't a good thing?"

"Sure it was. But that's not the point. It got me thinking about Talia."

"You had a *thing* for her."

"See? Now *you're* doing it," Garibaldi accused.

"Baloney. I saw it on your face."

"How do you know? How can you tell? Maybe when you *think* you're reading expressions you're really subliminally picking up on my surface thoughts. Maybe you've been associating the two for so long you don't know the difference."

"I doubt that."

"But you don't *know.*" He leaned back again. "She slapped me one time, you know. Talia."

"I bet you deserved it."

"No. I was looking at her—well, never mind what I was looking at. And I was thinking—no, never mind that, too. But she *knew,* even though I was standing so she couldn't see my face. That's not right. It's not what we *think* that's important, it's what we *do.* I'd go crazy if I thought my private thoughts weren't private, and anyone else would, too. As a telepath, you don't have that worry. *You* can sense those things—*you* can block them. I can't. So no, I wouldn't marry a telepath."

"And ninety percent of normals would agree with you. So why this objection to us marrying each other?"

Garibaldi looked at him frankly. "Because it's making us different species. Competing species. And competing species fight. Look, the big fallacy behind racism is the belief that people with different skin colors have different innate abilities, that one is superior to the other. That's not true, but people like to believe it because people generally like to think they're superior. But when one group of people has something that really *does* make them superior, it only gets worse. Pretty soon they get bored with treating their inferiors as equals."

"That's funny," Thompson cut in. He was becoming angry. "Of all of the violence and flat-out pogroms I can think of in the history of telepathy, not *one* has involved telepaths slaughtering normals. But I can think of a damned lot of mass killings of telepaths *by* normals."

"You're forgetting Bester; he and his thugs killed normals aplenty. And that was just the beginning for him, as the hearings proved. If the telepath war hadn't come along—"

"Bester is one man. You can't judge us all by him."

"There'll be more Besters. One day one of them will get the ball rolling."

"Really? More Besters? So why do you care so much about *this* Bester, who happens to be the real, actual Bester?"

Garibaldi grinned. "*The Three Amigos*? I knew I liked you, Thompson. Why *this* Bester? Look, I'm not Sheridan. I'm not out to save the universe or anything. I just call things like I see 'em and do the best I can for me and mine. Bester—you remember that telepath I was talking about? Talia?"

"The one with the nice 'whatever'?"

"Yeah. Nothing ever happened between us, but she was a friend. I thought she was. And yeah, if she had *wanted* something to happen . . . Well, like Londo, I was different then. But the Talia I knew wasn't real.

"Bester and his buddies had reamed her out, built a fake personality, hidden the real, nasty her way down deep. Or maybe it was the other way around. Maybe the woman I liked was the real person, and the buried creation ate her alive. Whatever the case, Talia, as I knew her, died because of Bester. And that was just the start of it. That was before he got inside of *me*. I won't try to pretty this up, because I don't think it needs prettying up. Revenge is a long and honorable tradition, in its own way. Nobody is going to cry over Bester."

"Are you saying—"

"I'm saying, Junior, that when the time comes, don't you be in my line of fire."

Thompson seemed to struggle with that for a moment, then nodded. "I understand."

"Good. I'm glad we're clear on that."

"So what about this war you see coming between telepaths and normals? You don't think separation is the answer, but you can't see your way clear to actually mingling your genes with ours either."

Garibaldi sighed. "I don't know. There was a time—" He remembered Edgars' telepath virus and shuddered internally. "I thought there was an answer. Now I'm just content to hope it happens after my time, and after my daughter's time. Maybe a miracle will happen and we'll all just learn how to get along."

"I think the new laws are a good start to that."

"Maybe. Or maybe they're just window dressing. Time will tell." He looked up. "Where's the damned waiter? I'm all for French atmosphere, but this is ridiculous. Hey, you! *Garçon!*" A narrow face turned toward him, and he belatedly realized that the server was female. Oops. He *was* getting old.

The server came over. "Yes, madame?" she asked, coldly.

"Sorry about that. We'd like some coffee."

"As you wish," she replied. "And you?"

"Just coffee," Thompson said.

"I will do my best to fill such a difficult and complex order," she said, and walked off.

"Anyway," Garibaldi said, rolling his eyes, "we got way off course. The question of the hour is, why has Bester broken his pattern? And why did he break it in Paris?"

"Why not? Who would notice him here? He grew up in Geneva, so he probably speaks French as well as he speaks English, if not better. Most of the landlords in this city won't bother checking into you as long as you pay your rent on time—minding your own business is an art form here. Plenty of places to go, if he has to run. Borders are pretty easy to cross these days, with the exception of those around planets. If he leaves Paris tonight, he could be anywhere on Earth by tomorrow morning."

"I want someone at every airport and train station and especially at the spaceports."

"Fine. So he'll rent a car and drive out. Or take a bicycle. You can't button up Paris with anything short of an army backed by martial law. And seeing as how you're trying not to let the EABI in on this—which I still think is a mistake—you can't muster a fraction of that kind of manpower, even if you have it."

"So we'll have to sniff him out. How close would you have to be to sense him?"

"You're kidding, right? I only met the man once, and anyway, I don't have any training as a tracker. What you need is a Metasensory tracking unit, and you know it."

"He has a man inside. I know he does. The minute Metasensory knows he's here will be sixty seconds before he's gone."

His coffee arrived. He thanked the girl and took a sip. It was good—damn good. Better than what he could usually get on Mars.

His tel-phone trilled. He took it out and opened it up. "Garibaldi," he said.

It was Inspector Girard. "Mr. Garibaldi, I have some good news for you, if you'd like to come hear it."

Garibaldi was more imposing in person than on the vids. Not physically—he was actually smaller than Girard had imagined. But he had an effortless presence, an energy, that made one feel rather—ordinary.

"So what's the big news?" he asked, draping himself onto the chair that Girard kept in his office to make his visitors uncomfortable. Somehow Garibaldi defied the hard wood and sharp angles, made himself look perfectly at ease.

"The thug who was killed in the pharmacy break-in, Jemelah Perdue. One of his neighbors saw a man visit him a few weeks ago. A man fitting Bester's description."

That got his attention. His eyebrows arched, his eyes widened—Girard could almost swear his *ears* pricked up.

"Do tell. This just in?"

Girard bit back a sarcastic comment. He was starting to wonder if having Garibaldi and his goon squad around was any better than having Metasensory straddling him. He settled for an icy "Yes."

"What does that mean?"

"Perdue ran a small-time organization in the Pigalle—drugs,

protection rackets, and so forth. He was very, ah, local. Didn't usually do things outside the boundaries of his territory."

"Let me guess. Except for the drugstore heist."

"Exactly."

"So let's assume this witness wasn't high on monkey grass or something, and he really saw Bester. That means maybe the man who got away was Bester himself."

"I wouldn't think so. More likely another of Perdue's people."

"No, it was Bester. You don't know him like I do. Bester isn't a coward. He's a real hands-on kind of guy. I'm betting he got what he came for—the inhibitor—and replaced the ampoules with water or something. I guess it's too late to check that now. But I bet he arranged for this Perdue fellow to die there, to throw you off the track. *Damn!* I almost dug deeper into that back then. Why didn't I?" He looked back at Girard. "So how did Bester know this man?"

"What do you think I am, the answer wizard from *Science Kingdom*?" Girard asked, irritably. He had had a hard night. Marie had called—called his *house*. He had tried to get rid of her as quickly as possible, but his wife had known, of course. Not that it was a secret anymore, and not that his wife would forgive him any time soon, but he had sworn to her that he wouldn't talk to Marie again. His wife had said nothing after the call, hadn't cried or raged. She just poured herself a glass of vodka and sat there, staring into space.

"He must have been involved with Perdue before," Girard heard himself saying. "They must have had some relationship before the pharmacy job."

"Would that mean Bester was a local? That he lived in the area?"

Flash. Two men confront each other, men from very different worlds. One is at the pinnacle of his short career, the leader of a pack of losers and thugs. The other was once something much, much more. They've met the way Jemelah— no, everyone called him "Jem," yes?—Jem always meets new people. When he threatens to break their arms. He's made a mistake, though, a bad one, and doesn't know it.

The other man is Bester, and he knows Jem has made a mistake. Jem has come to hurt him, or extort from him. Bester can break his mind. But Bester thinks, "This fellow might be of some use, down the road." Then, one day, Garibaldi cuts off Bester's supply of a needed drug, and Bester knows that the day has arrived, that it's time Jem paid in full . . .

"Yes," Girard said. "He might even be a shop owner, or something. Someone Jem tried to extort protection from."

"Jem? You guys on a first-name basis all of a sudden?"

"Perdue. Jem was what the locals called him."

"So this Pigalle, can we seal that off? Quietly?"

"With all of the men and equipment you brought? Maybe so." He made sure his disapproval registered, however.

Garibaldi was more perceptive than he seemed. In fact, Girard was beginning to think that when the man seemed to miss some insinuation, it was deliberate. "You're the one who knows the city. How do you think we ought to proceed?"

"With the local gendarmes, the ones who know the place back and forth. But we can set up a plainclothes perimeter, using some of that spying equipment you brought, establish an HQ in the area."

"My friend Thompson here is a telepath. He might be able to get a read just walking around, or something."

"Better we wait until we have something to read, yes?"

Garibaldi nodded reluctantly. "Yeah."

"Something wrong, Mr. Garibaldi?"

"It just seems like we're so close," he said. "Too close, too easy. Makes me nervous. And Bester as a shop owner? That's ridiculous. I wonder if this is another one of his elaborate false trails?"

"Well, we won't know until we find out, will we?"

"Nope. You can't break eggs without breaking a few eggs. Or something like that."

"Something *like* that, I should hope, since that made no sense at all."

Garibaldi shrugged. "Wait till you meet Bester. His sense of humor will *slay* you."

Girard grinned ruefully. "You Marsies. Sometimes I think

everything you say is explained on a need-to-know basis—
and I have no need to know."

Garibaldi's face went flat. "Is that a French expression?
Where did you hear that?"

Girard was taken aback by the violence of Garibaldi's reaction. "I suppose it's French. It's just a thing some people are
saying these days. I think it comes from a popular literary or
movie critic or something."

"A movie critic."

"Yes, I think so. Kaufman? Something like that. Why?"

Garibaldi's face relaxed again. "Nothing, I guess. Just
nerves. Well. Shall we go catch ourselves a telepath?"

— *chapter 8* —

They took Louise's sister to the train station the next morning, where the two women hugged and wept a little.

The major spared a hug for him, too. "Take care of my little sister," she whispered into his ear. "She's more fragile than she seems. But I think she's in good hands."

"I would never do anything to hurt her," Bester replied.

She released him from the embrace and stepped back. "You two will come visit me next, of course. Louise, this was too long. Let's not let it happen again, no?"

"No," Louise said.

The depth of what the two women felt for each other was almost more than Bester could take. It made him feel small, and it made the things he *felt* feel small. Fraudulent.

That's not fair, he thought as they walked her up to the platform. *I'm risking my very life for Louise. What could be more real than that?*

When the train left, he felt a sudden terrific urge to be on it.

"Let's take a trip," he told Louise, abruptly.

"What? To where?"

"Anywhere. The south of France. London."

"Oh, Claude, that sounds wonderful. When shall we go?"

"Now. This minute."

"You crazy man! I just got back from a trip."

"So?"

"And I'm not packed."

"I've got plenty of money, and I just got a raise from the paper. We'll buy what we need as we go."

She laughed and kissed him. "You *are* crazy. What a wonderful, romantic notion. But impossible. I was gone for a week, and I've neglected things while Genny was here. I need a few days, at least, to get everything back on track."

"We'll have lost the impulse by then," Bester argued. "When one has a romantic impulse, one must act on it right then."

She frowned prettily. "You *are* serious about this."

"Yes. Absolutely."

She hesitated, and hesitated longer. All he had to do was push her, just a little, just nudge the part of her brain that loved him, loved this idea. And then, and then, he would find some way to explain, some way that would leave her still loving him, and—

—and the moment passed. Her mind settled and set like concrete, so that it would have taken a *real* push to change it. "I'm sorry, love," she said, fondling his hand. "I just can't, right now. I don't want to. I want to sleep in my own bed, with *you* in it. I want to putter around the hotel. Can't we find some way to make that romantic?"

He laughed it off. "Of course," he said. "It was just an idea."

"And a sweet one. A wonderful one. I never knew you could be so spontaneous."

But he understood, suddenly, that one of the reasons she loved him was his normal *lack* of spontaneity. Her husband had been spontaneous, romantic, impulsive.

Those things could turn on you. The same childlike whimsy that could seem so charming when it suggested a sudden trip to Spain was much less charming when it turned into an impulse to go off alone, on foot, unburdened by marriage and commitments.

"I'm usually not," he said, to reassure her. "I think I was just going a little stir-crazy without you around, and then sharing you with your sister. But when we get back, it will be just the two of us, won't it?"

She smiled. "Why don't we just go see how that works out, right now?"

* * *

Later that night, when she was asleep, he got up and checked the messages stored in his tel-phone. There was one he was expecting. He keyed it up. It was his government contact.

"Your new papers are on the way. They'll arrive by special courier. Good luck, sir. Some of us are still rooting for you."

He smiled thinly, and without humor, then erased the message. Then he went back to bed.

Garibaldi looked over the rooftops of Paris, restless.

"Somewhere down in there," one of the local policemen told him. "That's the Pigalle."

"Huh." The streets looked like worm trails. He could see this because they were both on a hill, standing in a room on the top floor of a four-story building.

When you lay in wait for a telepath, it was best to keep out of any possible line of sight, let mindless electronic machines do the watching for you. Garibaldi kept this in mind, even though it was unlikely Bester even knew he was in the city. Banks of screens were reporting, focusing on each person they observed, comparing the images with lightning speed against a fund of possible ways in which Bester might have altered his appearance.

Chemical sniffers were doing their job, as well—everyone in the world had a different chemical composition, so everyone left a signature trail of compounds behind them. Of course, it was a blurry signature, since diet caused it to vary, and air pollution muddied the picture even more. So the sniffers put up a lot of false red flags, most of which could be discounted within seconds by cross-referencing them with the visual images.

Thompson came up, obviously excited. He had just been on the phone with Girard.

"What's the latest?" Garibaldi asked.

"One of the local cops thinks he knows Bester. He's staying at a local hotel."

"Why haven't we grabbed him yet?"

"He was out. The cop didn't say anything to the landlady

because apparently she and Bester have some sort of thing going."

"Really. I guess there really *is* someone for everyone. Especially if you're a telepath."

"What?" Thompson's excitement was replaced with equally apparent irritation.

"Hey, don't get touchy. I'm not talking about you, or any normal telepath. I'm talking about *Bester.* This guy doesn't hesitate in the slightest to screw with people's minds to get what he wants. How else would a dried-up bastard like him get a girlfriend? He probably thought it would be good cover."

"Didn't you tell me he had a lover before? One that the Shadows did something to?"

"Yep. She was a Blip, one of his prisoners. *You* figure it out."

"Sir?" That was one of his team.

"Yeah?"

"Possible positive from both chemical and visual sensors."

"Hot damn. Which location?"

"This one, sir."

"You mean right below us?"

"Yes, sir."

Garibaldi was in motion before the affirmative was even out of the man's mouth.

He took the stairs, bounding down four and five at a time. His knees might complain about it later, but for now they were just fine. He felt twenty years younger.

On the street he did a quick right-left-right. "Which one?" he asked to his link.

"The one in the checked shirt, about a hundred meters to your left, now."

Thompson burst from the stairwell behind him, puffing.

"Cover me," Garibaldi commanded. He palmed his PPG and ran up the street. The possible looked right from the back—the right build, right hair color.

A couple stepped from a side street, and he bumped the

woman. She shouted in outrage, and the man yelled after him. He didn't even slow. Surely Bester had heard that, and would bolt.

But he hadn't. He was just walking along like nothing happened, and then Garibaldi was on him, swinging him around—

The frightened face confronting him wasn't Bester. Plastic surgery?

No. Bester would be there, in the eyes. It wasn't him. Unless, unless he was playing some sort of fraggin' mind trick.

"Mr. Garibaldi. Stop. Stop it. That's not him."

That was Thompson, tugging at his elbow. Garibaldi suddenly realized he had the PPG pointed in the man's face, and that the man was gibbering in French.

"You sure, Thompson? Could he be screwing with me?"

"No. I'd know. I promise you. Put your gun away."

"Yeah," Garibaldi said. "Yeah. I guess I oughta do that." He released the man, who backed quickly away, shouting. They had drawn a small crowd, now—a disapproving one.

Man. I'm really letting this get to me, he thought. He put the gun back in his pocket. "Sorry, folks, show's over," he said, as jovially as he could manage. "Just a little mistake." He drew a deep breath.

"Are you okay?" Thompson asked.

"Yeah. Damn. Poor guy." From long habit, he scanned the street carefully. Getting shot in the back once in his life was plenty, thank you, and Bester was still out there, wasn't he? It would be just like him to send out someone matching his physical description, to create a distraction. He wished, now, he had questioned the fellow.

He laughed, suddenly. "Now *that's* paranoid," he said.

"What?"

"Hmm? I was just imagining Bester, when he was three, secretly manipulating the genes of some other kids, making Bester-look-alikes and smell-alikes. Planting them all over the world." He broke off again. "It's the waiting. It's getting to me."

A man in a magazine stand shouted something at him, probably for him to get moving. Garibaldi realized that people were still keeping their distance—who wouldn't, after all? He was a crazy man who'd been waving a gun. Crazy men with guns probably weren't good for this guy's business.

"Hey, sorry," he said, producing a few credits. "I'll buy something." Then he remembered Girard's comment from the day before. "Ah, which paper does that movie critic write for?"

The man looked as if he was going to pretend he didn't speak English, but apparently decided an answer might get Garibaldi to go away all the more quickly. "All of them have movie critics."

"You know the one. The 'need-to-know-basis' guy."

"Oh. *Book* critique," he said. *You idiot Marsie/American/ non-Frenchman* was only implied, but Garibaldi heard it, nonetheless. "Here." He handed Garibaldi a paper.

He found the column as he was walking back toward the building. No picture. *That* was suspicious.

"It's in French."

"Of course," Thompson said. "You want me to read it to you?"

"You know French?"

"No. But I thought I would offer anyway. Yes, of course I can read French. I'll translate it for you."

Garibaldi handed him the paper. Thompson studied it for a few moments, then cleared his throat and began reading.

"There are moments in literature, rare and wonderful, that stretch us as human beings, push us beyond our ordinary boundaries of thought and experience. *A Gift of Gratitude* is a novel filled with such moments. Unfortunately, the boundaries pushed and the epiphanies experienced by the reader are in no way intended by the author. Anyone who reads often has experienced the banal, the saccharine, the self-indulgently lachrymose, but never to the extent we experience it here. Through these pages we step beyond the ordinary to a sort of über-banality we never could have imagined, in our most sedentary dreams, ever existed." Thompson stopped to chuckle. "Jeez, this guy's a riot."

"That's Bester," Garibaldi said. "Jesus K. Copernicus. That's Bester."

At that moment he noticed someone coming up from the right, fast. He turned, reaching for the PPG.

"Michael Garibaldi? It *is* you."

It was a pretty young woman in a mini-suit. He had never seen her before in his life.

"What?" he said.

"Mr. Garibaldi, could you tell us what the altercation a few moments ago was about? What's a hero of the Interstellar Alliance doing accosting citizens on a Paris street?"

That's when he noticed the newstaper floating over her left shoulder and it all snapped into place.

"Hey, hey, hey! Turn that thing off!"

"If you could just answer a few questions—"

"How do you people *do* this? What, do have some kind of pneumatic tubes under the sidewalk, that just shoot you up wherever there's trouble?"

She motioned, and the red transmission light went out on the taper. "To tell you the truth, Mr. Garibaldi, I've been following you, hoping for an interview. You were spotted at the airport, and I got the assignment. This is better than I hoped for. What's going on here? I thought you had retired from military service, but you're still carrying a PPG."

"Look, you don't know what you're messing with here. You could screw everything up. Just please—hold off, and I'll make sure you're there for the *big* story. And when I say big, I mean Jupiter-sized."

"Ah, well, we were *live,* Mr. Garibaldi. I already got you chasing that man, too. It's been on the air." The red light came back on. "So if you could just answer a few questions—"

"Oh, jeez," Garibaldi muttered. "I'm on vacation. Lemme alone."

She followed him to the building, where he at least had the satisfaction of slamming the door in her face.

A second later, though, he changed his mind. After all, his cover was already blown, wasn't it? If Bester didn't already know he was in town, he'd have to be deaf, dumb, and blind.

It was time for plan B, then.

He went back down the stairs and found her—as he knew he would—still waiting.

— *chapter 9* —

Bester glanced at the clock and put down his pen. In an hour, the courier would be at the hotel. He should head that way—it wasn't as if he was getting anything done, anyway. All he was really doing, in staring at his notebook and gripping his pen, was avoiding the decision he was going to have to make soon.

Or thought he was. Things had been remarkably quiet since his talk with Lucien. That could be a good sign or a bad sign.

He switched his notebook to newsmode, another thing he had taken to doing every few minutes. So far, it had been an exercise in paranoia, but that didn't mean it wasn't a sensible precaution.

Which point proved itself instantly, because there was Michael Garibaldi's face, not nearly as big as life, but as ugly as always. Bester had set the device to search certain news items first, using keywords like *Bester, Psi Corps, Jemelah, Telepath(s)*—and of course, *Garibaldi*.

He keyed the story on, saw a brief vid of Garibaldi attacking some fellow on the street, a fellow he couldn't help noticing resembled Alfred Bester more than a little bit.

"Oh, no," he said. He recognized the place, too. Not far away. And Garibaldi not only had a PPG but some kind of link on. People didn't just wear links—tel-phones, yes, or collarphones. That was a police link.

I'm coming for you.

Well, so he was. And he was close.

Bester closed his eyes, trying to sort it all out, squeeze down the rising panic and the flood of attendant emotions. It was survival time, now. They must have linked him to Jem, somehow, maybe even to Ackerman's murder. It had just taken longer than he thought it would.

Fine. By now they would be showing his picture to people like Lucien. No—he checked the time on the story he had just seen. Only ten minutes ago. What else was queued up?

Just as he was wondering, his own face appeared in the priority column. An old picture, from back during the hearing. Probably the most famous picture of him, in full Psi Corps uniform, gloves and all. It seemed like a lifetime ago.

He keyed the story, kept it on mute mode, and watched the words scroll out.

Paris. Police have revealed that Alfred Bester, the fugitive war criminal indicted for numerous crimes against humanity, may be at large in Paris. He is apparently living—and writing—under the name of Claude Kaufman, a name that will be familiar to readers of Le Parisien. *This recent picture was taken in the offices of* Le Parisien *only weeks ago.*

Anyone with any information on the whereabouts of this man is urged to come forward. Michael Garibaldi, CEO of the Edgars-Garibaldi pharmaceutical empire, is offering a one-million-credit reward for information leading directly to his capture. This is in addition to the one million offered by the high crimes tribunal.

Alfred Bester's story is a long and lethal one, and it begins in Geneva—

He switched it off. He knew the popular version of his life well enough.

He had to assume they knew where he lived, or would in a very short time.

On the way out of the café he tossed his credit chit to a beggar who hung out every day on the corner. "Buy yourself a hot meal and some new clothes," he said. He wouldn't be using Kaufman's credit again. If the bum used it, it would at least pull the search in the wrong direction for a few minutes. Minutes and seconds would be crucial now.

Garibaldi thought he had him trapped, but as usual, Garibaldi had made a mistake. He hadn't meant to be noticed by reporters, that much was certain. That's why Bester's face was everywhere, now—though the pieces of the trap weren't all in place, and now Garibaldi would be desperate.

His tel-phone blipped.

"Yes."

"Mr. Bester? This is Sheehan. They're on to you."

"Tell me something I don't know. Is the Bureau involved yet?"

"Yes, sir."

"Are you with them?"

"Yes, sir."

"Have they located my residence?"

"The hotel? Yes."

"Okay. This is what I need you to do."

The Psi Cops had changed their name, the color and cut of their uniforms, and some of their tactics, but they were still unmistakable when they arrived. They came in a pack, eight of them, dripping arrogance.

"Well," Garibaldi said, as they swept out of the elevator and into the search headquarters. "That took longer than I thought it would."

They didn't waste any time with pleasantries—another thing that reminded him of the bad old days. The leader was a woman, perhaps thirty-five, very professional looking, with closely cropped brown hair. She wore a lieutenant's insignia.

"Michael Garibaldi, you are under arrest," she said. The other teeps were fanning out briskly into the adjoining rooms, except for a hulking fellow who might have been a Viking if he had been born in an earlier era. He was a lieutenant, too, but there was no question which of the two officers was in charge.

"You don't say? What's the charge?"

"Criminal obstruction of an ongoing investigation."

"I think if you'll check out my clearances—"

"Oh, we will. For the moment, however, you may consider yourself my prisoner. If you could hand over any sidearms, please, and your link."

"You're arresting *me,* with Bester out there?"

Her eyes flared. "Did you really expect to capture a telepath of Bester's power and training without *us*? Thanks to you, we almost lost him."

"Almost? You mean—"

"We have confirmed sighting at Gare du Nord. A team of hunters is on it right now."

"Why haven't I heard about this?"

"Just who do you think you are, Mr. Garibaldi? I don't care who you *were,* or who your friends are. At the moment you are a private citizen, with no jurisdiction in this matter whatsoever."

"Funny. You guys didn't take that attitude when I was supplying you with funds and weapons during the war. You seemed to think I had a legitimate interest in these matters then."

She ignored that and turned toward Girard. "I don't know how he managed to bully you into this," she told the Frenchman, "but there will be a full investigation of your department by an independent authority, I can assure you."

"I don't doubt that," Girard replied. He sounded doleful but not exactly repentant.

"As of now, I have EA authorization to take control of this mess. I want all of your men and equipment off the streets, *now.*"

"That's insane," Garibaldi snapped. "You don't *have* him, yet."

"We will. I suggest you start being concerned about yourself. Call your lawyer. Monsieur Girard, I suggest you consult with your department. I think you'll find that the order to stand down is already in the system."

"Look," Garibaldi said, "if you really think I trust you guys—"

"I don't care *what* you think, Mr. Garibaldi, or who you trust. You're done here. Your link and your gun—this is the last time I'll ask."

"This is a mistake."

The Viking—Garibaldi mentally dubbed him "Thor"—raised his own weapon.

Garibaldi hesitated for a long moment. Something wasn't right here.

But then he sighed, took out the PPG, unhooked his link, and handed them over.

"Thank you. Please take a seat, somewhere. I'll want to question you in a moment."

Bester watched until he was sure all of the men staking out the hotel were gone, along with their equipment. By that time it was dark, and keeping to the shadows, he moved quietly into the building, glyphing himself as a nonpresence.

He was a little worried—he hadn't seen anyone who looked like a courier. They might have been scared off by the surveillance, or they might have been captured. Or, if they were smart, they were inside, registered as a guest.

He had to take the chance that the courier was in there. It would be too difficult to get replacement papers at this late date.

The front office and café were dark and quiet when he entered, but he immediately felt Louise's presence, and his guts knotted up. He wasn't looking forward to this part.

"Claude?" She was sitting in her usual place, a large envelope in front of her. "Or should I call you Alfred? Or Robert?"

"Louise—" He stopped. The impact of her saying his real name was almost staggering.

"Were you going to tell me about this? Or were you just going to leave without saying good-bye?"

"I was going to say good-bye."

"Really? Or were you just coming for these papers?"

"How did you get those?"

"A boy came by with them. The men watching the hotel tried to take them, but I insisted they were mine. Your courier had a choice of giving them to me or to the police. He wisely chose to give them to me."

She didn't sound angry. She didn't sound *anything*.

"I know you don't believe me," he said, softly, "but I do

love you. I had hoped this was all behind me. I had hoped to spend the rest of my life here."

"This is why you wanted to leave yesterday. Why didn't you tell me? You know I would have gone."

"You—would have?"

"Of course, you stupid fool." Now she *did* sound angry. "Do you think I didn't suspect something like this? Do you take me for a complete idiot? I don't care what you've done, or who you've been. Whatever you were like then, I know who you are *now*. You're not the same man they're talking about on the vids. You're a good man, a loving man. I—" Her voice caught. "I don't understand all of this. I don't know everything that's happening. But I do know I love you, and I think . . . you need me."

He realized he hadn't moved a muscle. He unfroze and walked slowly over to the table and lowered himself into a chair.

Her eyes were red—she had been crying. He reached out to touch her cheek, and she didn't stop him.

"You don't know what you're saying," he said, softly. "You don't know what it's like to run from world to world, having to leave everything at a moment's notice. I couldn't ask you to do that."

She raised her chin defiantly. "I think you were *going* to. What changed your mind?"

"Reality. It's not make-believe anymore, Louise. This is the real thing. I fought a war. I fought it for good reasons, and I'm not ashamed of anything I did. I wish I had won, but I didn't. Now I'm just a reminder of everything they want to sweep under the rug. They'll hunt me until they catch me, or I die."

"They can hunt us together, then. I want to go with you."

And there it was.

Once he had been briefly stranded in hyperspace, floating in that miasma that the human eye perceived as red but which serious studies proved ought to have no color at all. In hyperspace, telepathic power extended toward the infinite, and he had felt like an expanding star, as if his mind was becoming everything and nothing.

He felt like that now. Of all the reactions he had imagined from Louise, this wasn't one he had dared. And yet here it was, the simple, elegant answer to everything.

"You *do* love me," he sighed, reaching to touch her face again.

"I do," she said, taking his hand. "I want to stay with you, be with you." He gripped her fingers, knew it was the truth.

He also knew it would never work. She loved him, yes. But could he count on her? When it fully sank in that he had really done the things he was accused of, would she truly understand? How could she? She was a normal. When it really hit her that she would never see her family again—this family that she was rediscovering, her love for them just reawakening—how would she feel then? When she understood that in harboring him, in going with him, she was becoming as much a criminal as he, that her only doorway to a normal life would be his capture and conviction, what would she do?

It might be days, or hours, or months, but she would turn on him. She had to. She was in love with him, but love wasn't rational. And it was fragile, so very fragile.

But if he left her here, they would question her. They would scan her. She knew his new identity, she knew where he was headed.

"Okay," he said, softly. "You can go with me. I love you, Louise." He bent over to kiss her, savoring the feel of her lips, the emotions that spoke through them, the surge of joy and relief. He wasn't going to leave her, not like everyone else . . .

She went rigid, when he started, and then she struggled. "Claude . . . Claude . . . something's wrong—" She didn't know yet that it was him doing it, but then, in an instant, she guessed, and her eyes widened like a child's, full of betrayal and incomprehension. "What are you—*no!*"

But by then he had her paralyzed, her defenseless mind opened like a ledger. *It'll be okay,* he told her, *this is for the best.* He felt sick, though, almost to the point of throwing up. This was *Louise.* Each part of her he cut out was like cutting out a part of himself. But it was too late, now. It had always been too late.

Snip their summer afternoons together, their long walks along the Seine. *Snip* the day playing tourist, their love-making, their laughter at an old movie. *Snip* their quiet talks, washing dishes together, arguing playfully about who would cook supper.

It was all going too fast. He didn't have enough time. Soon the ruse his insiders had set up would be at an end, and the hunters would be back here, for him. Garibaldi would be back for him.

He was trying to be careful, but it was hurting her. She moaned almost steadily, and all of the sweet light disappeared from her eyes, leaving only pain, and loss, and still that awful incomprehension. *Why are you doing this to me? I love you!*

Snip him posing for her, the sun shadowing his face. *Snip* their first kiss. *Snip* the comfort of body against body, in the dark of night, when nightmares woke her.

The artist in the square. The fight with Jem. Tasting wine together and complaining about the vintage. Everything. She passed out long before it was done, thin streams of blood leaking from her nose.

He collapsed onto the table, every nerve raw, utterly exhausted. He felt dead. He wanted to be dead.

But Louise would live. There were holes, of course, things torn, but they would heal, and she would have no memory of him. To her, he would never have existed. But she would live, and with help she could be rebuilt into a normal, functioning, *safe* human being.

He staggered to his feet. One more thing.

Going up the stairs took almost all of the energy he had left. The loft was locked, but he had her key. He used it and entered the room where he had fallen in love with her. The easel and the canvas were still there, quiet, awaiting her hand, her presence. He almost saw her there, hair pulled back, paint smudging her face.

For too long he stood, locked in place by emotion. But it was too late. It was done.

He walked across the room, stood where she had stood when she painted, and at last saw it.

It was finished, and it was him. He wobbled slowly to his knees, almost as if praying.

Because it *was* him. All of him.

How had she done it, with nothing more than a brush and paint?

The face that stared back at him was lonely, and hurt. And yes, there was cruelty there, and cold purpose. She had seen that. She had always known. But she had also seen the compassion he hid, the love that came so hard, his deepest desires and most profound wounds, the ones that remained unhealed from his earliest childhood. The boy, the man, the torturer, the killer, the poet, the lover, the hater, the fearful, the hopeful. All there, in loving brush strokes.

She had known everything important about him, and loved him still.

He had known grief before. But he had never known *this*. A sound came up from his throat that he didn't even recognize, a sort of whimper, a tearing.

"What have I done?"

He had been wrong. Louise would have followed him anywhere, and loved him. She would never have betrayed him.

He took the can of turpentine and emptied it over the painting. He struck his lighter to it and stood there, watching the face dissolve in flame, a damned soul burning in hell.

When it was ash, he ground out what remained of the fire, the smoke stinging his eyes. When he was sure it was out, he went downstairs and got his papers.

He checked Louise's pulse. It was weak, but steady.

He wanted to say something. He couldn't. His throat was tight. *I love you,* he 'cast, knowing it would mean nothing.

Papers tucked under one arm, he opened the door, and went out into the night.

— chapter 10 —

After an hour, Girard began seriously worrying about what Garibaldi might do. At first he had railed against Sheehan and her people, then he had grown sulkily quiet.

Now his muscles were starting to twitch.

Girard, he was pragmatic. He had seen this coming all along, and it didn't surprise him. What did surprise him was Garibaldi's arrest. The EABI might not like what he had done, but they had to know they wouldn't be able to make any charges stick. The arrest had to be purely for the purpose of annoying Garibaldi.

It was working, maybe too well. Any minute now, the ex–security officer was going to try something rash.

Was that what they wanted? They hadn't cuffed him or anything. No one seemed to be watching him. But they were telepaths, so they knew better than Girard did that Garibaldi was about to explode. Were they giving him an opportunity to hang himself?

He walked over to where Garibaldi sat, fuming.

"They're letting him get away," Garibaldi said, softly. "Intentionally, deliberately."

"They seem to have the matter in hand."

"They're going through the motions, chasing a ghost. Have you been watching them? They *know* they're chasing a ghost. Sheehan does, anyway."

"You think she's the insider?"

"One of them. There may be more. Hell, they may all be Bester's chosen few."

"How can that be? I thought they were all monitored."

Thompson, a few feet away, nodded. "Sure. But that can be pretty pro forma. Besides, it's not impossible to condition yourself to respond the right way—or *be* conditioned, by someone as strong as Bester."

"Or maybe it's rotten right to the top, like it always was."

"I don't believe that," Thompson said. "For one thing, some of these people are pretty excited about catching Bester—I can feel it. He's the boogie man for the younger generation of teeps."

"You scanned them?"

"They're leaking it. But you're right about Sheehan. She's up to something. She's sweating it, too."

"They're chasing a decoy and they pulled all of our men off the streets. You know what that means."

Girard nodded. "Of course. It means he's still in the Pigalle, tidying things up."

"But not for long." Garibaldi lowered his voice even further. "We have to get out of here."

Girard laughed bitterly. "Mr. Garibaldi, I have exactly two things worthwhile left right now. One is my life, the other is my job. I don't particularly feel like risking either."

"Thompson?"

The younger man hesitated. "What about that call you made to your lawyer? It can't be long before they release you."

"It doesn't have to be long," Garibaldi grunted. "Just long enough for Bester to vanish. Why else would they even arrest me? Why would they keep me here?"

"The inquiry will show what happened," Girard said. "Sheehan and her cronies will be discovered, surely."

"I don't give a damn about that," Garibaldi said. "It has to be now, not later." He cocked his head at Thompson. "You really think the rest of these guys are straight?"

"I'd bet my life on it," Thompson said.

"Glad to hear it," Garibaldi replied.

"What do you—"

"Hey!" Garibaldi yelled. "I want to call my lawyer again. Somebody bring me a phone."

Sheehan turned from her task of "monitoring" the chase to scowl at him.

"Call him, then."

"You took my link. I need it back."

She grinned, not in a nice way. "I'm sorry, you aren't authorized to use a link. Use your phone."

"I don't *have* one. That's why I had a link."

"Too bad."

"Let me use yours."

She looked more annoyed than ever, but then walked briskly over, producing her phone.

As soon as she got close enough, he leapt.

Girard was impressed by the speed of the maneuver, by the way Garibaldi's limbs uncoiled, straightened, snapped out all in the same breath. He was impressed, too, by the speed with which Sheehan understood what was happening and reacted, dodging back while simultaneously chopping a knife-hand at Garibaldi's throat.

Finally, he was impressed at how quickly it was over, with Garibaldi's forearm clenched tightly under Sheehan's chin and her gun in his hand, pressed against the side of her head. Every telepath in the room had produced a weapon as well, and they were all aimed at Garibaldi—for a moment. Then, as if in response to a silent agreement, several of the muzzles slowly moved, to cover Thompson and himself. He raised his arms, slowly.

"Drop it," the Thor look-alike said.

"Hang on. Everybody just calm down. I want to try a little experiment. If it doesn't work out, I'll let her go. If it *does* work out, I'll let her go. But you're going to let me try it, or so help me God I'm going to splatter her brains on that wall over there."

"Let her go," Thor repeated, but none of them moved.

"Thompson, get her phone."

Thompson did so, moving slowly and deliberately so as not to excite anyone.

"What's your encryption key, Sheehan?"

She didn't answer. Two of the telepaths shifted a bit, presumably to get a better shot at Garibaldi.

"Come on. I don't have all day. I say your boss, Sheehan, here, has something to hide. I say she's been making and receiving calls from the man you're supposed to be chasing."

"That's insane," Sheehan managed to gurgle.

"Is it? Do any of you really think your team is chasing the real Bester? Even if you thought that, why would you pull surveillance from the one place you *know* he was? That can't be procedure."

"What are you talking about?" Thor grunted.

"He's trying to—" Sheehan gasped as Garibaldi tightened his grip.

"It's insane? Then you shouldn't mind giving us your encryption keyword. Prove me wrong."

"I don't take orders from you," Sheehan snapped.

"Thompson, scan her—get it from her."

"No." Thompson said it quietly, but firmly.

"What?"

"I may work for you, Garibaldi, but you can't make me do that. It's not legal and it's not right."

"Of all the—"

But Thompson wasn't finished. He looked squarely at Thor and the other telepaths and addressed them. "*You* can do it, though, if you think she's lying. *I* think she is. It comes off her like a stink, even without me scanning her. Whoops—feel that? She just blocked up. Why would she do that?"

Thor raised an eyebrow. "Mr. Garibaldi, let Sheehan go and drop the gun. Then we can talk about this."

"Sorry," Garibaldi said. "No can do. Not until we hear the last few conversations she had."

Thor took a step closer.

"Stop," Garibaldi said.

"No. I won't. And you won't kill her. I can tell you won't."

"She's lying to you. She's working for Bester."

"We'll see about that. After you let her go." The big man took a step closer.

"Don't try anything," Garibaldi warned. "Don't try a damn thing, or—" he broke off, midsentence, his lips quivering.

For a moment, no one moved, and then Girard noticed something that sent cold chills up his spine.

Garibaldi's finger, spasming on the trigger. Not quite hard enough to discharge the weapon.

Thor took four big steps, reached down, and carefully removed the weapon from Garibaldi's fingers. Then he placed the end of his own gun against Garibaldi's head.

"I'm going to let you move again," he said, "and you will remove your arm from around Sheehan's neck."

Garibaldi's hand suddenly clenched, and he let out a tortured gasp. Then, slowly, he raised his arms.

Sheehan wriggled out of his embrace.

"Bjarnesson, give me my sidearm," she snapped.

"Just hold on a minute, Lieutenant," Bjarnesson said. "I'd like to know—"

"Bjarnesson, that's an *order*."

The big man stared at her, his blue eyes steady. "Lieutenant, for the record, I think it's best that I temporarily relieve you of duty until I can—" His voice suddenly caught, as if there were something in his throat, then he slapped both hands to his head and groaned. The gun in his hand went flying.

So did Sheehan.

She got it and fired from the floor, hitting one of the younger cops—a young Chinese man—an inch to the left of his heart. The return fire from the remaining four all went wide, and then it got confusing for Girard because he was diving for cover himself.

He had a glimpse of Garibaldi, in motion again, a pantherlike form. Of the muzzle flash from Sheehan's weapon leaping out to meet him halfway.

He heard three, maybe four more shots, and when he got to look again, there was Garibaldi, clutching his shoulder, standing straddled over an unconscious Sheehan. The whole left side of her face was an angry red.

Thor was getting shakily to his feet, blood running out of his nose and from the corners of his eyes.

Garibaldi bent over and very deliberately picked up the PPG.

"Thompson, call an ambulance," he muttered. "And somebody cuff her. Bjarnesson, are you in charge now?"

"I—ah—" He nodded his head. "Yes."

"Get a squad together. We're going hunting."

Thor hesitated for another second, then chopped his head up and down. One of the cops was tending to the wounded one—probably not for long, given the nature of the wound.

"Derben, you and Messer stay with Li. Inform the Bureau of what's happening. The rest of you—you heard Mr. Garibaldi. Get your gear. We have a monster to catch."

The last time Garibaldi had hunted with a telepath, it had been with Bester himself. The two of them had gone after a dust dealer on Babylon 5. Sheridan, never one of Bester's fans, had forced the then–Psi Cop to take the sleeper drug, to temporarily cancel out his powers. Even without them, Bester had proved a hell of a hunter.

After all of it was over, Garibaldi had developed a grudging respect for Bester. He was a vicious, arrogant man, but what he did, he did well, powers or no.

He still respected Bester, the way you might respect a snake. That didn't mean he thought the man ought to go on breathing.

These cops were good at what they did, too. It was spooky, the way they deployed without speaking a word, each scanning a different sector as they made their way quickly up the narrow streets toward the hotel where Bester was supposed to have been staying.

"I've called my men back," Girard said. "You think he's still there?"

"I can smell him," Garibaldi grunted.

"How's your shoulder?" Thompson asked.

"Nothing I can't live with," Garibaldi answered, grimly.

* * *

Bester had only gone a few steps from the hotel when he felt a gun pointed at him.

"Hello, Officer d'Alambert," he said.

"Hold it right there, Mr. Bester." D'Alambert's features appeared as he stepped into the light of a streetlamp.

"I'm unarmed."

"You don't fool me. I know what you are."

"Well, you are either very brave or very stupid. I can switch your brain off like a light."

In point of fact, he couldn't. The effort of wiping Louise, without seriously hurting her, and in such a short time, had taken its toll. He could barely sense the policeman's surface thoughts, much less do anything about them.

"If you've hurt Louise, I don't care what you do to me."

"Ah. I thought you protested too much. You do love her."

"What have you done to her?"

"She's in there." He nodded toward the building. "She's not hurt. And I'm out of her life. You ought to be happy."

"Yes, you are out of her life. I'm taking you out of it."

"You'll have to kill me."

"I'll do it."

Bester cocked his head, aware that his time was running out. It almost seemed as if he could hear the hounds coming, in the distance. "You've never killed anyone before, have you, Lucien?" he said softly. "I envy you."

"Shut up."

"No, I do. There's this moment, when they die, when you know you've taken everything from them, and they know it, too. It's an awful moment. People pretend I have no conscience, because they want to pretend they could never do what I've done. The fact is, their ghosts never leave me. I see their eyes, in the dark. I hear the last, sucking gasps. Every man or woman I've ever killed follows me. It sounds unbearable, doesn't it? But it is bearable—it just takes practice.

"In fact, it only takes one time. The first time you kill, and you watch the lights go out, you understand how terrible it is. But at the same time you know you can do it again. That's the worst thing about it: you can never be clean again, never get the blood off your hands, and so a little more doesn't matter, does it?"

The gun wavered. "You're just trying to fool me."

"Stop you, yes. I don't want to die. But fool you? No. You know what I say is true. And Louise, you know her, too. She still loves me, you know. She wanted to go with me, but I wouldn't let her. But if you shoot me down, me, a defenseless man, her lover, how will she feel about you? Intellectually she might understand, but in her heart she will never forgive you."

"You bastard."

Bester took a step forward. "I'm leaving. I'm not going to hurt you, Lucien. With me gone, Louise will need every friend she has, and she doesn't have many—you know that. I won't take you away from her, too. So you have a decision to make. I hope for all of our sakes you make the right one."

With that, he very deliberately started walking past the policeman. The gun tracked him, and then he could feel the man's gaze, boring into his back, wavering, wavering.

Gone. A moment later, he heard the door of the hotel open. He started to run.

chapter 11

When they reached the hotel, the hunters clumped together and then broke like a rack of billiard balls, some darting up side streets, others covering the windows and roofs around them. Two drew a bead on the door.

"Is he in there?" Garibaldi asked Thompson.

"Somebody is," Thompson replied. "I don't feel Bester, but I don't have line of sight, either, and he would be blocking anyway."

"I'm going in."

He sidled up to the door, and with a quick, explosive motion, kicked it open.

In the murky room beyond, someone moved, and he drew the PPG around. "Hold it!" he shouted. "Whoever you are, hold it!"

"I'm not him," said the figure, hunched in the darkness. He spoke in heavily accented English. A man.

Garibaldi kept the man covered while he fumbled for the light switch.

The light revealed a small café. A middle-aged man in a policeman's uniform knelt beside a woman slumped across a table.

"He did something to her," the policeman explained. "He lied. He said he hadn't hurt her. But I can't get her to wake up."

Garibaldi didn't let his aim waver. Who was to say this wasn't another of Bester's tricks, another of his hollowed-out robots? The moment he turned his back, this guy might gun him down.

"Drop your gun and kick it over here," he commanded.

195

Around him, Thompson, Girard, and Bjarnesson covered the stairs and the various other exits. The policeman complied, putting his pistol on the floor and then giving it a good nudge with his foot.

"Is he here?" Garibaldi demanded, retrieving the weapon.

"No." The cop looked back at the woman. "I've called an ambulance, but . . ."

Bjarnesson holstered his weapon and strode over to the two. He knelt by the woman, took her pulse, then concentrated for a moment.

"I think she'll be okay," he said. "She's been wiped—a very professional job, probably Bester's work."

"No? Really?" Garibaldi asked, voice sopping with sarcasm. Then a bit more thoughtfully, "She must have known something. Can you get anything from her?"

"Not right now. She's in a delicate state."

"Try."

"No!" The policeman was suddenly on his feet, eyes blazing. "She's been through enough. Leave her alone. Leave her alone, or so help me—"

"Don't worry, sir," Bjarnesson soothed, with a glance toward Garibaldi. "I won't touch her. Like I said, she's in a delicate state."

Garibaldi absorbed that silently. Was Bjarnesson telling the truth, or was this just another delaying tactic? Maybe he was one of Bester's, too—just more subtle about it than Sheehan.

"I'm checking the rest of the place out," he said.

He moved from room to room, switching on lights, knocking down doors when no one answered them. Thompson and Girard trailed behind him, calming and questioning the hotel guests as he eliminated hiding places.

The whole time, he felt Bester slipping away. But maybe that's what Bester wanted him to think, as he hid gloating in some little corner of the building. He had to search it.

Behind one door he found the remains of an AI, stinking of ozone, probably from a deliberate overcharge. He searched the room quickly, found a weird dressing-robe sort of thing and a rack of mostly black clothes. And tacked to the wall, next to the mirror in the bathroom, a charcoal drawing. Bester's eyes stared from the sketch, mocking him.

"Damn it!" he snarled. He tore the picture from the wall, then went to flip over the bed, rifle through the dresser drawers. Nothing, of course. The AI might still have some information of use in it, though he doubted it. More frustrated than ever, he continued his search.

When he reached the topmost floor, he smelled smoke, and went more carefully. The door to the loft apartment was cracked; he eased it open and peered cautiously in. After he assured himself no one was inside, he went to look at the smoldering pile on the floor, near an easel. The resiny scent of turpentine tingled along the back of his throat. He stared, puzzled, at the burned painting.

Something about that scene convinced him, though he couldn't say exactly what. Bester wasn't hiding in the hotel— he really was gone.

Garibaldi hurried back down the narrow stairs.

The rest were already gathered in the lobby. "Four of the guests recognized his picture," Thompson informed him, "though none of them have seen him lately. But the cop—" He quickly related d'Alambert's story.

Bjarnesson was talking over a link. He glanced up at Garibaldi. "Trang and Sloan think they've picked up his trail," the agent reported. "They've gone ahead."

Garibaldi remembered the canvas, still smoking. "He can't have too much of a lead," he said. "We've wasted enough time here."

Outside, the ambulance had arrived, and they were loading the unconscious woman into it. D'Alambert, the cop, looked on, wringing his hands.

"You had him, didn't you?" Garibaldi said. "And you let him go."

"I couldn't stop him," the man said, miserably. "I tried."

Garibaldi would have felt sympathy if he'd had time for it. He didn't. The colder the trail got, the harder it would be to follow. Bester might be only a few steps ahead of them, but he had the advantage of knowing where he was going.

"No. I won't get this close and fail," he said, under his breath. "Let's go," he told the telepaths.

"My men have almost all of the streets closed off," Girard informed him, "and we have choppers and hovercraft up, too. We'll get him."

"I'll believe it when it happens," Garibaldi replied.

Bester leaned against a building and drew a deep, calming breath. Panic wasn't going to get him anywhere. Panic triggered reflexes that were too ancient, reflexes that knew nothing of the helicopters he heard buzzing about, of infrared cameras, of telepathic hunters. Panic might have been an asset in the days when it helped a naked monkey-thing scramble up a tree, three steps ahead of a pack of hyenas, but it was no help to a teep in his present position.

He couldn't count on his insiders, anymore. By now they had unmasked themselves, outlasted their usefulness. He was on his own.

He clutched his new identity to his chest. It wasn't that bad. All he had to do was get out of Paris. A small area could be searched intensively, but expand that area to France, to Europe, and beyond, and he would be safe again, for a while.

And he wouldn't repeat the same mistakes again. No, he just needed a little distance, and more importantly, a little time. He was too weak, now. A few hours before he would have been able to penetrate a police barricade, like the one he saw a few streets ahead, simply by willing it so. Now he would be lucky to fool a single normal.

He still had one advantage. He still had the Shadow chip. He couldn't cloud a man's mind, but he could cloud a machine's.

There was a department store on the next corner, wasn't there? He slipped toward it.

He used the Shadow chip to make the security system stupid, but locks were another matter. Like those of the pharmacy, they were independent mechanisms. He took off his jacket and placed it against a window, which fortunately turned out to be glass. He couldn't hold the jacket up with his crippled hand, so he leaned against it and punched with the other. The window shattered inward without much fuss, and he stepped in. Was there a live guard here? Probably, but he didn't remember. He waited, crouching for a few seconds, straining his worn-out abilities to the maximum.

Yes, there was a guard.

When he had him in line of sight, he jolted the fellow, which was the best he could do, and followed that with a vicious uppercut. He was physically weakened, too, but achieved the desired result. The man—no, woman—fell sprawling, her shock stick bouncing on the floor. He picked it up and hit her with it, twice. Then searched her. No gun. What kind of guard didn't carry a gun?

The kind that didn't think she needed one, obviously. He shocked her again, then knelt, pinched her nose, and covered her mouth.

"Sorry," he said, "but if I just cuff and gag you, they'll feel you when they come by. Can't have that."

So much for his promise not to kill anyone else. Of course, they would notice the broken window anyway—maybe a little sooner if they felt the guard. But how much time would her death actually buy him?

Swearing, he let her breathe again, took her phone, cuffed her hands behind her and around a column.

He was in the women's lingerie section, so he balled up some panty hose and shoved them in her mouth. Then, still cursing at himself, he made his way toward sporting goods.

He had come shopping here with Louise. It was where he had gotten her the dress.

What would she think, when she looked in her closet? She wouldn't remember getting it, but she would know, by then, who had given it to her. Would she throw it away? Or would she keep it, sensing that there must have been something true between them, something real?

It doesn't matter. Concentrate.

He wove through the darkened racks, trying to think of something else. He remembered playing cops and blips with

the other kids in his cadre, when he was only six or so. He had
always wanted to be the cop, the hunter, the good guy, but
more often than not they had made him play the Blip, the
rogue on the run.

He remembered an argument he had had with one of the
boys in the cadre—Brett—when they had played Blips together. Brett had insisted that Blips always acted stupid, always made obvious mistakes. Bester had wanted to play as
smart as he could, because he hated being beaten, even if he
was supposed to be. He had sacrificed Brett to the others that
day, made Brett lose, so he could win. He had been punished
for that, for turning against one of his own brothers in the
Corps, even in a game.

Now he was the Blip, for real. But no, that wasn't right. He
wasn't a Blip—he was the last Psi Cop. It was the world that
had gone rogue.

For an instant, he was that six-year-old all over again. It
was so real, and so vivid, that the intervening years seemed
dreamlike, unreal. As if the thing that connected him to the
child wasn't a linkage of years, or the passage of time, or personal evolution, but that single, unchanged desire to win.

In sporting goods he picked up a target pistol, a small-
caliber weapon that fired fléchettes. Anything heavier would
be locked up someplace, and he didn't have time for that. He
also picked up a Bowie knife, night vision goggles, and several motion detectors of the sort that campers used for
perimeter alarms. He placed one by the broken window and
another near the front door.

Then he slipped out the back door and into an alley. They
didn't know how weak he was. They would waste time
searching the store for him, assuming he was creating a psychic shadow for himself.

He hurried down the darkened street, feeling a little better
with a weapon in his hands. He was also regaining his
strength—the background babble of Paris grew clearer with
each passing moment. Soon he would be able to face his
hunters on a more even footing.

Or so he was thinking when he turned a corner and ran

square into one of them. It was a young fellow, scarcely out of training. He was as surprised as Bester—Bester could feel his shock like a grenade going off.

The hunter's weapon was already out, and up. He fired.

He missed.

Something whined by Bester's shoulder as he sidestepped left and fired the fléchette gun once, twice. The boy got off another shot, too, but Bester felt a diffraction of pain. It wasn't from being hit himself, but from the darts punching holes in the hunter. The second one hit bone in the shoulder, and the young man gagged on his own tongue. Bester finished putting him down with the guard's shock stick.

He searched the still body, quickly. Oddly enough, the boy was using some sort of fléchette gun, too, and not much better than his own. He traded shock sticks—his own was nearly out of charge—took the gun, and then quickly scanned the boy.

He had a partner, working around the other side of the building. Bester flattened against the wall and waited.

A moment later the second man came around, warily. Bester hit him in the neck with the fléchette gun he had taken from the first hunter.

The response surprised him. The man roared in pain, but was not otherwise deterred, pulling his gun up to fire. Bester had only one choice—he leapt forward inside the extended arm, swinging the shock stick. The hunter reacted too quickly, however, and they were suddenly grappling.

The hunter struck—not physically, but with all of the power of a young P12.

Long ago, Bester had studied shaman battles.

The human brain had evolved to process data derived from sensory input. The recent mutation that had produced telepathy hadn't changed any of the other hardwiring. Telepathic input was complicated, it circumvented the sensory nerves, went straight to the brain. Still, the brain, being as it was, interpreted psionic attacks as sensory input. The result seemed eerily optical.

In short, a battle of minds was, on the perceptual level, a battle of illusions—like those described in ancient myths and legends. For Bester, there was nothing mystical about the process, but "shaman battle" was as good a name as any.

His enemy launched a multilevel attack, aimed at pain centers, voluntary muscle control, and at the cerebral cortex more generally, triggering some random and some specific neural firings in Bester's brain. Mechanically, that was what happened.

How Bester perceived it, however, was somewhat less clinical.

A cloud of wasps surrounded him, condensing from the air like dew, tickling his naked flesh from head to foot. Their stings dug into him everywhere simultaneously, and he suppressed a shriek. They crawled into his eyes, his nose, his mouth, his ears, and with them brought agony that curled him like a withering leaf.

Bester gathered what strength he had left and wreathed his tortured flesh in flame, searing the insects away. Their charred bodies fell from him by the thousands, and he tasted the stink of them on his tongue. Even before the last of them were gone, biting hard rain and hail drove into him, quenched his fire. Grimly, he clothed himself in heavy combat armor, but he knew that it would last only an instant.

If he kept playing this defensive game he was going to lose.

His enemy's mind was a spinning disk, a buzz saw, then a jagged globe turning several directions at once. Bester engulfed it in viscous fluid, clogged it. The hunter responded almost instantly, crystallizing the fluid and shearing through it, sending sharp fragments flying back at his opponent. But Bester's move hadn't really been an attack—it had been a feint.

Beneath that assault—really a broadscale isolation of neurons—he had slipped in a jolt to the motor nerves. Bester couldn't see how effective it was, but he felt an uncontrolled trembling that he imagined was a point for his side.

But he was still too weak, and the wasps were back, more of them than ever. Repetition was crude—in fact, all of the hunter's attacks relied on sheer brute strength of mind. Unfortunately, it was a strength the fellow had, and which

Bester, at the moment, lacked. Sure, in top form he could beat this kid hands down, but—he was losing. His responses were slow, and inadequate.

He twisted the wasps inside out, but they exploded as they did so, turning his once again naked flesh into a sheath of agony. He gritted his teeth and swore, lashing back without finesse, and without much strength, either. Like a man in the last stages of being throttled, slapping weakly at his killer's face.

And then, weirdly, all of his opponent's power went out of him, sucked down some drain Bester could not see. When Bester sparked out his cortex, he was able to raise only the flimsiest of barriers. The man collapsed, spitting up blood.

Bester reeled against that wall as reality snapped up around him again. He hit the man with the shock stick, just to make sure he stayed down.

A nearly blinding light shone in his face, and for an instant he thought he was still in the mental combat zone, that this was all an elaborate ruse setting him up for the real, final blow. Then he understood. He was standing in the street, in the path of a car.

A man stuck his head out of the car. "Hey, old-timer. You okay?"

"They attacked me," Bester groaned, indicating the bodies. "They—" He lifted the gun and pointed it between the man's eyes. "Do exactly what I say, and you will live."

"*Sacré merde!* You are the fellow on the news."

"So pleased you recognized me," Bester said. "Step around and open the passenger door. Around, not through the car." He sidled closer.

The man was probably in his fifties, greying, with a long, solemn face. "No problem," he said. "Just take it easy with the gun, yes?"

"Yes. As long as you follow my instructions."

Obediently, the man went around and carefully keyed open the passenger door. Bester followed him.

"Now, slide through to your side and shut your door."

The man did so, and seconds later they were both in the vehicle.

"Head north," Bester grunted.

"Whatever you say."

They traveled east for a block, then north. Bester clenched and unclenched his good hand. Where to go? There must be barricades everywhere.

He glanced out the window, and with a dull shock realized that they were on the same street as Louise's hotel. In fact, they were passing it.

He threw his blocks up, built a nothingness around himself. The darkness should help protect him from a physical sighting.

There was quite a crowd in front of the hotel, he noticed. Policemen, an ambulance—had he hurt Louise more than he thought? He might have. He might—

"Keep driving," he told the driver. "Do nothing suspicious."

"Stay calm," the fellow said.

Bester saw a familiar face. Garibaldi. Of course.

They cruised on past, unnoticed. Three blocks later, he began to breathe easier.

"Back north," he directed. "Try to get on the Rue de Flandre."

"I passed a roadblock coming in here," the man said. "I'll bet they have things blocked up north, too."

"You'd better hope they don't," Bester told him.

But at least he had broken the trail—that was the important thing. Even if he had to get out of the car soon. And he knew, for the moment, where Garibaldi was, and more or less what he was up against.

The Rue de Flandre *was* blocked off, and so were the next few streets. They weren't substantial blocks—often just one man—but in his state, Bester knew he couldn't risk it.

But what *did* that leave him with?

"What's your name?" Bester asked the driver.

"Paul . . . Paul Guillory."

"Paul, you live around here, don't you? Inside this perimeter they've set up?"

"No. I live across town."

"Don't lie to me. Why else would you come here?"

"I—okay, I'm sorry. Yes, I live just a few blocks away."

"Do you have a wife? Kids? A girlfriend?"

"I have a wife and a little boy. Please don't drag them into this."

"Sorry, Paul, but I'm afraid I have to. Take me there." He prodded Paul with the gun.

"Yes, sir."

"No need to be so formal, Paul. After all, I'm going to be a houseguest. Call me Al."

Garibaldi noticed the funny look on Thompson's face.

"What is it?"

"Just felt somebody walking on my grave."

"What?"

"Bester." He turned his head, slowly. His gaze settled briefly on the taillights of a passing groundcar.

"He's in that car," he whispered.

"You're sure?"

"Yeah. You were right, about me being able to sense him. His tinkering with my brain left a kind of—wound. It just started hurting again. When I look at the car, it hurts even more."

"That would be like Bester," Garibaldi said. "Driving by the scene of the crime, so he could watch us all shaking our heads in confusion. So he could gloat."

"Shall we go after him?"

"On foot?"

Girard spoke up. "I can have a car here in a few moments."

Garibaldi shook his head. "No. No car chase. Look, we know where he is right now, and he thinks he's pulled one over on us. This is the best break we've had." He looked sidewise at Thompson. "You're *sure* it isn't some sort of decoy?"

"Sure as I can be."

"Okay. Girard, can you have that car followed?"

Girard nodded briskly, pulled out his phone, and spat some French into it. Garibaldi recognized the make and model of the car, and the identification number. "It ought to have a transponder," he explained. "Most people have them put in, in case of theft."

He got some sort of answer a few moments later.

"Yes. They have a lock on its signal," he said.

"Good." Garibaldi rubbed his hands together. "Now about that car you said you could get *us* . . ."

— *chapter 12* —

"Nice place you have here, Paul. Good day, Ms. Guillory."

Guillory's wife was a stout, pleasant-looking woman with very dark hair and very pale skin. She nodded at Bester politely, though clearly she was puzzled.

"Paul should have told me he was bringing company. I just got off work, and picked up some dinner, but I'm afraid there isn't very much. I hope you like Chinese food."

"That sounds wonderful," Bester said.

"Papa!" A boy, perhaps five years old, came scuttling out of an adjoining room and leapt into Paul's arms. Bester strolled over and glanced in the boy's room, as father and son hugged.

"Pierre, this is my friend Al. He's going to be visiting with us tonight, and I want you to be good, yes?"

"Ha!" the mother said. "He's not only good, he's excellent—at getting into trouble. Pierre, tell papa what happened in school today."

"Oh, eh, well nothing really happened, Papa. Nothing, really."

Bester stepped into the boy's room. The floor was strewn with toys, books, coloring books, and random bits of paper. He found a single window, shuttered with venetian blinds. He lifted the blind and peered out. The view was of the second floor of another, very similar apartment building across the street.

"Now, Pierre, either you tell him or I tell him—excuse me? Can I help you?" The woman suddenly noticed what he was doing.

"Sorry," Bester said. "It's just been so long since I've been in a child's room, and I didn't want to interrupt what you all were talking about." He smiled. "It sounded important."

"Well, that's okay, but I would have made Pierre straighten up if I knew you were coming."

"So what did you do at school, Pierre?" Bester asked, reentering the room and squatting next to the boy.

"I, eh, I put some glue in this girl's hair. Jesse."

"Oh, dear. Why did you do that?"

" 'Cause she's dumb." He looked down at his feet. "I dunno."

Bester smiled and mussed Pierre's hair. "Kids," he murmured. He looked up at the mother. "I'm sorry, what was your name?"

"Marie," she answered. "And you were Al?"

"Yes. Marie, I think Paul has something to tell you. Pierre, why don't you show me some of your toys while they talk?"

"Okay."

"What?" Marie asked.

"Do as he says, dear," Paul told her, his voice strained.

Bester followed the little boy back into his room as a hushed conversation followed in the kitchen.

"I think I'm in trouble," the boy confided, shuffling through his things. He extracted a toy Starfury from an agglutinated mass of clothes and crumpled paper. "Here's a toy."

"Yes, it is," Bester said. "I used to fly one of those."

"Nu-uh!"

"Yes, I did."

"In the war?"

"Yes. In several wars, actually."

"No, you didn't."

"Sure I did," Bester replied.

"I want to fly one one day. Do you think I can?"

"Well," Bester replied, "that depends upon your parents. And whether or not you stop putting glue in girls' hair. They frown on that kind of thing in EarthForce." He noticed Paul and Marie were back in the living room. "Oh, hello. Done talking?"

Marie's face was paler even than when he had first seen it. "Pierre—" she said, her voice rattling.

"Why don't you get that Chinese food ready?" Bester said, softly. "I'll be fine with Pierre. Which reminds me, Paul, didn't you have some errands to run?"

"Oh, yes. I clean forgot. I'll, ah, bring back some more food, too."

"Why don't I kick in for that?"

"No need. You're our guest."

"Well, thank you. I must say, you make me feel very welcome."

After Paul left—his reluctance and worry were actually almost painful in Bester's reviving senses—Bester turned back to the boy. "Pierre, let me tell you about flying a Starfury, and you show me the rest of the house, okay?"

It was a small place. The master bedroom had a window with the same view as Pierre's bedroom. The combined kitchen–dining room was decorated in a cheerful eclecticism, with a vase of tulips, a cheap imitation Aztec wall calendar, a bowl of papier-mâché fruit, and a laughing Buddha carved from Martian hematite. Marie was forking kung-pao chicken and lo mein from cardboard containers onto yellow ceramic plates. She glanced up at Bester, often.

"Go wash your hands, Pierre," she said.

"Oh, yeah!" the boy responded, and ran off to do so. Then he turned, and bouncing on one foot, beckoned to Bester.

"I forgot to show you the best thing!" he said.

With a what-can-you-do? shrug to Marie, Bester followed Pierre into the cramped bathroom.

"See? See?"

What Bester saw at first was that the wallpaper had come off one of the walls and hadn't been replaced. But the boy was gesturing at something more specific—a sort of drawer set into the wall. He pulled it open, revealing a shaft that dropped straight down and then curved off after a few feet.

"What is it?" Bester asked.

"Dad says these apartments are real old, and in the old days they used t'put their garbage down this. He said this must have been part of the kitchen before they made smaller rooms."

"Huh." Bester peered down the shaft. "So that probably goes all the way to the basement somewhere."

"Yeah. I wanted to slide down—"

"Supper!" Marie called from the next room. "Are your hands washed?"

"Better wash them," Bester said.

"What about you?"

"I'm grown up. I don't have to if I don't want."

He went back to the kitchen. "What do you want with us?" Marie whispered.

"I just need a place to rest for a little while," he said. "You'll hardly notice I'm here."

She started to say something, hesitated, started again. "We aren't political here," she said. "I mean, we don't—"

"Don't what? Vote? Why should I care about that?"

"All I mean is, I know they're after you, but it's something political, and we don't care about that. Just don't—don't hurt my son."

"Dear me. Why would I do a thing like that? And to someone showing me such hospitality?"

"I—guess you—wouldn't?"

"Let's say I'd *rather* not, and leave it at that, shall we?" Bester replied.

"See? Clean!" Pierre said, running back in from the bathroom.

"Well," Marie said, composing herself. "Let's eat."

"There he is," Garibaldi grunted. "You guys cover me." He got out of the car and crossed the street to where another man was just leaving his car, the same tan Cortez sedan they had followed to these apartments, then back out to a grocery store and a train station, then back here.

"Hey, buddy. You speak English? Can you help me out with something?"

The fellow looked up warily. "I'm in a hurry," he said, shouldering a backpack.

"Sure, sure. I just need some directions."

"Where are you trying to go?"

"To wherever you've got Alfred Bester stashed. *Shh!*" He made sure the man—Paul Guillory, his registration called him—noticed the PPG.

The man froze. "I don't know what you're talking about. He's that war criminal they're looking for, no?"

"He's that war criminal *we're* looking for, *yes,* and he's up in your apartment."

"No, I don't think so. That's silly."

"Sorry, buddy."

The man heaved a deep sigh, and to Garibaldi's mortification, a tear slipped from one eye. "Monsieur, he has my wife and my little boy up there. He has a gun. He will kill them if anything goes wrong, I am quite certain of it."

"What's this?" Girard asked. "I'm Police Inspector Girard. He has your family as hostages?"

"Yes. He sent me out to get some things. He said if I wasn't back in an hour, he would start to hurt them. It's been almost an hour."

"What did he send you for?"

"Train tickets. Some food. Please, I have to take them to him."

"I'll help with that," Garibaldi offered.

"No!"

"Look, we've already got your place surrounded."

"Don't you hear me? He'll *kill* them."

Garibaldi looked at Girard. "Gas? What? There's gotta be some way to get him out of there."

"Without endangering the family?" Girard replied. "I much doubt that. Why not wait until he leaves, in the morning? We know what train he's taking, now."

"Just one problem with that. He'll scan Paul here when he gets upstairs and get an instant replay of this whole conversation. Who *knows* what he'll do then?"

"You did it on purpose," Paul said heatedly. "Spoke to me on purpose. To trap me."

Garibaldi shrugged. "It ain't pretty. But look, this guy just mindfragged his *girlfriend* for Chrissakes. You think he's gonna even blink with you guys? Man, every *second* he's with your family they're in danger. You think he's just gonna walk away from the three of you, especially after he sent you to get train tickets for him? No way. All three of you are dead or as good as dead without us. We're the only thing between you and Bester, and you'd better believe it."

"That's the problem," Paul said. "You *aren't* between us. There is *nothing* between him and my little boy. Nothing."

"Well, then. Let's put our heads together and see what we can come up with, then. And, considering your deadline is almost here, I think it oughta be pretty fast, don't you?"

Bester felt a sudden flash of heat that had nothing to do with the kung pao sitting uneasily in his stomach. It felt more like a hot wind in his skull, followed by a contrasting cold that lingered.

He'd felt it before, just before walking into Lyta's trap. He'd felt it on Mars, seconds before a terrorist bomb had depressurized his office.

There was an old exercise for picturing how gravity worked. You imagine space as a sheet of rubber, extending in all directions. You put a ball bearing on the sheet, and it creates a small dimple. You place a cannonball on the sheet, and it makes a large one. Place the ball bearing near enough to the cannonball, and it rolls down the large dimple to join the cannonball. The lesson is that mass warps space, and that the "attraction" of gravity is merely a by-product of that warping.

Bester had long ago used that same visualization to think about telepathy, with the ball bearings and cannonballs and what-have-you representing minds. A normal made a tiny dimple, a P12 a deep one. But it was more complicated than that. The older a telepath got, the more experience he acquired, and the more he learned from his instincts, the stronger his telepathic gravity became and the more the plane of thought curved around him. The deeper his imprint became, so to speak.

At the same time, he became more and more sensitive to other perturbations on the imaginary rubber sheet. Yes, real telepathy, the transfer of coherent ideas from one mind to another, depended upon proximity and, ideally, line of sight. But there were older senses that telepathy could engage, senses that worked below the level of rational thought.

He had felt Lyta, that day. Her Vorlon-enhanced abilities had made a huge dent in the fabric of psi-space, and his back-brain had fairly shrieked *Get out*! What he felt now was no less compelling—a bunch of little ball bearings were rolling toward his cannonball, and the deep-warning-system of his brain was yammering for attention. *This* was an instinct he had learned to trust.

Yes, something was wrong.

"You can keep us covered all the way up?"

"Yes," Bjarnesson said, matter-of-factly. "Telepathy works on line of sight, and he won't have that until we open the door. It's easy to disguise the faint impressions he might feel until then."

"So I've heard," Garibaldi answered.

Girard had begun to wonder just what the hell he was supposed to be doing here. His investigation had spiraled completely out of his control. Just like his life. First Garibaldi had horned in, then the EABI, now Garibaldi again.

Looking back on it, it had almost been a relief. When he, Girard, was in charge of things they tended to go wrong, especially lately. When he learned that one of the century's worst war criminals was the object of his pursuit, he had talked himself out of the case. He had been a coward, in that way, ready to let outsiders take the risks, even if it meant they would also get the prize.

Now things had gotten damn muddy, though. Who was in charge? Garibaldi, clearly, mostly by the force of his bullying, but also because he had been *right*. And because Sheehan's betrayal had mired the EABI forces in uncertainty.

Parisian citizens were paying for all of this, though. His citizens. The people Girard was sworn to protect—the people Garibaldi and the rest didn't give a damn about.

He took Garibaldi aside. "I'm going through the door," he said, mildly.

"It's okay, Girard, I've got that covered."

"No, it's not okay," Girard said. "There's a woman and a little boy up there in danger. I will not let you burst in, guns blazing."

"Look—"

"No, *you* look. You aren't an officer of the law, Monsieur Garibaldi. You are just a man with an unhealthy obsession and far too much money, who thinks he's a cowboy from the American West. We'll do this my way. Period."

"What's your way?"

"I go in with Paul, alone and unarmed. I explain to Bester that he's surrounded—"

"Oh, give me a break," Garibaldi said, rolling his eyes. "He'll just take one of them hostage. Or maybe you."

"He already has them hostage. He won't get far if he tries to leave with them."

"But with the element of surprise—"

"Now you give *me* a break. We haven't surprised this man yet, and despite assurances all around, I'm not confident he *can* be surprised. My way. If he isn't amenable to reason, *then* you can do what you wish."

"This is a bad idea."

"Right now, my men outnumber yours ten to one, even if we include the telepaths, who don't seem to know who they're working for anymore. I can have you arrested again, and I won't make the same mistake they did. I'll have you hauled down to the station and held until this is all over. Understand?"

Garibaldi was a man who was used to getting his way, but that had been a relatively recent development. Deeper than that, beneath the veneer of the rich tycoon, there was a man who had spent most of his life following orders. He nodded reluctantly. "I still think it's a mistake."

"So noted. But that's how we're doing it."

"Your funeral, buddy. And it probably will be."

Girard smiled ruefully. "I just have this image of you and

Bester—one man made of matter, the other of antimatter. If I let you rush into that room . . ." He shook his head. "I won't let that happen."

Girard checked to make sure everyone was in place. Snipers in the apartments across the streets, men below the windows, several on the roof. All were told to stay out of line of sight and let their surveillance equipment do the watching for them. Once he felt secure, he waved Paul over.

"I'm going in unarmed, to talk to him. I'll do my best for your family, I swear."

Paul just shook his head. "We should hurry," he said. "I told him I'd be back."

He positioned two teeps and two normals at the base of the stairs, then let Paul lead him to the lift. There were eight of them in all: Paul, Garibaldi, Thompson, Bjarnesson, another teep named Davis, and three special-ops policemen armed for bear.

He tried not to pause when they reached the door and the others took their positions. Then, screwing up his courage, he knocked.

"Who is it?" A woman's voice.

"Police Inspector Girard," he answered, in a loud voice. "I'm unarmed. I'd like to talk to Alfred Bester, please."

A pause of several heartbeats followed before she answered.

"Come in."

— chapter 13 —

"The door is locked, madame," Girard said.

"I can't come to the door," the woman replied.

"It's a trap," Garibaldi hissed. "Break it down."

"I would rather use Monsieur Guillory's key."

"Oh. Yeah. Well, if you want to be lazy."

"Don't follow me in," Girard warned. He took the key and opened the door.

Guillory's wife and child sat on the couch, watching them.

"Monsieur Bester, I wish to speak to you," Girard called. He didn't see Bester anywhere. "I am unarmed, but there are armed men in the hall and surrounding the building. I want to come to some accord that will settle this without any more violence."

"He's gone," the woman on the couch said.

"What? Impossible. And if so, why didn't you answer the door?"

"He told us not to."

"But if he isn't here . . ." Girard walked slowly around the living room. Nowhere to hide there. He looked in the kitchen next, checking the cabinets even though he didn't really imagine a grown man could fit into them. He looked in the bedroom, the boy's room, the bathroom. No one there, not even behind the shower curtain.

When he came back into the living room, the two were still sitting there. Garibaldi peeked around from behind the door.

"He doesn't seem to be here," Girard admitted.

"He went down the garbage chute," the boy said.

"What?"

"In the bathroom," the woman said. Paul had called her Marie, yes? It wasn't a name he could hear without experiencing some troubling thoughts just now.

"No way." Garibaldi grunted. "I'm coming in."

"Watch it," Thompson called from out in the hall, "he *might* still be in there. He might just be telling you he's not."

"Can he do that?" Girard asked, incredulous.

"Yes, against normals, certainly."

"Okay. Let's all search, then." He noticed that Marie and the boy were both sitting exactly as they had been, and little spider legs tickled up his back.

"You can get up now," he said.

"No, we can't," Marie said, tears starting in her eyes. "He *told* us not to."

"He compelled them," Bjarnesson said. "Should be easy enough to fix. He couldn't have had much time."

That was too much for Garibaldi. He entered the room, and *he* wasn't unarmed.

"Where's the garbage chute?"

The boy pointed the way with his eyes.

Garibaldi gazed in dismay at the dark shaft.

"Damn it. Where does this go?"

"We don't know," Paul called, from where he knelt with his family, soothing them, telling them that everything would be all right. "The basement, I guess."

"Perimeter reports no one went out the window or exited from the building by the doors," Bjarnesson relayed. He paused. "I think he *is* gone. I don't think he could fool all three of us working together."

Garibaldi looked back down the shaft, speculatively. The inside was filmed with dust, and what looked like fresh scratch marks.

"I'm going in," he muttered.

"I've sent a detail to try and find the basement, so that end is covered," Girard said. "If you want to follow the cobra into its den, more luck to you."

"Just call me Ricky-Ticky," Garibaldi replied.

Bester was smaller than Garibaldi was, that was clear from the start. He'd known that, of course, only it was hard to think of Bester as small, at least until he was confronted with the fact that he, Garibaldi, fit into the shaft like a cork just a micron shy of a perfect fit. There was little he could do other than wriggle and let gravity do the work. As it was, he had to stretch his arms out above him.

It wasn't until he'd managed, catching and bumping, to descend about ten feet that he considered what might happen if Bester was still at the base of this thing. He would be a perfect target, coming out legs first. A sitting duck.

What the hell did that mean, anyway, a "sitting duck"?

He slid down what he estimated to be another ten or fifteen feet. Then the chute angled sharply. Until that point, he hadn't been able to see how far down it went, but he figured the building was two stories, with a generous basement. So he ought to be about two-thirds of the way down.

Good, because he was getting itchy. The chute was too damned small, and he couldn't *move* . . .

But he had dropped only another five or six feet before his feet came to rest on something solid. He kicked around, and found that the chute simply came to an end. Which was stupid, but . . . come to think of it, he'd never known anyone who lived in a building with a garbage chute. It had never occurred to him it might not be functional. On Mars, you didn't build something unless you were going to use it, and if you decided you weren't going to use it you took it out, to free the space for something else.

Of course, on Mars you weren't dealing with three-hundred-year-old buildings that had been tinkered with incrementally over the years.

"Nice insight, Garibaldi," he muttered to himself. "Now how are you going to get out of here?"

A couple of minutes of frantic wiggling proved to him he wouldn't be able to reverse the process that had brought him down. He couldn't get any leverage with his arms up over his head, and his elbows didn't have room to flex out.

He felt panic rising and batted it down. He didn't like tight places. He *hated* not being able to move his arms and legs, scratch his nose.

"Hey! Get something you can use to pull me out of here," Garibaldi called up. "Hey! Somebody!"

No answer. And he was hit by the sudden, terrible image of Bester, standing among the corpses of Thompson, Girard, and whoever else had remained in the apartment. Bester, grinning as he heard Garibaldi's voice, trying to decide whether to toy with him or cut right to the chase.

He looked up, but all he could see was the smallest sliver of light. Enough of a window for someone to pump a few bullets or PPG blasts down?

Sure.

The light flickered as a shadow crossed it.

"Did you call, Garibaldi?" It was Thompson.

"Yeah. Get me the hell out of here. This doesn't *go* anywhere."

"That means—"

"Yep. It means he's still up there, somewhere."

"Oh, shit. I—" Then Thompson made an odd noise.

"What was that, Thompson?"

Silence. Then a sort of muted chuckle.

"Well. Mr. Garibaldi. We meet again. And under very odd circumstances, I must say. I always knew you were beneath me, but to have it brought home so graphically, well, it's really quite amusing."

"Bester. Damn you, I'll—"

"Sorry. No time for chit-chat. I'll be back in a few minutes, though."

Bester closed the garbage chute and surveyed his handiwork. Thompson was down but still breathing, and would probably continue to. The big telepath wasn't so lucky. He had shot him in the head, first thing, while he was concentrating on taking the inhibitions off Marie and Pierre. Crude and amateurish, but he was a P12 and Bester still wasn't as strong as he ought to be.

Bester had sparked out the police officer and Paul—they

would recover any moment now. Only Thompson had given him a minute of real worry. Someone had removed the fail-safe he had planted in the ex–EarthForce officer, so he'd had to clobber him. Fortunately, the teep had been busy talking to Garibaldi.

Garibaldi, who would die next. But first Bester had something else to attend to.

It had all worked out pretty well, really. It had taken him only a few moments to do what was needed to Marie and Pierre—both were pretty weak-minded, and after all, he didn't do much to them. He planted the very strong suggestion that he had gone down the garbage chute, forbade them to remember his real exit, then forbade them to get up and walk around. None of these suggestions bore the force of permanence, though quick had also meant brutal. At the very least the two were going to suffer bad dreams for a few weeks.

What he had actually done, before his pursuers had arrived, was leave the apartment, cross the hall, and knock on a neighboring door. The sleepy tenant who answered had been easy to control, and better yet, single. The door had been shut, his new host down for the count, for about ten seconds when he heard the lift open.

For several long moments he could do nothing but wait, and hope, and make himself appear as an empty place in the universe.

When he heard some of them come tearing back out, and the lift went down, he knew his plan had worked. Yes, part one had gone very well—it was good to know he could still improvise.

Time for part two.

He found a roll of heavy tape in the kitchen and used it to bind up everyone who was still alive. He taped their mouths shut, too—everyone except the cop, Girard. He prodded Girard awake, scanning as he did so.

"What a complicated life you have," he said to Girard, as the cop's eyes flickered open. "Not one woman, but two. I've never really understood that, myself. I've never been able to be in love with more than one woman at a time. Here you have two, and you may lose them both because of your greed. You should be ashamed of yourself."

"Murderer."

"Ah. You want to change the subject. Good enough, I don't have time to be polite. We're going to use your link to make a call. You're going to tell them that Paul admitted it was all a ruse, that I've been gone for hours, and that I'm on the train to Amsterdam. I'll give you all of the information. Now, before you can object, let me tell you *why* you are going to do this, and why you'll do it just as I say.

"See, I could make you do it, but that would be very painful for you, and more important, fatiguing for me. On the other hand, I can easily slip into your mind, hear your every word before you say it. I'll know if you plan to betray me. If you try that, not only will you not have a chance of succeeding, but I'll kill one of these people and then we'll try again. And again, until you get it right. Do you understand?"

The policeman looked at him with a weary sort of comprehension.

"Yes."

"Good. Here's the information. And make it believable."

Girard performed flawlessly.

"Perfect," Bester told him, patting his head. "You've just saved a few lives." He wrapped a piece of tape around Girard's head. Then, carrying the dead teep's pistol, he went back into the bathroom to kill Garibaldi.

Garibaldi had felt like a sucker plenty of times in his life, but this was going to stand out as the high point—the Olympus Mons of suckerhood—if he managed to survive it.

And Lise wasn't going to like this story, not at all. Best not to tell her. Of course, when it hit the papers—well, that might take a while. If Bester killed everyone who knew he'd come down here, they might just miss the body until the smell started percolating.

That did it. Yep, he was panicking. He always got silly when he panicked.

He strained at the chute again, as if by some miracle the physics of the situation might suddenly change. But the mechanical problem stayed the same. Try as he might, he couldn't climb up.

He might get better purchase if he dropped his PPG, but at the moment that was his one and only chance. Bester might not know he had a gun, and he might get off the first lucky shot.

He doubted that Bester would leave something like that to chance, though. He'd probably heat up a pan of oil and dump it on him first, something like that.

He rolled his eyes. Perfect. He was thinking of things to help Bester out, just on the off chance Bester hadn't thought of them himself. Could he be scanned from up there? Did a tiny glimpse of him constitute line of sight? Probably.

Even in a straight-up exchange of gunfire, he would lose. PPG shots were globs of superhot phased helium plasma. Once they made contact with any surface they began to lose integrity. With this angle, he might be able to sort of blister his enemy's face. Meanwhile, Bester had a variety of weapons to choose from, including slug throwers, which would work much better in this situation.

He couldn't wait for that. He had to do something. It had already been too long—what, five minutes? Ten? Bester wouldn't hang around much longer.

He couldn't go up. He had tried to flex like Hercules and break the chute with the mighty strength of his limbs—no luck there, not even the slightest reason to hope. He couldn't go down, either.

"Wait a minute," he breathed. Why couldn't he go down? What was he standing on, anyway? Not the foundation—he hadn't dropped far enough for that.

He raised his right heel the full five inches he could manage, and kicked down. Kicked again.

Something gave, slightly.

He kicked with the other foot, then punched down with both feet.

"Making a lot of noise down there, Mr. Garibaldi." Bester's

voice sounded as if it were right in his ear, and for an instant he thought it must be telepathy. His skin crawled to think Bester might once again be in his head. But, no, it was just the acoustics of the shaft.

He fired up the chute without looking. Jumped and kicked, fired again. Jumped and kicked.

The air grew warm in the chute, thanks to the dispersing plasma. But something was certainly giving way beneath him.

He fired again, and this time the PPG didn't recharge. He dropped it, and used his arms as best he could to shove down, down, against the weakening floor of the shaft. At least he desperately hoped it was weakening.

Something finally broke beneath his feet, and he fell until his upper body caught in the too-small opening, nearly dislocating his arm. At the same moment, something like an angry hornet stung his ear. He wriggled frantically, his feet kicking free in a large, open space, his upper body still stuck in the shaft. Then something hammered unbelievably hard into the top of his shoulder, and he was through, falling free.

Then slamming into something that broke with a lot of noise. That part wasn't even so bad; all of the air had been knocked out of him by whatever had hit his shoulder.

He grunted and sat up. He was on the ruins of a coffee table, in the middle of someone's living room. The someones, an elderly couple, gaped at him from a dingy sofa. "Hi. Sorry," he managed.

A dizzying wave of pain hit him as he stood. His left arm hung like a noodle, and he realized that he was bleeding, though not heavily. A bullet had shattered his collarbone, but not penetrated any further into his body. He looked up at the gaping hole in the roof of the apartment, then, thinking better of remaining beneath it, moved aside. With Garibaldi's luck, even a blind ricocheting shot might hit him right between the eyes. Or maybe Bester had grenades, who knew?

Bester. A floor or two above him!

He picked up the drained PPG and popped another charge into it.

The old people were yelling at him, now—in French, naturally.

"Okay, okay. Keep your shirts on. I'm not here to hurt you. And I'm going. If I were you, I'd do the same, at least for the next hour or two."

He didn't wait to see if they understood him or not, but found their front door and left as fast as he could, which, given the fact that the world was doing a slow spin, wasn't too fast.

Back in the hall, he located the stairs and stumbled toward them.

— *chapter 14* —

Bester left Paul's apartment in a hurry, cursing and wondering exactly where Garibaldi had gone. The ancient shaft must have ended in someone's ceiling, which probably meant he was a floor or two down.

Bester's second shot had drawn a flash of pain, but he couldn't tell how badly he had hurt the ex–security officer. Not badly enough, in all likelihood.

He decided to take the stairs. At least there he could reverse direction quickly, and he wouldn't be trapped in a box. Of course, Garibaldi would be thinking the same thing.

The disadvantage was that he had to pocket his weapon briefly to open the stairwell door, which was precisely when the lift opened.

He spun and reached for his weapon at the same time. Then, to his vague surprise, he saw that it wasn't Garibaldi, but a uniformed young man with a mustache and close-cropped hair, accompanied by a similarly dressed, dark-haired, pretty woman. The man's eyes widened, but he acted quickly, pushing the woman down and firing well before Bester even had his pistol out. Bester heard a dull hiss and something struck him sharply in the chest.

It didn't stop him from returning the fire. His first shot missed, but the second took the fellow in the thigh as he ducked back into the lift. The doors closed again.

Bester took the moment to pocket his weapon and yank the stairwell door open again. Only then did he examine his chest. A small hypo-dart stood out from it. He yanked it out. What was it? A knockout drug?

225

Bester ran down the stairs, determined to get as far away as possible before the drug took effect. He could only hope that Girard's orders had been taken seriously, that the cordon around the neighborhood at least had some holes in it now.

He was almost to the ground floor when he heard the first-floor door above him open, and then a hoarse, familiar shout.

"Bester!"

He looked up to see a bloody Garibaldi taking aim. He threw himself to the left and fired just as a PPG burst sizzled by. Though his arm was grazed, Garibaldi stood his ground, ignoring Bester's shot, and fired again.

Bester leapt over the rail, dropping five feet. It felt like twenty might have, in his prime. His knees didn't like it at all. Behind him, Garibaldi said something colorfully slanderous about Bester's sex life.

Well, I hit him, at least, Bester thought, as he kicked the door open to the ground floor corridor and made for the outside door. *It should slow him down, and we seem to be even in the arm department.*

No one seemed to notice him as he bolted out onto the street, and he didn't wait around to give any remaining hunters a chance.

He ran, thinking how odd it was that he was running at all. If the dart had contained something to knock him down, it should have done so by now. Could it have been empty, by mistake? He was feeling a little queasy, but that was all.

He turned a corner, changed direction as often as he could.

He needed a goal. Where was he going? For the time being, he would simply settle for getting out of the immediate area. Then he would have a little more opportunity to think.

His lungs started to burn, and between one footfall and the next something turned around in his mind. He was fifteen again, racing through the same darkened city. He had broken the academy rules, set out after a dangerous rogue on his own, and tracked her to Paris. It was the first time he had been in a city other than Geneva, where Teeptown was located, and Paris had come as a revelation.

That was when he learned that the city had its own mind, of

sorts, a voice that was really millions of voices. That was where he had met Sandoval Bey, the mentor who had changed his life.

And now, so many years later, he was running through these same streets. And again his lungs were burning. Of course the first time, they had burned because one of them had a hole punched through it, not because of his age. Still, that boy of fifteen would have been caught long before now. What he had lost physically was more than made up for by what he had gained in experience. And Paris still sang to him.

No—it didn't. He realized that what had put him on that train of thought was the itchy feeling that something was missing.

It was. He couldn't *p'hear* anything. *Anything.*

Even at his weariest, he should be getting a background hum. But the silence in his head was as profound as if he were in space, solo, a light-year from any other mind.

The answer came to him like a cold, frozen hand on his chest. He remembered his psychic duel with the teep, earlier that night, the one he had shot with his partner's hypo-gun, the one whose power had just suddenly drained away. Sleepers. The hypos contained sleepers.

Once before he had taken them, as a condition for conducting an investigation on Babylon 5. It had been unpleasant, but he had dealt with it. This would be much harder to deal with.

He turned another corner. The darkness seemed to be wrapping around him, collapsing of its own dead weight. Dead was a good word—the world felt dead, lifeless around him. And he was alone in that dead world. The first time, he had at least had someone to talk to—Garibaldi, in fact, of all people.

They had actually been a good team. That had been when he first realized how useful Garibaldi could be to him. But now he had no one, just the silence, the claustrophobic, sticky silence. And the terrible knowledge that if death found him now, he might not even feel it coming. He had to remind himself to keep looking back over his shoulder.

How could normals live like this? Why didn't they just shoot themselves, become as dead as the world they inhabited?

Garibaldi's legs buckled as he stepped out onto the sidewalk. The initial shock was wearing off, and his injury was really starting to hurt.

Bester wasn't anywhere in sight. Which way? If he made the right choice now, he stood a chance of catching the bastard. If he chose wrong, it was all over.

Superstition at least as old as ancient Rome won out. He went left, the sinister direction. And as he entered the alley, he caught a glimpse of a Human silhouette against the next, dimly lit street, running, favoring one arm.

Yes. His legs tried to fail him again, but damn that. He remembered the last time he had tried to kill Bester, the sickeningly helpless feeling of wanting to pull the trigger, *trying* to pull the trigger—and being totally unable to do it. There Bester had stood, laughing at him, that stupid smirk on his face, talking to Garibaldi as he might to a little child. He explained that he had "Asimoved" him, put a little subroutine in his head that wouldn't allow him to harm Bester, or permit him to come to harm.

Eventually, Lyta had been the key to his release. They had struck a bargain. He had helped her rogue telepaths, and she had removed the block. Good old Lyta. Good old scary-as-hell-there-at-the-end Lyta. Her death was another thing he owed Bester for. But who was counting?

He was. It was what kept him going, when his body told him to just lie down. For Sheridan, and the torture he had endured. For Talia, dead even though her heart was probably still beating, somewhere. For himself. For himself.

For himself.

It worked. His arm jangled like a live wire, but he picked up the pace.

Girard rubbed his mouth. The tape *hurt* coming off.

The young man who had untied him didn't look like he was in good shape. He had left a trail of blood on the way in.

"We have to do something about your leg," the young woman with him said. Girard remembered the man—he was EABI. The woman he had never see before.

The young man sat down heavily. "I won't argue," he grunted.

The tape was still lying where Bester had left it. It would do for the moment, until he could get an ambulance here. "What's your name, son?" he asked.

"Diebold, sir. Benjamin Diebold."

"I think he saved my life," the woman explained. "He pushed me out of the way."

"That was Bester, wasn't it?" Diebold gasped, as Girard cut his trousers away with his pocket knife.

"Yes."

"But we got orders to break the cordon . . ."

"I know. Hold still."

Diebold said something else, but Girard didn't hear. A sudden flash exploded in his head.

Two men, running. Old enemies. Garibaldi chasing Bester. No question what will happen when they meet. There will be no arrest, no capture, no trial, no prison. One of them will die, or both.

"Bester!"

Garibaldi's shout sounded strangely tinny, depthless. Words were the tips of icebergs, and Bester was used to seeing the mountain that lay beneath the waves, the really dangerous mass of emotion and cognition that thrust words up for the ear to hear.

Normals talked and wrote of being able to "hear" anger or desperation in a voice, but like the parable of the blind men describing an elephant, they had no idea what they were talking about.

He didn't care what Garibaldi was thinking, per se— he could guess that well enough. But it would help to know how badly his foe was injured. He *did* seem to be favoring one arm.

Bester stopped, turned, aimed, and squeezed off a shot.

Green fire answered him, but missed by a yard, and he ducked around a corner.

Something cold and wet struck him on the cheek, and he turned the weapon up toward the sky. Another drop of water hit his forehead.

It was raining.

Bester remembered a duel he had read about. A young man had challenged an older. They had started with swords, but when it became clear to the other fellow that the young man was no match for him, he had thrown down his rapier in disgust and suggested something different. So the two got into a carriage, each tying a hand out of the way so that they couldn't use it. Wielding knives in their free hands, they fought while the carriage was driven around and around a park.

Bester seemed to remember both men had died. Probably Garibaldi would be happy with that. Bester was starting to think it would satisfy him, too. After all, how much longer before the other hunters came? The gunfire and smell of blood would bring them running back. With his psi he might have been able to deal with them. Not now.

Fine. If Garibaldi wanted a duel, he would give it to him. If nothing else, Bester would kill the man who had brought him so much misery. He ducked into a recessed doorway and waited.

The rain started as a few isolated drops, but within seconds it was hammering the avenue in undulating sheets. Garibaldi bit back a string of colorful expletives. Telepaths could hear you better when you spoke out loud, right? Or was it just more clearly? Whatever, Bester had more of an advantage than ever. Garibaldi was half-blinded by the rain, and the telepath would be able to *feel* him coming.

He took the next corner a little more cautiously, but he didn't want to slow up too much. Water was running into his eyes. Squinting, he did a slow pan of the street with the PPG, wishing he'd had time to stop and collect some night goggles. But of course, if he had, Bester would be gone.

If he wasn't already. He was nowhere to be seen. Had he had time to make the block? It didn't seem so, but adrenaline, pain, and the weird susurrus of the rain were doing funny things to time.

Prickles crawled across his scalp. He was here someplace, wasn't he? Masking himself, screwing with his mind. An invisible man.

The hand holding the PPG was shaking. It might have been shock from his wound, it might have been that little voice in his head that reminded him that Bester always, always won. *He's smarter than you,* the voice said. *He's always one step ahead.*

Feeling like a blind man surrounded by snipers, he flattened against the wall, his heart hammering.

Bester, blinded by the downpour, didn't notice Garibaldi until he was a few feet away. Tightening his jaw, he stepped out from the door, found his target—a vague man shape in the dark and wet—and pulled the trigger.

Someone stepped quickly from a doorway. Garibaldi didn't think at all. His finger squeezed the contact of the PPG.

The result was spectacular, and not at all what he expected. A green ball of fire seemed to explode in front of him as the rain refracted the coherent plasma into sudden incoherence. Murderous heat singed his eyebrows, and a dragon's tongue licked his hand. He dropped the PPG and hurled himself to the side.

Rain. He *knew* the damn stuff was dangerous. He blinked his eyes, trying to clear them.

A wave of steam and cooling plasma slapped Bester like the palm of a sun god. He lost his weapon in a moment of agony. He might have even blacked out for a second.

When he managed to look up, through the spots in his eyes, he saw Garibaldi rising up between him and the next streetlamp. With an inarticulate cry, Bester scrambled to his feet

and launched a punch with his good arm. His face felt
scalded. Maybe he was already dying.

The fist connected, but all wrong, and he nearly broke his
wrist. Still, Garibaldi grunted and fell back. Bester dropped
and swept, and had the almost religious satisfaction of feeling
the impact, of seeing Garibaldi leaving the ground, hearing
the meaty thud as he struck pavement. He kicked out again,
catching Garibaldi in the ribs, and again.

The third kick met only rain. Garibaldi was in motion
again, back on his feet, advancing.

They circled each other warily.

"Still a loser, aren't you, Garibaldi?" Bester sneered.
"What's the matter, do you need a few snorts of Dutch
courage?" He had to keep the ex–security officer off-balance,
mentally and emotionally. Garibaldi had a greater reach and
was three decades younger than him. "Or are you just too
dumb to know when you're outmatched, with or without the
booze?"

Garibaldi laughed harshly. "I'm not the one running like a
jackrabbit. That would be you."

"I'm not running anymore," Bester returned. "I'll admit
I'm in a hurry, but I figured if you wanted me so bad, I could
do a favor for an old friend. Especially one with whom I've
been so . . . intimate."

"Don't even try to play that," Garibaldi said. "You're
caught. Admit it. I've got you."

"You and what army? Oh yes, you *do* have an army, don't
you? You didn't have the guts to come after me on your own.
Afraid I'll turn your mind inside-out again?"

"They aren't here now. It's just you and me."

"You know why you hate me so much, Mr. Garibaldi? It's
not anything I've done to you, like you pretend. It's because I
know too much. I'm the only one who knows how dirty you
are in there, in your private little hell. I've seen it all, and you
can't stand the idea of anyone walking around who has even
had a peek at it."

"Shut up."

"I didn't make you anything you weren't. In fact, I had to

do remarkably little to turn you against Sheridan. You always resented him. You resent anyone who's stronger than you, with more strength of character than you. Like Sheridan. Like me." Garibaldi *was* favoring his arm—and badly.

"Don't even say your name in the same breath as his."

"You know it's true. Congratulations, by the way—I see you've had my Asimov removed. Lyta? Of course, Lyta. Only she would have been strong enough. Funny, Mr. Garibaldi, how your bigotry takes a backseat when it serves your own interests. Letting another dirty telepath into your mind must have been—"

Garibaldi lunged, and Bester was ready. After all, *he* had been living and fighting with only one arm for almost half a century. Garibaldi, for all of his size and training, was clumsy.

Bester sidestepped, snapped a hard jab into Garibaldi's wounded shoulder. The ex–security chief choked out half a scream, which cut off when Bester snapped a vicious knife-hand into the base of his skull. Garibaldi dropped to the pavement.

"What, did you think this would be easy, Mr. Garibaldi? You have to *work* for revenge. I could tell you things . . ."

Garibaldi was on his hands and knees, coughing. Bester kicked him as hard as he could, angling his toe up to catch the solar plexus.

Garibaldi felt ribs crack and tasted blood in his mouth. Stupid. He'd been stupid. Again.

If you let Bester talk, you lose, he thought grimly. He could feel your fears, play you like a harp, know your every intended move. His words would soften you up, and then he had you.

He felt rather than saw the next kick coming, and he took it, only this time he curled around it, caught the foot. Bester tried to twist away, but Garibaldi held on. Clawing for the rest of the leg. Somewhere, he found a hidden reserve of strength, and yanked.

Bester went down.

They got back to their feet at the same time. This time, Garibaldi didn't let him talk. He lowered his head and charged like a bull, letting his reflexes do the fighting rather than his brain. Bester hammered at his broken shoulder, and he felt the sickening scrape of bone against bone. But he didn't care anymore. Now that he had his hands on the teep, Garibaldi wasn't going to let go.

The wall stopped them both, but Bester took most of the punishment. The telepath's hand came up, clawing at Garibaldi's eyes, but he slammed him into the wall again. Then he unwrapped his arm and dealt Bester an uppercut. Hitting him felt good. He did it again, for good measure, with all of the strength that he could muster.

Bester kicked him in the crotch. It hurt, of course, but he really didn't care what happened to his body anymore. All he could see was Bester's face; all he could hear were his taunts. He got a good handful of hair and cracked Bester's head against the wall again, again, again. The telepath moaned and slid to the ground like a sack of potatoes.

Garibaldi, swaying, stepped back. He walked a few feet to where he had dropped the PPG. The rain had slackened, but he wiped the muzzle thoroughly, and to be sure, he placed it against Bester's head.

The telepath's eyelids flickered open. They had ended their brawl near a streetlamp, so it was light enough to make him out, but his eyes were black, like holes in space. Like Lyta's in all her unholy glory.

"Go ahead," Bester murmured. "It's what you want. But you know I'm right. I know how sick you are inside, and you can't stand that."

"You *are* right," Garibaldi said. "You're always right, aren't you? But you don't know me anymore, not like you think you do. Yeah, maybe on the inside I'm a bastard—we all are, one way or another. Maybe I can't blame it all on you. Maybe I do have to shoulder some of it. I'm willing to try. But you—you were responsible for the death of thousands. Millions, for all I know. And you don't have any remorse at all."

"No," Bester said, quietly. "I don't. There are things in my life I regret, but none of them would mean anything to you. And listen to yourself. All you're doing is trying to work yourself up to killing me, to justify it. Just *do* it, you pitiful gutless coward."

Garibaldi's finger trembled on the contact. "I don't need to justify it," he said, softly. "I can do it because I want to."

He counted five, then squeezed the trigger—or tried to. He found that he couldn't.

"Who has you Asimoved now, Mr. Garibaldi?" Bester asked, mockingly.

Garibaldi didn't let his weapon waver. "You owe me, Bester. You owe it to me to die like the dog you are. No, strike that, I *like* dogs. But as much as you've hurt me, as much as you've wronged me, there are a thousand others who you owe more. I'm not going to deny them, just to satisfy myself. I thought I could, but I can't. Your life belongs to everyone you've screwed, not just to me."

Bester managed a weak laugh. "Nice speech. You *are* a coward."

"Maybe. Maybe I am. But I'd rather be that than what you are. What I would be if I pulled the trigger."

With relief, Girard sagged against the wall and lowered his gun, still not sure what he would have done if Garibaldi had gone through with it.

No, he knew. He wouldn't have stopped Garibaldi, but he would have arrested him, and then turned in his own badge. He was flexible on certain points—cynical, some might say—but down deep, he believed. Believed in the law, believed in *right*.

What he had done to Paulette—yes, Paulette, he could think of her by a name other than "my wife"—hadn't been right. That was the crux of the problem, the thing he had been dancing around. He could pretend that her reaction was extreme, that he was only upset because he'd been caught, that Marie was being a nuisance, that it was the inconvenience of the whole thing that bothered him. But those were lies. He was upset because he was *wrong*, and he had to look it full in the face.

But first things first. He took out his cuffs and went to help Garibaldi.

—— chapter 15 ——

The War Crimes tribunal facilitation committee met today, to discuss the feasibility of acceding to the demand of the French government that the trial of Alfred Bester be conducted in Paris and not in Geneva.

Speaking before the committee, French President Michel Chambert reiterated his claim that since Bester was arrested on French soil he should be tried there. Senator Charles Sheffer of the United States vehemently opposed this position, calling it a "cynical ploy on the part of the French government to exploit what will surely be the trial of the century.

"Bester stands accused, not by France, but by the Human race," Sheffer went on, "and should be tried in EarthDome."

A number of other Earth senators protested as well, but by the end of the day, it was clear that the committee would likely agree to French demands. Dr. Eugenia Mansfield, a professor of law at Harvard, pointed out in testimony to the rules committee that, if denied the larger venue, France could press for trial on local charges, which process might take months—after which every other jurisdiction with some grievance against the infamous telepath could well press to do the same. This could delay the EA War Crimes trial indefinitely, something EarthGov is not likely to permit.

Senator Nakamura seemed to sum up the majority opinion when he said, "After waiting for so long for a final resolution to the telepath crisis, the world is hungry for justice. We should not deny the people that justice simply because France chooses an inappropriate time to assert its sovereignty."

* * *

Garibaldi watched the vid images come and go, fiddling with the controls from his hospital bed. He was thankful that, for the most part, the hospital had managed to keep the reporters at bay. Oh, one would appear outside of his window now and then, pleading soundlessly for an interview, but only two had managed to actually get in disguised as doctors. That had been a bit disturbing, since Girard had a couple of uniforms outside, just in case Bester had any vengeful allies left. On the other hand, letting them through might have suited the Frenchman's idea of a prank.

The result was that there were exactly five shots of him that repeated endlessly on the vids: his attack of the Bester look-alike and subsequent dismissal of the reporter, a brief shot of him being loaded into the ambulance after he collapsed at Girard's feet, and two views of him in the hospital bed, puffy-faced and looking incredibly old. In one he simply scowled and pushed the call button. In the other he made a six-word statement summing up his feelings. They were unfortunate words to become famous for. He wasn't exactly Churchill or Sheridan, he thought wryly.

He had hoped to hear from Sheridan, but the president of the Interstellar Alliance seemed to have dropped out of known space again. He had a way of doing that.

"Well. I'm glad I found you here, and not in the morgue, at least."

Lise stood in the doorway, more beautiful than ever.

"Hi, honey." He tried to look calm.

Her lips compressed, and he prepared for the worst, but after a moment or two, she walked over to his bed and took his hand. "Are you okay?"

"Broken ribs, shattered scapula, ruptured spleen. Bester in custody. Never felt better."

"You left without telling me where you were going. You won't do that again." She didn't qualify it. She didn't even say "or else," but he was left without any doubts.

"I won't do that again," he said, and meant it.

She nodded, then smiled, briefly. "You didn't kill him."

"No. I couldn't."

"The Michael Garibaldi I love wouldn't kill him. I'm glad to know you're the man I thought you were."

"I try to be, Lise. The man you see in me is the best of me. It's just the rest that's a mess."

"Not a mess—just a little untidy."

"Where's Mary?"

"Outside. I wanted to see you first. I wasn't sure how you would be, how I'd react." She brushed his cheek. "Now that this is over—"

"It's not over yet. There's still the trial, and the sentencing, all that good stuff. I want to stay for the trial."

"But for you, it's over," she said, firmly. "And now that it's over there's going to be a hole in your life, Michael. You'll have to be ready to deal with that."

"No hole. Just a wound, finally closing up. I knew that, when I finally had him." He squeezed her hand. "You think I don't have enough?"

"You aren't a quiet man, Michael. You aren't comfortable just with happiness."

He laughed. It hurt. "I bet if I put enough effort into it, I can be," he said. "And believe me, I intend to put a lot of effort into it."

She smiled a little skeptically, then kissed him.

"By the way," she said, when they came up for air. "*You* can explain to our daughter what those words mean. The ones they keep playing on the newscasts."

Bester felt as if he were looking down on the courtroom from a great height, as if the witness stand were Olympus. For weeks, others had sat here, but they had seemed small to him, lost in the crowd of humanity, in the humming of newstapers, there in the almost baroque splendor of the French hall of justice.

Small. Even Garibaldi looked small, perched in that place that demanded the truth. Old enemies and old friends came, spoke, and went. A few struggled, unwilling even now to betray him in an entirely unqualified way. Most of these were already in prison.

Others were glad to proclaim him a monster, to paint him as something more removed from humanity than the Drakh or even the Shadows. He listened to them, watched them shrink into history even as he felt himself grow larger, a towering shadow. People would remember Alfred Bester, yes, but these others were mere footnotes.

It might have been different, he mused, if Sheridan had come. Perhaps Sheridan would have even said something good about him. After all, Sheridan understood, as the rest of these insects did not. Understood about the sacrifices one made for the common good, the stains one would accept on one's own soul when something higher was at stake.

Yes, all of this was inevitable. Oh, his lawyers tried. Hadn't Bester been an appointed official of an organization created and overseen by the EA Senate? Had he really been doing anything more than implementing the policies of Psi Corps, the president, EarthGov itself?

All of that was just marking time. The prosecution was full of answers. Nothing in the Psi Corps charter allowed for the murder of unarmed civilians, the blackmail of EA senators, unauthorized experiments on detainees, torture, distribution of illegal substances. No, Bester had taken matters into his own hands, creating a government within a government, and had gone to war against not only the law, but everything that was right and decent.

Inevitable.

Now he sat in the chair himself, the place of truth. He wore a black suit. He didn't wear his telepath's badge. He smiled when the mouthpiece for the prosecution—a young EA senator named Semparat—stepped onto the floor. Semparat looked . . . small.

"State your name, please, for the record."

"My name is Alfred Bester," he replied. He paused, cocked his head slightly to the side. "Or would it make you feel better if I said my name was Hitler, or Stalin, or Satan?"

"Alfred Bester will do," the senator said, dryly. "I think by the end of this we will see that it will do quite nicely."

"Oh, but you knew that coming in, didn't you?" Bester asked. "You had no need of a trial, did you?"

Semparat frowned, but ignored that last.

"Mr. Bester," he continued, "you have heard all the charges against you before, at your hearing. At that time, you maintained that you were innocent. After all of the witnesses that have come before us, do you still so maintain?"

Bester raised his eyebrows. "Of course I do."

"Really."

"I do."

"You deny, for instance, the murder of forty-three unarmed civilians connected to the telepath Resistance on Mars?"

"I deny their murder, yes."

"You deny the evidence brought before this court that you ordered their executions and killed three yourself."

"I don't deny killing them. I deny the charge that it was murder. And I applaud your semantic games, Senator. What you now call the telepath Resistance was at the time universally recognized as an illegal, subversive organization of terrorists. The normals involved were also terrorists and subversives."

"But they weren't armed, were they? Did they try to resist you?"

"Frankly, I did not care to give them the chance. Their activities had already resulted in the deaths of at least sixty-four of my colleagues. Senator, it was a war. However you look at it, those people fought in that war and they were casualties of it."

"Who declared this war? You?"

Bester raised an eyebrow mildly. "The terrorists declared it when they bombed our facilities on Mars. Everything we did after that was response, kind for kind."

"We've heard evidence that you, Alfred Bester, murdered civilians long before the beginning of the telepath conflict. Are you going to claim that that was war, as well?"

"Of course," Bester said.

"I, for one, am confused by that statement, Mr. Bester, and my guess is that many of this court are equally confused. Would you care to explain?"

"I would be delighted to, Senator," Bester replied.

"Please do so then."

Bester took a sip of the water next to him. "One hundred and fifty-eight years ago, the existence of telepaths was known to almost no one. One hundred and fifty-seven years ago, it became common knowledge thanks to an article in the *New England Journal of Medicine*.

"By the end of that year, eighteen thousand telepaths were dead. No war was declared by any government. They were killed one at a time, they were killed en masse and buried in pits, they were aborted when DNA testing revealed what they were as fetuses."

"Mr. Bester, I'm sure we all know the history."

"Really? Funny, I've never heard a word about it during this trial. You asked me to speak—I'm speaking. Don't I have that right?"

"This isn't a platform for your political views."

Bester laughed, sharply. "It seems to be a platform for *yours*. More than half of the so-called crimes you're accusing me of were committed with the consent of the legitimate government of the time. You represent the new order, so of course you would like nothing better than to discredit the old one, in order to legitimize yourself.

"This entire trial is nothing more than the final step in rewriting the last century-and-a-half of history to suit those of you who are in charge now. And yet you claim that this trial is not a platform for political views? Senator, your hypocrisy and the hypocrisy of this court sickens me. Either afford me my right to speak without interruption, or send me back to my cell. Frankly, I don't care which this kangaroo court sees fit to do. But do one or the other."

That drew a deep murmuring from the audience, and not all of it sounded negative. What he felt was still overwhelmingly hostile, however.

"Very well, Mr. Bester." The senator sighed. "Just get on with it."

"Thank you. As I said, once telepathy was discovered, the murder of telepaths began. It hasn't stopped. I could draw your attention to last month's case in Australia, or the one reported this week in Brazil, but there really is no need for a list of examples, is there? Each of you know it's true. To grow up telepathic is to grow up with the constant menace of death, the vague but real threat of dying at the hands of someone who doesn't even know you, only knows what you *are,* what you represent to them. *I* grew up with it. The first time I left the academy grounds, to go on a hike with my friends, I was attacked. The *first* time."

He paused. "This undeclared, unrecognized war has been fought for a hundred and fifty-seven years. Its casualties—have always been on *my* side. And when this killing began, what did EarthGov do about it? They built a telepath ghetto called Teeptown, and they gave us badges to mark us, separate us. They gave any normal who wanted to kill a telepath the means to find us and identify us. Then they used telepaths to control telepaths. Why? The implicit threat was always there—ask any telepath old enough to remember. *Either you control yourselves, or we will control you.*

"That was the choice I grew up with. Hunt down and sometimes kill my own kind, with the blessings of EarthGov and every normal citizen who voted for it, or be subjected to the same uncontrolled genocide that was visited on us in the beginning.

"You made that, each and every one of you. Oh, you might try to pawn it off on your ancestors, but you reified it each generation, gave it the nod. I spent the first seventy-two years of my life being told what a *good* little boy I was, how *well* I served humanity by hunting down my people. I have the commendations to prove it, a drawerful.

"Now, suddenly, you've decided that maybe Psi Corps wasn't such a good idea, and you want to sweep it all under the rug. You want to pretend it just went bad, somehow, and that it was *my* fault. You also know that isn't true.

"You blame me for continuing to fight the war that started in 2115? You blame me for defending my people? I suppose you do. Psi Corps was developed to keep telepaths in their place. An act of war, of suppression. You want to know who the real telepathic Resistance was? It was *us*. Protecting ourselves against you. Sure, along the way we protected you, too, whether you knew it or not, and more than you will *ever* know.

"But in the end, all of us inside knew what was coming. That one day some bright boy would hit upon the 'final solution' for the 'telepath problem,' and there we would be, all caged up and ready for the gas. Only we didn't play the game that way.

"Now you're upset. Who can blame you? Hitler would have been upset, too, if the Jews in Warsaw had turned out to be armed to the teeth and ready to fight."

"Oh, come on—"

"No, Senator. *You* come on. You want to pretend a century and a half of continual violence against telepaths never existed? Fine. You want to pretend that Psi Corps wasn't created by the EA Senate? Fine. You want to silence me, lock me away, maybe even kill me? Well and good. But you know the truth. In your hearts, all of you do. This isn't over. You've divided and conquered, scattered my people. And yet, they still wear the badges, don't they? They still have to report to be examined, don't they? They're still registered at birth, marked more certainly and permanently than anyone who ever wore an armband with a star—because that, at least, you could take off.

"In fact, the *only* thing that has changed is that you've taken away our ability to fight back, when the time comes. And, boys and girls, the time is coming. All of your wishing and hoping and praying won't stop it. The mass of humanity won't tolerate our existence. Tomorrow, in ten years, in fifty—it's coming, and this playacting, my trial, its context will become abundantly clear.

"So, yes, I have killed, like any good warrior. I have fought the good fight, and I lost. I regret nothing. I would change nothing in my power to change, I would—"

His tongue stumbled. As he spoke, he had been sweeping his gaze over the crowd, and from camera to camera. He wanted every single person watching to know he was speaking to *them,* personally. To let them know they *all* shared the blame.

And there, six rows back, toward the center . . .

Louise, staring at him with those eyes he knew so well, a faint wrinkle in that forehead he had kissed. Her hair—he could almost smell it, feel it between his fingers.

I regret nothing. She rebuked him, by her mere presence, made him the liar. For in her eyes, there was nothing about him. No recognition, no love, only faint puzzlement, perhaps a hint of revulsion. Nothing.

If he hadn't cut her up, she would love him still, and her eyes would be an anchor, her words a safe harbor, even in the midst of all of this.

He suddenly felt very old, and very tired, and very, very alone. He *had* killed—the one person in the universe who might have spoken for him. For that, if for no other crime, he deserved whatever came.

"Mr. Bester? Are you through?"

Louise realized he was looking at her, and her brow creased angrily. Even if she didn't remember him, she knew what he had done to her. Even if he could start over, she wouldn't love him again.

"Mr. Bester?"

"I've said everything I'm going to say," he murmured. "You'll do what you want anyway. I'm through. I'm through."

— chapter 16 —

In his dreams he heard the singing mind of Paris. Sometimes Geneva, sometimes Rome, or Olympus Mons or Brasilia—but mostly, usually, Paris. In his dreams, he sat watching the sky wrap up in watercolor shrouds as it died for the evening. He sipped coffee and thought about how much of his life lay ahead, how many possibilities.

Or sometimes, in his dream, he sat with Louise, thinking how much of his life was gone, but how good the rest of it would be. And still Paris sang like an immense choir, with Louise the featured soloist, the brightest, loveliest voice among them.

He awoke knowing that it was the city and its sighing mind he had truly loved, and Louise, who represented it, personified it. But both were gone now, forever.

In dreams, in dreams. He preferred them. Awake, the world was dead, a cave of bone.

But wake he must, at times. He rose that morning as he did every morning, splashed water in his face, went to the window, and looked out upon his childhood. Teeptown.

In the distance, he could just make out what had once been the cadre houses. Just below him, clearly visible, was the quad common with its statue of William Karges, which he and his friends had called the "Grabber."

Of course, the Grabber was no longer grabbing. There was nothing left of him but a pedestal and part of one leg. The statue of Karges had been blown up, along with much of the quad, during the wars.

Just as well. Karges had been a secret telepath who had

246

saved President Robinson's life at the cost of his own. When Bester had been little, they had taught him that Psi Corps had been created by Robinson to honor that sacrifice. That wasn't true—the Corps had existed in essence, if not in name, for decades. It had never been one of the lies he liked—it suggested too much that only by sacrifice did telepaths prove they had the right to exist.

So good-bye, Grabber, and good riddance.

They had tried to shut Teeptown down, as they had the Corps, but it hadn't quite worked out. The scores of private academies that had sprung up to instruct young telepaths hadn't worked very well, just as he had predicted they wouldn't. Over the years, he had watched the Psionic Monitoring Commission gradually reimplement almost all of the old Corps institutions, though in darling new baby-doll clothes. Once again Teeptown was a campus, a center of telepath life and activity. Many older teeps never left their quarters there—life among normals had proved too hard, too uncertain.

And so Teeptown remained a ghetto. Again, as he had predicted. It gave him some small comfort, to be right. It gave him little, though, to know that this maximum security facility was his own creation. He had built it to hold telepaths—and so it did. War criminals.

He heard footsteps in the corridor. "Good morning, James," he said.

"Morning Mr. Bester," James said, in his faintly mocking tone. "How're the memoirs coming?"

Bester glanced over at the simple AI on his bed.

"Pretty well," he said.

"I have some news for you."

"Oh?"

"Olean passed last night."

Bester absorbed that silently for a moment. "How did he manage to kill himself?" he said at last.

"It was pretty clever, but I can't tell you, of course. You might imitate him."

"I'm not going to kill myself. I won't give you the satisfaction."

James, the jailer, shook his head. "I get no satisfaction from it. I think you know that."

"The world, then. They'd love it. It's what they want. Life sentence—absurd. I was sentenced to death, death by suicide. I just refuse to carry out the sentence."

James hesitated. "You may be right, there. But you condemned thousands of teeps to the same fate—you made *them* take sleepers."

"I never did that and you know it. I enforced the law, I didn't write it."

"You understand me, then, why I have to give you this." He indicated a small gun-shaped device at his belt.

"Skip it this week. Just once."

"I can't."

"Just once. You know I can't escape. I just want to *feel* again."

"So did Olean, and Brewster, and Tuan."

"Once. One week."

James shook his head. "If it were up to me—"

"It *is* up to you," Bester said, gritting his teeth.

"Be a good boy and take your medicine, Mr. Bester."

And so he did, stood still while the needle pricked his arm and the sleepers went in, as they had for ten years now. He barely felt the stupid feeling spread. He had never had the extreme reaction to the sleepers that some did—the listlessness, the deeply drugged feeling. No, they left his mind pretty much intact, so he could be acutely aware of how crippled he was.

James left, and Bester fought the gloom by working on his memoirs. He was nearly done with them, had been nearly done with them for years. He just kept fiddling. He liked to fiddle with his history—it was the only thing he still had control of, his version of things. Let the historians wrangle endlessly about what was true and what wasn't. *He* knew, and they didn't, and it was the only power he still had.

Well, that and the power of his predictions, of his insights. Those would validate him, one day.

Two days later, a week from Birthday, he got an early present. The vidcom on the ceiling came on, unannounced. It did that rather rarely—he could request programming and sometimes get it, but it usually took awhile. When it came on of its own accord, it usually meant bad news, some new announcement from the prison director.

This time, however, as he watched and listened, a ghost of his old smile returned to his face. The smile broadened when he understood that most everyone else in the world was starting to weep, or denying reality, or cursing softly. They would look back on this day and everyone would remember where they were, what they were doing. Garibaldi, for instance, probably was not taking it well.

Yes, they would all remember where they were when Sheridan died.

Of course, Bester would—how could he forget? *"Let me see,"* he imagined himself telling someone. *"That day I must have been—why, yes, I was in prison . . ."*

Sheridan had been no friend of Bester's and he'd been a hypocrite besides. They said the best revenge was living well; it wasn't. It was *much* simpler than that. It was seeing your enemies die.

Now if he could just outlive Garibaldi, then even *this* life would have a certain sweetness.

He listened intently, in the hopes that Garibaldi had been involved and perhaps had died as well. No such luck. Ah, well, he would settle for Sheridan for the moment.

They were putting up a new statue where the Grabber had once stood. At first Bester thought they were clearing away the pedestal and its pitiful half-leg altogether, but they were just cleaning it off for a new occupant.

This interested him, as nothing had for some time. He entertained himself by speculating who it might be. Lyta? Byron? More likely Byron—he had been the martyr, the one who had acquired everyone's sympathies. Lyta had led them, too, but she had been frightening even to her allies. Still, it was she who had struck the real blows, wasn't it? Ultimately, Byron had been a coward.

A few days later he awoke to find a crowd gathered, and the statue in place, covered by a tarp. He put his face against the monomolecular glass, his heart working oddly in his chest. *Oh, come now,* he thought to himself, disgustedly. *You don't really care that much.*

But he did, somehow. The symbol that the slowly re-forming Corps chose for itself would tell him much about its character, about its leaders. Would they choose the warrior queen, the mystic martyr—or perhaps even himself, a sort of dark reminder of what *not* to become?

He watched the crowd, wishing he could *p'hear* them. He had heard that when a normal lost a sense—vision, for instance—their other senses sharpened, to take up the slack. Not so with telepathy. His other senses were only fading. Not that any normal sense could begin to replace his birthright.

Speeches began, but he couldn't hear them. The crowd applauded—he couldn't hear that, either.

He hit his call button. After a long delay, James answered. "Yeah?"

"I wonder if I could get the audio for the ceremony outside."

"The dedication? Sure. Don't see as how that would hurt anything."

A moment later the sound cut in. The speaker was winding up.

". . . dark days, but they represented hope, created it, held it aloft like a candle. It was their memory that carried us all through to the liberation, their sacrifice that represents the best in us."

Bester nodded sullenly. He thought it had looked like two statues. Byron *and* Lyta, then.

"And so, all of you, it's my great honor to present our ancestors. Not in fact—for their only child, their great hope, vanished or was killed in the vicious raid on their hidden camp. But spiritually, and morally—" The speaker paused.

"Those of us who grew up in the Corps were taught that the Corps was our mother, and our father. But if we must look to a common, spiritual mother and father, let us look to those who represented freedom, not oppression. Tolerance, not intolerance. Hope of liberty, not the despair of repression.

"My friends, my kith, my kin, I give you Matthew, Fiona, and Stephen Dexter."

The shroud came off. Time slipped for Bester, a weird plummet between heartbeats.

He sat in a tree, at the age of six, watching the stars, searching for the faces of his parents. Sometimes he could see a hint of them, of his mother's eyes, a suggestion of auburn hair, an echo of her voice.

He was older, on Mars. The oldest and most successful of all the rogues, Stephen Walters, lay crushed against a bulkhead, one leg bent under him in a very strange way, one arm missing at the elbow. He still had his mask on, but Bester had the distinct impression the eyes behind it were open.

I know you, Walters psied.

The hairs on the back of Bester's neck stood up. *I was in New Zealand,* Bester replied. *I tracked you here.*

No. Before that. I know you. Oh, God in heaven. It's my fault. Fiona, Matthew, forgive—

It paralyzed Bester. The sense of familiarity was like a drug. It wasn't pleasant, it was horrible, but he needed it somehow. Somehow—somehow it was a piece of him that was missing.

What are you talking about?

I know the feel of you. I saw you born—after all I had done, after all the blood on my hands, but they let me watch you come into the world, and you were so beautiful I cried. You were our hope, our dream—

My name is Alfred Bester.

We called you Stee, so you wouldn't be confused with me. They gave you my name, made me your godfather. Your mother, Fiona, how I loved her. Matthew, I loved him, too, but

God— a terrible spasm of pain stopped him then, and almost stopped his heart. Bester felt it tremble. *It was me that lost you,* Walters went on. *I thought I could save them, but they knew they wouldn't make it. All they asked was for me to get you out, keep you free, and I failed them. Failed—*

Matthew and Fiona Dexter were terrorists, Bester replied. *They died when the bomb they were planting in a housing compound went off early. The bomb they set off killed my parents.*

Lies. He was getting weak. *They fed you lies. You are Stephen Kevin Dexter.*

No.

Walters cocked his head wearily, and then he reached up to Bester's face. With a trembling hand he pulled his breather up and off. In the gloom, his eyes were colorless, but Al knew they were blue. Bright blue, like the sky. A woman with dark red hair and changeable eyes, a black-tressed man, both all smiles. He knew them. Had always known them, but he hadn't seen their faces since the Grins had banished them. They were looking down at a baby in a crib, talking baby talk. And Bester could feel a love so strong—was it love? He had never felt anything just like it, because there was no hint of physical desire, no desperate need, just deep, abiding affection, and hope . . .

He was seeing through Walters' eyes, through the filter of Walters' heart. But then, horribly, another image superimposed itself. The same two people, but looking down at him, and he was the baby in the crib, and behind Mother and Father stood another man, a man with bright blue eyes, as bright as the sun . . .

They loved you. I loved you. I love you still. Psi Corps killed them and they took you away. I tried to find you . . .

Bester wasn't aware of finding the PPG. Suddenly it was there, in his left hand and in front of him. His hand clenched on it, and Walters' face turned bright green, uncomprehending.

Shut up.

His hand clenched again, another viridian flare.

Shut up.

The mind images were dropping away, but not fast enough. He tried to shoot again, but the charge was gone. He tried and tried, squeezing the contact, throttling the lying glyphs in his brain.

Fiona . . . Matthew . . . Walters was still there, pulling the images about him in a blazing cloak. His eyes were still there, too, resigned, full of gentle reprimand. He stood near a gate, the doors of which were just beginning to crack open. *You can't destroy the truth.*

And he was gone, and finally the images shredded, a thousand visions of his parents, dancing, fighting, embracing, holding him . . .

No! He took it all in his fist and he squeezed until it went away.

His fist had never opened again. Never.

He shook his head, becoming aware of his cell again.

There they were below—the man and woman he had never known, save in dreams, and visions, and from the mind of a dying man. Matthew and Fiona Dexter, the mother and father in bronze. And in their arms, the lovingly held bundle—

Of course it was true. Of course he had always known it.

It felt like a cough, at first, so long had it been since he laughed. He hacked up another, and had to sit back on his bunk.

James must have thought he was dying, because he showed up a few minutes later, looking worried. "Bester?"

"It's nothing," Bester managed, waving him away. "Just the universe. Don't believe anyone when they tell you irony is just a literary convention, James. It's a universal constant, like the coefficient of gravity."

"What are you talking about?"

But Bester shook his head. Another thing that only he knew. No one else on Earth or in the stars knew what had happened to that baby, immortalized in bronze. That the symbol of hope for the brave new world was none other than the most hated criminal of the old.

Maybe there *was* hope for them, after all.

Still smiling, he lay down on his bunk, trying to frame what to do about it. Would that go in his memoirs? Maybe, but it might be better, more delicious, to never let them know, to never tell *anyone*.

For now he was tired. He would think about it in the morning. He sighed and closed his eyes, and felt an odd softness in his arm, his left arm. A sort of warmth. And movement, like something unfolding.

And he dreamed—maybe it was dream—that his left hand opened like the petals of a flower, and the fingers wriggled, and he laughed in muted delight.

When James found him the next day, it was the first thing he noticed, the hand. Palm up, fingers only lightly curled, free of the fist that had trapped them for so long.

Bester was free, too, a faint weird smile on his lips, his face looking somehow younger. He really did look like he was just sleeping.

—— *epilogue* ——

Girard wondered again what, exactly, had brought him to
the graveyard. It was raining lightly, not a nice day even if you
were somewhere pleasant, somewhere that didn't remind you
that you were shuffling ever faster toward the off-ramp of the
mortal coil.

He looked out over the garden of marble headstones and
shrugged. Well, he had been in the neighborhood, and he
rarely got to Geneva. That he should be here when his most
famous case died—it seemed, somehow, that he was fated to
watch them put Bester in the ground. And he didn't like to
argue with fate *too* much.

Few others seemed to have felt so compelled. Some thirty
people accompanied the body to the graveside, but of those,
most were clearly with the press, come for photographic
Grendel-heads to assure the world that the monster was dead
at last. There were four or five people who might have been
family members of Bester's victims, here to find that assur-
ance in person. Another four or five simply looked curious.

The only weeping was from the sky. No one had come to
mourn Bester, only to bury him.

There was no graveside service. After the press had been
run off, a man in EA uniform checked the coffin. Girard saw
him lift the lid, nod, and speak briefly into a recorder. The lid
came back down, four men in prison uniforms put the box in
the hole, a fifth in an earthmover covered it over, and that
was that.

He had half expected that woman to show up—what had
her name been? Louise? She had looked Girard up, years

255

later, to ask him what he knew about *her* role in things. He had thought she would eventually talk to Bester himself, but maybe that hadn't been allowed. Surely she knew—his death had made the news everywhere, and even now the sordid details of his life were being rehashed on the networks.

But no. The men did their work in almost eerie silence. No words, gentle or harsh, were spoken. No benediction, no blame. He almost felt as if he should say something himself.

But he didn't. Girard watched until the men left. He wasn't in any hurry. His wife was shopping, and he had nothing to do for several hours. He stayed, thinking that surely, *surely* someone else would come.

He realized he was still waiting for the woman, Louise. After all, it was Bester's love for her that had gotten him caught . . .

Merde, but I'm a romantic! Girard thought. Yet here was the proof, love *could* be destroyed, cut out as if it had never been. And a man really *could* go to his grave ungrieved. It made him feel better about his own life, his own choices. Despite himself, Girard had people who loved him.

As he was finally walking away, some instinct made him look back. He had just passed into a small copse of trees, and a breeze mingled the scent of clay with the green scent of the leaves fluttering wetly around him. Life mingled with death. It was nearly dark, and at first he thought he had turned for nothing, for some ghost in his own brain.

But then his peripheral vision made out a shadow approaching the grave. As Girard watched it move into the open, it became more distinct. A man, not a woman. The man knelt by the fresh earth, staring at it for a long time. Then he lifted something—Girard couldn't make out what—and put it on the grave. He got up and strode away without looking back.

Girard recognized him then, by his walk. Garibaldi.

He almost went after him, to say hello, if nothing else, but somehow felt it would be inappropriate. There had been something solemn, almost sacred about Garibaldi's movements, something inviolable.

Still, when Garibaldi was gone, Girard walked over to see what he had placed on the grave.

When he saw it, he shook his head and chuckled softly. It was a wooden stake, pushed into the yellow clay as far as it would go.

"Amen," Girard whispered. And, "Peace." Then he left the dead where they belonged.

When he reached the street, he flipped his phone open and ordered flowers for his wife. As he walked to the hotel, he began humming to himself. The rain kept up, but it didn't bother him in the slightest. There were worse things in life than a little rain.

And now, an excerpt
from the next dramatic chapter in the
Babylon 5 saga . . .

LEGIONS OF FIRE

Book One
The Long Night of Centauri Prime

by *New York Times* bestselling author
Peter David

Based on an original outline
by J. Michael Straczynski

The Drakh felt sorry for him.

Londo Mollari would have been surprised to learn that such considerations went through the Drakh's mind. If the sentiments the Drakh possessed had been relayed to him, he would have been even more surprised to learn precisely *why* the Drakh felt sorry for him.

But he did not know, so he faced the Drakh with his jaw set, his shoulders squared, obviously doing everything within his ability to look cool and confident in the moment when his keeper would bond with him.

The Drakh, however, could already sense the accelerated heartbeats, the forced steadiness of the breathing, the general signs of rising panic that Londo was pushing back by sheer force of will. All of this was clear to the Drakh, for the bond upon which he and Londo would operate was already beginning to form on a subliminal level.

His name was Shiv'kala . . . and he was a hero. At least, that was how the other Drakh tended to speak of him, in whispers, or when they communed in silence, having abandoned the need for verbal speech.

Among the Drakh, there was none more brave, more diligent, more pure in his vision of what the universe should be. Nor was there any who was more sympathetic to his fellow creatures. This was what served to make Shiv'kala so effective, so pure, and so ruthless. He knew that in order to accomplish what was best for the galaxy, he had to be willing to hurt, terrify, even kill if necessary. Anything would be justified, as long as he never lost sight of the common good.

Shiv'kala loved the common Drakh. He had the common

touch . . . and yet, he also had been highly regarded by the Shadows. With equal facility and consistent equanimity, Shiv'kala was able to walk amid the mundanity and move among the gods. He treated the gods as mundanes and the mundanes as divine. All were equal. All were of a piece, and Shiv'kala could see all, understand all, and love all. He loved the cries of creatures at birth. And when he wrapped his hands around the throat of a creature he was sending to its own personal afterlife, he could glory in its death scream, as well.

He was one of the most soft-spoken of the Drakh, and his mouth was pulled back in an almost perpetual smile. Or at least that was how it was perceived by others.

That wasn't how Londo Mollari, imminent emperor of the great Centauri Republic, perceived him now. That much Shiv'kala could tell, even without the tentative connection that already existed between them. In all likelihood, Londo looked at that curious rictus of a smile and saw the satisfied grin of a predator about to descend on its prey. He did not know; he did not understand. But Shiv'kala understood. Understood and forgave, for such was his way.

The keeper was stirring within him. Londo would never have known it, but the keeper was fearful, too. Shiv'kala could sense that as well. This keeper was relatively new-born, spawned from its technonest mere days before. Shiv'kala had attended to this one personally, for he knew of the great fate and responsibility that awaited it.

When the keeper had opened its single eye for the first time, blinking furiously against the light, it had been Shiv'kala's face into which it had gazed. It hadn't been able to see clearly, of course; Shiv'kala had appeared as a hazy image at first. But full vision hadn't taken long to develop.

The keeper was born with a high degree of awareness, but was not quite certain what its purpose was in the broader scheme of nature. Its tendrils, mere stubs upon birth, had flickered around aimlessly. They momentarily brushed against its parent, but the parent was already a small, black-ened husk, as was always the case. It had no soft thoughts to offer, no guidance to give as its offspring tried to determine just what it was doing and how it was supposed to do it.

"Calmly, little one," Shiv'kala had whispered, and he extended a grey and scaly finger. The keeper had tried to wrap its tendrils around the finger, and Shiv'kala had gently lifted it from the technonest. As he had done this, he had drawn aside his robe and placed the newborn keeper against his chest. Operating on instinct, the keeper had sought nourishment there, and had found it. Shiv'kala trembled slightly and let out a deep, fulfilled sigh as the keeper burrowed in, sucking and drawing sustenance from Shiv'kala's very essence.

In doing so, the keeper had burrowed not only into Shiv'kala's soul but into Drakh Entire. Shiv'kala would always have a special status with this particular keeper, would always be the most sensitive to its needs, wants, and knowledge. And the keeper, now that it was attuned, would be able to commune with any of the Drakh Entire at any given moment.

A magnificent creature, the keeper. It had nursed within Shiv'kala and had grown to maturity within three days. Now it was ready . . . ready to assume its most important job. Yet as prepared as it was to do so, and as much as its nature suited it for the task, when Shiv'kala opened his vest to extract it from its nourishing pouch, he was amused to discover that the keeper, likewise, was apprehensive.

What troubles you, little one? Shiv'kala inquired. Across from him, a few feet away, Londo Mollari was in the process of removing his coat and loosening the collar of his shirt.

He is very dark. He is very fearsome, the keeper replied. *What if I do not keep him properly? What if I fail in my task? Can I not stay with you, in the pouch, in the warmth?*

No, little one, Shiv'kala replied gently. *We all serve the needs of the universe. We all do our part. In that way, I am no different than you, and you are no different than he. He will not, cannot hurt you. See how he fears you, even now. Reach out. You can taste his fear.*

Yes, the keeper said after a moment. *It is there. He is afraid of me. How odd. I am so small, and he is so huge. Why should he fear me?*

Because he does not understand you. You will explain yourself to him. You will make him realize what is to be done. He thinks you will control him, always. He does not understand that we will not deprive him of free will. He does not understand that you will simply monitor our mutual interests. You will not force him toward what he must do . . . you will simply help us to guide him away from what he must not do. He fears not being alone.

This is strangest of all, said the keeper. *The one time I felt any fear . . . was when I was alone in my nest. Why would anyone or anything desire to be alone?*

He does not know what he desires. He has lost his way. He moved toward us, moved away, then toward and away again. He is without guidance. You will guide him.

But he has done terrible things, the keeper said with trepidation. *He destroyed many Shadows. Terrible. Terrible.*

Yes, very terrible. But he did so because he was ignorant. Now . . . he shall learn. And you shall help teach him, as will I. Go to him. See how he fears you. See how he needs you. Go to him, so that he may start his new life.

I will miss you, Shiv'kala.

You will not, little one. You will be with me always.

With that parting sentiment, Shiv'kala removed the keeper from its nourishment pouch. Its tendrils had grown marvelously during its sustenance period and were now long and elegant. Moving with the grace that was customary for its species, the keeper glided across the floor and wrapped itself around Londo's legs. Shiv'kala could sense the tentativeness of the keeper. More, he could feel the rising terror in Londo. Sense it, but not see it. Londo's face was a mask of unreadability, his brows furrowed, his eyes . . .

There was fury in his eyes. They bore into Shiv'kala, and had they been whips, they would have flayed the skin from his body. Shiv'kala decided that it was an improvement over fear. Fear was a relatively useless emotion. Anger, fury . . .

these could be harnessed and directed against an enemy and be of great use to the Drakh. Furthermore, such emotions were far more alluring to the keeper and would make it much more comfortable with its new host.

Above all, Shiv'kala wanted to make certain that host and keeper blended smoothly, for they were a team. Yes. That was what Londo did not yet grasp; they were a team. Although the creature was called a keeper, implying a master-slave relationship, the reality of their binding went much deeper than that. It was almost . . . spiritual in its way. Yes. Spiritual. Others, including Londo's predecessor, had not understood that. He had not had enough time, or had simply been too limited in his perspective.

But Londo . . . Londo possessed a much broader view, had much greater vision. Hopefully, he would comprehend and even come to appreciate what he was undergoing.

Londo's back stiffened as the keeper crept up toward his neck. He had potential, Shiv'kala was certain of that. Perhaps the most potential any associate of the Shadows had ever shown. Perhaps even more than Morden had offered. Morden had been an excellent servant and had proven himself superb in carrying out orders. While he had been capable of actualizing the dreams of others, he had been noticeably limited. Morden had glowed brightly but only because he had been basking in the dark light generated by the desires of Londo Mollari. Now Londo himself was in thrall to the Drakh, serving in turn the great philosophies and destinies of the Shadows, and that opened an array of new opportunities and possibilities. What was most important was the dreamer himself, and Londo was just such a dreamer. Yes, it promised to be most exciting indeed. Shiv'kala only wished that Mollari was capable of sharing in that excitement.

The keeper dug into Londo's shoulder, and Shiv'kala sensed the bonding. He smiled once more, reveling in the joy of the moment. Londo's emotions were a snarl of conflicts, fear and anger crashing into one another like waves against a reef, and he shuddered at the feel of the keeper's tendrils as they pierced his bare skin. That was all right though. He would adjust. He would learn. He would see that it was for the best. Or he would die. Those were the options, the only options, that were open to him, and Shiv'kala could only hope that he would choose wisely.

As for the keeper, Shiv'kala was pleased to sense that the creature was calming. Its initial trepidation was dissipating, as the Drakh suspected it would. Furthermore, Londo's thoughts were coming into clearer focus, the blinders and shields falling away.

Londo stiffened slightly, as Shiv'kala eased himself into the Centauri's mind the way that he would ease his foot into a comfortable shoe. Within seconds, he inspected the nooks and crannies, studied Londo's deepest fears, viewed his sexual fantasies with morbid interest, and came to a deeper and fuller understanding of Londo's psyche than Londo himself had been able to achieve in years. Londo wasn't fully cognizant of everything the Drakh had already discerned. His mind was still reeling and disoriented, and with a gentle push, the Drakh steadied him, helped realign his focus.

Deciding that he would ease Londo into casual telepathy, he said out loud, "You will be all right." He spoke with his customary low, gravelly whisper that forced people to listen closely. It was an amusing display of his power, albeit a minor one.

"No," Londo said, after a moment's consideration. "I will never be all right again."

Shiv'kala said nothing. There was no point in trying to force a realignment of Londo's state of mind. Sooner or later he would learn and understand, and if it was later rather than sooner, well, that was fine. The Drakh had great and impressive plans, long-term goals that spanned decades. The instant comprehension, understanding, and cooperation of a single Centauri—emperor or no—simply was not necessary. They could wait.

So Shiv'kala just inclined his head slightly, acknowledging Londo's remark.

Londo tried to sneak a glance at the keeper, but then

where the voice had come from, and then he looked at the Drakh. His lips drew back in anger, and he snarled, "Stay out of my head!"

But the Drakh shook his head and, with that same damnable smile, thought at Londo, *We will always be there.*

Then he extended a hand to Mollari. He did so as a symbolic gesture, for he did not truly expect Londo to take it. Instead, he stared at the hand as if it were dried excrement. Shiv'kala then stepped back and allowed the shadows of the early evening to swallow him up.

In a way, it felt as if he were returning home.

looked away. Instead, he started buttoning his shirt, pulling his vest and coat back on. "It . . . does not matter, in any event," he said after a moment. "Whether I am all right. It is my people that matter now. It is Centauri Prime, only Centauri Prime."

"You will rebuild. We will help," said the Drakh.

Londo laughed bitterly at that. "Unless, of course, you choose to blow millions of my people to pieces with your fusion bombs."

"If we do . . . it will be because you have chosen that path for us."

"Semantics," Londo said contemptuously. "You act as if I have free will."

"You do."

"One choice is no choice."

"The Shadows you killed when you destroyed their island . . . they had no choice in their fate," Shiv'kala said. "You do. Do not abuse it . . . lest we give you as much choice as you gave the Shadows."

Londo said nothing to that, merely glowered as he buttoned his coat. "Well," he said briskly, "we should begin this sham, eh? This sham of leadership. I, as emperor, with you guiding my every move."

"No." Shiv'kala shook his head ever so slightly. Everything he did, he did with minimal effort. "Not every move. Simply keep in mind . . . our goals."

"And your goals would be . . .?"

"Our goals . . . are your goals. That is all you need remember. You will address the populace. They will be angry. Focus that anger . . . upon Sheridan. Upon the Alliance."

"Why? What purpose would that serve?"

Shiv'kala's skeletal smile widened ever so slightly. "The Alliance . . . is the light. Let your people look upon it in anger . . . so that they will be blind to the shadows around them." As always, Shiv'kala spoke in a low, sibilant tone of voice. Then, ever so slightly, he bowed and thought at Londo, *Good day to you . . . Emperor Mollari.*

Londo jumped slightly at that, clearly not expecting it. Reflexively, he looked around, as if trying to figure out